THE PERFECT
LIAR

Published by Bookouture in 2020

An imprint of Storyfire Ltd.
Carmelite House
50 Victoria Embankment
London EC4Y 0DZ

www.bookouture.com

ISBN: 978-1-83888-957-9
eBook ISBN: 978-1-83888-956-2

THE PERFECT LIAR

BEVERLEY HARVEY

Bookouture

CHAPTER ONE

Tunbridge Wells, July 2019

Susanne

Susanne paces and hunts for a stain to punish. It's been three days since her son boarded a British Airways flight to Edinburgh and already separation anxiety and cabin fever have set in.

'Give him some space, Susanne. Cody's fifteen, for god's sake. Do you think for one nanosecond that I'd let anything happen to him? Please, love, don't phone every day, it smacks of you checking up on him – on *us*.' Colin had been emphatic during their second phone conversation in twenty-four hours.

Deflated, Susanne had agreed. Col is right of course. Her handsome, smart and independent boy will be just fine with his father during the summer holidays. If only she could convince her heart.

She picks up her mobile phone, thumbs the app for her local gym and books a Pilates class for noon. Rule Number One while Cody's at his dad's: *keep busy*. Which shouldn't be a challenge: she's got an autumn 10K to train for, her regular midweek Pilates class with Evie and boot camp with her sadist of a personal trainer, Andreas, on Thursdays.

Then there are her landlady duties to contend with. It always amazes Susanne how much admin and running around two small cottages in the next street actually generates – especially after a tenant changeover when there are always teething troubles, however respectable the family.

So, work and fitness, then. She sometimes wonders who she's keeping herself in such marvellous shape for.

She looks around her spotless kitchen – a dream kitchen, worthy of any interiors magazine – and is satisfied that there's truly nothing left to clean; even the windows sparkle in the morning sunshine.

Susanne heads upstairs, twists long, nut-brown hair into a claw and steps into the shower where the warm, scented water has a calming effect. Then, after marching through her skin care routine, she goes to her dressing table and opens her leather jewellery box, ignoring the expensive trinkets gifted by Colin over the years, choosing instead the gold St Christopher bought by her Grandma Amy for her twenty-first birthday.

'Miss you, Gran,' she whispers to the mirror as she fiddles with the tiny catch.

After a quick trawl of her wardrobe, Susanne pulls on leggings and pictures Cody in his favourite T-shirt and faded denims, and hopes she has packed enough clothes to last him all summer.

With over an hour until she's due at the gym, Susanne eschews a third mug of coffee for a cup of Earl Grey and forces herself to sit at the kitchen island and read her favourite magazine.

Exercise: Lifeline or Addiction, screams one headline; *Loneliness on the Rise*, warns another; then, over the page: *Teenagers: When to Let Go*.

Feeling like a living cliché, Susanne slams the magazine shut, pushes it aside and wonders how on earth she'll survive the summer alone.

When her mobile phone shudders beside her she smiles, expecting the text to be from Cody, but it's Evie, checking she's still on for Pilates and whether she's free for coffee afterwards.

Need class and coffee today. See you there. Susanne texts back a reply, adding a smiley face emoji at the end. As she's got to know

Evie, she's learned that texts without kisses or smiley faces are deemed brusque in Evie's eyes.

Despite her recent lecture from Colin, Susanne messages Cody. *All OK? Miss you xx.* It's all she can do to stop herself texting 'Mummy loves you, angel, come home at once'.

Car keys in hand, and gym bag over her shoulder, Susanne is about to leave the house when Cody replies to her message. She's crushed when there are no words, just the slow download of a photograph of her son cuddled up to a liver-and-white spaniel, its eyes huge and a fuzzy blur where its tail should be.

A second message arrives: *Melissa's dog Banjo. So cute!*

The dog is indeed as cute as Christmas, but Cody's economy with words has done nothing to lift her mood. There's no love, no kisses – and no 'miss you mum'. She scrutinises the photo. Cody looks happy, playing with the dog (Melissa's dog), his smile goofy and natural.

So, Melissa is still on the scene. When Col hadn't mentioned her for a while, she'd begun to wonder if things had fizzled out between them. But Cody's playful text has sent an entirely different message. The fact that her ex-husband has introduced his girlfriend to his son tells Susanne that they are serious about each other, and for reasons she can't fathom, tears well in her eyes.

*

Still in leggings and trainers, Susanne steers Evie towards a window table overlooking the outdoor pool. A handful of people are swimming hard, putting their lunch hour to good use, while others bask in the sunshine, stretched out on plastic loungers, fooling themselves that they're on holiday.

Feeling despondent, despite the punishing workout, Susanne pastes on a bright smile and focuses on Evie, who stirs her Americano, an expectant look on her flushed face.

'So, how are you, Evie? What's going on with you?'

'I'm well, Susie. Actually, I'm feeling a bit better. More…' Evie pauses, head cocked while she searches for the right word, 'hopeful,' she adds with a positive nod.

'Well, hopeful's good, isn't it? I mean, you've been through so much recently…' Susanne trails off, unwilling to upset her friend with painful reminders of the last few months. She diverts the conversation in another direction. 'By the way, have you thought any more about going back to work?'

Evie grimaces. 'It feels too soon, too many loose ends still to sort.'

'Of course. You've probably got enough on your plate without job hunting.' Susanne falls silent, her thoughts drifting back to Cody.

Evie is watchful, her expression full of concern. 'Are you all right, Susie? Only you don't seem quite yourself today.'

'I'm fine. Just feeling a bit sorry for myself and missing my son terribly; it's only been three days. I'm pathetic, aren't I?'

'Pathetic is the last thing I'd call you, Susie. You're bound to miss him. He might be as tall as you, but he's still your child.'

'You're right, I suppose – and there's other stuff that I won't bore you with.' With a stab of irritation, Susanne thinks of the adorable spaniel photo. *Melissa's* dog.

Evie frowns. 'Love, you can tell me. For months you listened to me endlessly going on about my problems.'

Susanne scoffs. 'Yes, I know, but that was different. Your situation was a lot more serious than me feeling a bit miffed because my ex-husband has wheeled out his new girlfriend. And maybe not so new. It's been at least a year since he first mentioned her, so I guess it's time.' Susanne picks up her phone and swipes the screen until she finds the photo of her son playing with Banjo.

'This came from Cody earlier. Her name's Melissa and that's her dog.'

Evie purses her lips and runs a finger around the rim of her coffee cup. 'Now I'm not a mum, but I can imagine it's painful to think of Cody spending time with someone else. Don't beat yourself up, Susie, any mother would feel the same.'

Susanne squares her shoulders. 'Maybe. God, Evie, all this doom and gloom; I need to get a grip.'

There's a lull in the conversation while they watch the swimmers thrash up and down, doing their best to avoid each other in narrow lanes.

'What are you up to this weekend? Do you fancy getting together? We could certainly do with a laugh,' Susanne says, her tone brightening.

Evie's face clouds over. 'Nothing really. I thought I'd make a start on mum's things. I've been putting it off for ages.'

'Oh, Evie. I'm so sorry. Here's me banging on about nonsense when you've got that to deal with. Why don't I come over and give you a hand? It'll be easier with two of us.'

Evie sits up straighter. 'Thank you, but I think I'll just potter through it – go at my own pace.'

'Okay, well if you change your mind…' Susanne says, feeling spare and useless.

'Thank you, but I won't,' Evie says, her round face set.

CHAPTER TWO

Evie

Evie heaves herself into black leggings and an orange Lycra vest before stuffing a bottle of water, purse and house keys into a small rucksack. She never showers at the gym and today will be no exception – although as time has passed, she's become less self-conscious, so perhaps she'll feel brave enough soon. Anyway, as far as Evie's concerned, nobody even looks at her, certainly not in the way they actively gawp at Susanne.

Once, they'd been leaving Costa Coffee in Tunbridge Wells when a woman had stopped dead in her tracks and looked Susanne up and down with such unconcealed venom that Evie had half expected scorch marks to appear on her friend's face.

To her shame, Evie had felt that way once, too, the first time she saw Susanne in the locker room at the gym – bra-less and wearing just the tiniest scrap of lace that passed for knickers and not an ounce of cellulite on her body.

Spellbound, Evie had watched Susanne walk straight to the front of the class where she'd thrown herself into the workout with total abandon, while Evie had hidden at the back, red in the face and breathless, embarrassed by her size.

That was the day she'd decided to do something about it – to change. Walking in alone on that first day had been excruciating. But after a few weeks, it was Pilates every Wednesday lunchtime that kept her sane – and not just because she'd begun to lose weight.

The gentle routine of seeing the same faces at the same time every week had soothed Evie, giving her a simple structure to cling to while everything else spiralled out of control. On the day she broke down in the changing room after class, the entire group of around fifteen women had filed straight past her as she'd sat blowing her nose and wiping away hot, panicky tears, but only one woman had asked if she was okay.

Still glowing from exercise, Susanne had squatted beside her, her clear, tawny eyes full of concern.

'Oh dear, lovely. Are you all right? Can I help with anything?'

Evie had been mortified – she hadn't meant to make a fuss, but the night before, over fish and chips destined to be abandoned and left to congeal in their waxed paper, things had come to a head.

'We need to have a proper talk, Evie,' her mum had said gently, before dropping the bomb that her cancer had spread, despite a harrowing course of chemotherapy.

'The thing is, love, it hasn't worked. All that pain and sickness, losing my hair… all for nothing. I don't think I can handle any more. It's time I let nature take its course, Evie – it's for the best.'

They'd argued, of course, but Jean had dug her little size four heels in, and in the end, Evie had had no choice but to accept her decision.

The following week, she'd resigned from the solicitors, which had felt hard; Evie loved being a legal secretary and took great pride in the way people trusted and relied upon her. Then three weeks later, she'd given notice on her flat – which had been even worse – and moved back in with her mother. Rent-controlled and in a quiet house near the station, with good neighbours and a narrow strip of garden that Evie had lovingly filled with terracotta pots which were a riot of colour all spring and summer long, her flat had been her haven for seven years. Evie wept the day she gave back the keys.

And somehow, she'd ended up leaking her personal disaster all over Susanne, a complete stranger, sitting in the snack bar at the health club, mocked by its cheerful lemon-and-lime walls, her sniffles drowned out by the hiss and roar of the coffee machine and the perky banter of a dozen other gym-goers.

After half an hour, Evie had dried her eyes. 'Sorry. I bet you wish you hadn't asked now,' she'd said with a watery smile.

But Susanne had shaken her head. 'Don't be daft. Shit happens to all of us, and it helps to talk. The way you're looking after your mum is amazing. Not everyone would take that on, you know. You're tougher than you think, Evie – never forget it.'

Months, and a dozen or so Pilates classes later, on Evie's thirty-ninth birthday, Susanne had taken her to a swanky department store for a manicure and a sleek blow-dry. Then they'd taken the lift to the rooftop café for smoked salmon sandwiches and champagne. Susanne had even organised a neighbour to sit with Jean while they were out. It was a level of kindness unknown to Evie.

They'd made an odd pair, standing at the front of the chilly crematorium, the air heavy with the scent of lilies and carnations, on that crisp March day. Evie was braced between Susanne and her auntie Cath, her Uncle Ken and her cousins filling the rest of the pew, whilst behind them was a sea of faces, blurred by Evie's tears, who'd come to say goodbye.

And as the visceral, gaping grief began to give way to something flat, grey and ordinary, Evie had assessed her situation.

She was alone now. She had no choice but to get another job; experienced legal secretaries were hard to find so at the very least she could temp for a while.

But there was no rush, because to Evie's utter astonishment, thanks to her mum's parsimony in life, as well as inheriting the small terraced house in Calvert Street, she'd gained a modest nest egg to renovate it with. It excited her to think of putting in a sleek modern kitchen and a pristine new bathroom; of taking down her mum's twee wall prints of sunflowers and teapots, and kittens in baskets, and painting over her dusty and dated wall colours. It gave Evie a little rush of optimism to imagine replacing the busy, tired carpets and to put up cheerful new curtains and blinds, and when she thought of filling window boxes and the little garden at the back with vibrant geraniums and petunias, she could almost smell their perfume. No. 9 Calvert Street was her house now and she would work hard to make it her own.

The flare of a car horn blasts through Evie's thoughts; she'd better get a move on or the class will start without her. Cheered by the thought of seeing Susanne, Evie shoulders her rucksack, steps into the late morning sun and power walks to the gym.

CHAPTER THREE

Dale

Dale snaps her laptop shut and strides out to the fire escape which doubles as a balcony. The insistent throb of a neighbour's drum and bass music and the early evening humidity only adds to her ill humour.

Shit! How dare the woman? Five! Five fucking messages on Facebook, in addition to the three unanswered texts on her mobile. Helena has jogged past keen, sailed right by persistent and has now entered stalker territory.

What part of 'I'm not into you' doesn't she understand? Dale hadn't meant to be so blunt, but it was a case of being cruel to be kind. After all, Helena hadn't responded to Dale's initial – and gentler – attempts to say goodbye.

Fuming, Dale stomps inside and picks up the phone, but it's not Helena's number she dials.

'Susie, it's me, can you talk?'

'Dale. Hello, darling. Are you all right? Only you sound a bit cross.'

'Ha! That's one word for it. Actually, no – I'm not all right. You remember Helena, that girl I was seeing?'

There's a pause on the line. 'No, I don't think you mentioned her,' Susanne says.

'Ah, well there you go – that's because it was just a fling.' Dale is triumphant, adding 'Just a… thing… that meant nothing, and now the woman won't leave me alone!'

Cradling the phone against her shoulder, she opens the fridge, removes a bottle of pinot grigio and sploshes some into a large glass.

'That's better,' she sighs after taking a big glug of the chilled wine. 'Okay, Susie – where was I?'

'You were telling me about your stalker. So, let me get this straight. Helena is some woman you saw a couple of times and now she won't take no for an answer. Ooh, you callous heartbreaker, you.' Susanne chuckles softly.

'It's not funny! She's a barista in my favourite coffee shop. I'll have to go elsewhere for my pre-school flat white now… or… or settle for bloody instant in the staffroom, yuk!'

Susanne giggles. 'Oh, Dale. Sweetheart, I'm sorry – but you're such a drama queen!'

'What can I say? Guilty as charged; it's my job. Oh, but what am I going to do about this girl? Seriously, she's left me about ten messages and we only met twice. Once we went to some tedious book fair on the South Bank, and the other time we had a drink and I… slept with her. And, Susie, believe me when I say, it wasn't good. So, I said I'd made a mistake. That's it. End of.'

'Not for her, apparently. Your place or hers?' Susanne asks.

'What? Oh, hers of course. I mean, I'm not stupid, she doesn't know where I live. Yet. But she knows where I teach, because I told her on our first date – and I'm worried she'll rock up at school. Thank god we break up for summer in a couple of weeks.'

'Okay, just don't give the woman any oxygen. Ignore her.' Susanne's tone is firm.

Dale drains her glass, refills it. 'You don't think I should tell her to bog off?'

'No, do nothing. Remember that guy I had problems with last year? The muscly one from the gym… anyway, we didn't even go out, let alone shag – but all my polite, wheedling refusals just gave him the attention he craved. He soon stopped contacting me when all he got was silence. Dale, you still there?'

Dale takes another swallow; the wine is beginning to take effect. 'Yes, just thinking. Anyway, sorry, I haven't even asked about you. How are you? When does the boy wonder leave town?'

'He's already gone. Cody left three days ago. I felt sick putting him on the flight. I know he's with Colin and I'm being ridiculous, but I miss him so much. Now I'm rattling round this big house, wondering how I'll get through the holidays.'

Dale's mood softens. 'Bless you, Susie. I'm sorry. Do you want me to come down?'

'Would you? A visit would be fab. In fact, why don't you come for the weekend? Get away from what's-her-name. We can go out in Tunbridge Wells on Saturday night, let our hair down a bit. Shall I pick you up halfway? Sydenham to here is a right faff by train.'

'It is, but don't worry, I'll borrow Mum's car, she won't mind. Shall we say sevenish? It'll be great to see you. Sorry for being a grumpy cow. Lots of love, honey – keep your pecker up.'

Mollified by the wine, Dale slumps on the sofa. Outside, the sun is sinking below the stucco-fronted flats on the other side of the park where she'd meant to cycle for half an hour before marking essays on *Macbeth*. Now she's too lethargic to do anything more productive than forage for a ready meal in the freezer and find a drama serial on TV.

She reflects on the weekend. It will do her good to get out of London, and anyway, a stay at Susanne's swanky pad is never a chore.

Even at school, it was a standing joke that with her looks, Susanne was bound to do well for herself: that she'd meet a rich man and live in a big house somewhere smart and leafy.

Marrying Colin Campbell, an Edinburgh-born fund manager, and buying a period town house with a view of the common in Tunbridge Wells had ticked several boxes in one hit. But the dream hadn't included divorce, nor failing to get pregnant a second time. Dale of all people knew that as perfect as it appeared, Susanne's

life was as flawed as anyone's and that she nursed her own brand
of pain and disappointment in private.

Aware she has already drunk two thirds of a bottle, Dale exca-
vates her freezer and is digging into an indeterminately flavoured
pasta bake when her mobile pings with another text from Helena.
Fuck you bitch is all it says. Dale hurls her phone across the sofa,
then casts the remains of the gloopy red mush into the bin, her
appetite vanished.

She rakes long fingers through her floppy blonde crop. 'Roll on
the weekend and getting out of Dodge,' she says aloud, draining
the last of the wine and switching on the television.

CHAPTER FOUR

Evie

Outside the master bedroom, Evie hesitates. She pushes the door open; it drags on the pile of the rose-patterned carpet. She rarely comes in here: the room where five months earlier, Jean's eyes had fluttered open for the last time, moments before she'd taken her last breath. Evie stands within its peach-coloured walls and feels the sadness weigh upon her like an old eiderdown.

A dry smell, like stale biscuits, has gathered now, not helped by the heat. She heaves up the sash window which has stiffened from lack of use. Dust motes dance in the sunshine as fresh air pours in.

She pads to the wardrobe where Jean's best wool coat hangs beside a row of tweed skirts, slacks and cotton blouses; a beaded dress shimmers beside a Nehru velvet jacket – both bought for a theatre trip organised by Evie on Jean's sixty-fifth birthday.

On the dresser, shrine-like, her mother's toiletries have garnered a thin layer of dust. A zipped floral bag, crammed with cracked palettes of eye shadow and face powder, tubes of worn-down coral lipstick and a pot of rouge, sits beside a barely used bottle of Lalique that has begun to cloud. Evie picks up Jean's hairbrush, still laden with her DNA, and a sob escapes her throat. She tears a bin liner off a roll and gets to work.

*

By five o'clock, Evie is tired, hot and dirty. On a whim, she calls Susanne.

Susanne's tone is gentle. 'Hi Evie, how did it go today?'

Evie puffs out her cheeks and exhales slowly. 'It was hard, Susie. But I'm glad I finally got over myself and dealt with it. Mum's house is mine now and I have to move forward. So, anyway, I filled at least a dozen bin liners for the Sue Ryder shop, put some things in the loft and packed a little suitcase of all the bits I want to keep... you know, jewellery and photos and so on.'

'Well done. Bet you're relieved, aren't you? Look, why don't you jump in the shower and come over? It'll do you good to kick back a bit. Dale's coming later, my old school friend. I've mentioned her before – the one who teaches at the big comp in south London.' Susanne's laugh tinkles across the phone line. 'Dale's feisty but great fun and she can cheer anyone up.'

The company of happy, shiny, good-looking people holds little thrall for Evie. But the thought of another Saturday night spent alone in the shadows of her mum's house, wallowing in memories, is worse.

'If you're sure I won't be gatecrashing your evening, that would be lovely.' The words are out before Evie can think them through.

'Absolutely not! Get your lippy and some high heels on and we'll hit a couple of bars. Dale's fab – honestly, you'll love her.'

Evie feels guilty as she showers away the day's misery, spritzes on perfume and slips easily into her best jeans and wedge-heeled sandals. She pats her shrinking midriff. There's no diet like the Grief Plan, she muses. A slick of lip gloss and two coats of mascara later, she totters across town in the direction of Susanne's.

*

Outside the grand townhouse, Susanne's white Range Rover dwarfs a red VW Polo that Evie has never seen before. As she stands there gripping the tissue-wrapped bottle of white wine she bought en route, Evie fights the urge to creep away unseen. But before she can escape, the sound of a sash window opening rumbles overhead. Susanne leans out, her hair falling around her face. 'Hi! I'll come down.'

Seconds later, there's a clack of high heels behind the front door. Evie takes a deep breath and smiles.

Susanne glows, sleek in midnight blue jeans and a silk vest top.

'Hey! You look gorgeous,' Susanne says, giving Evie a hug. 'Is the wine for me? Bless you, you shouldn't have. Come and meet Dale.'

Stomach knotted with anticipation, Evie follows Susanne into the tiled hallway, passing beneath an exquisite chandelier and into the kitchen which leads to an orangery. Slouched against the island in the centre of the room is a coltish-limbed blonde in a silver vest top, black jeans and battered cowboy boots. She straightens up, beams at Evie and extends one slim brown hand.

'Hi Evie, I'm Dale. Susanne's been filling me in. So sorry to hear about your mum – must have been awful. You need a drink!' Right at home, Dale fills a glass from an already open bottle and hands it to Evie.

She'd struggled across town in high heels, her feet swelling in the heat as she walked, but now Evie wonders why she's even bothered; the top of her head could tuck under the chins of both women. Her confidence flounders. Why is she here, in the company of these glamazons? They are not her tribe.

Susanne raises her glass. 'Cheers, girlies. Thanks for coming over. We've all had a pig of a week and we've bloody earned this,' she says, taking a large swallow of wine, and adding, 'Our cab is booked for eight, so drink up.'

Embracing the party mood, Evie smiles gamely then splutters on her wine as she attempts too much at once.

Susanne giggles. 'I thought I was the only one who did that,' she says, handing Evie a tissue to wipe her eyes.

They hover by the island exchanging small talk for a while, ignoring the nibbles that Susanne has put out as though they're only for decoration.

When their car arrives – a gleaming new Mercedes – Susanne and Dale fold themselves into the cavernous back seat. Evie hesitates then sits in the front, wondering whether or not she should chat to the driver.

In sensible shoes, the distance to The Gallery would be walkable, but Evie is glad of the lift. Her pink puffy feet have already rebelled and it's a huge relief to sit down at a window table.

Dale announces she's starving after a long bike ride in a south London park. Susanne agrees and soon they are ordering an array of tempting platters to share and topping up each other's glasses with prosecco.

'Is it naughty to order another bottle?' Susanne asks, her face a picture of innocence.

'Naughty? Bollocks to that!' Dale replies with a wave of her hand and a mimed exchange with the waitress. She leans forward and lowers her voice. 'So, Evie, what would *you* do in my shoes?' she begins, launching into a complicated story about an obsessive barista with a crush on her.

Susanne giggles and rolls her eyes. 'Oh, not this again. Dale, I told you what to do; just blank her, you know it makes sense.'

Evie hesitates. 'Sorry, Dale, I'm the last person to ask. Nothing exciting ever happens to me, so I've got no experience of… stuff like that.' Embarrassed by Dale's candour, Evie feels her cheeks redden, but by the time they are on their third bottle, she has hit her stride and all three women are screeching with laughter – to the point where the manager asks them to tone it down a bit – which only makes them laugh harder.

'Oh, I've loved tonight, it's been brilliant,' Susanne says. 'We should do this more often.'

'Oh, yes please,' Evie agrees, her stomach sore from laughing. 'I wasn't really in the mood for tonight, but I've had the best time.'

'Hey, you know what we need?' Dale says, her expression thoughtful.

'More prosecco?' Susanne suggests.

'Good point, but I was thinking more of a holiday. A bit of R and R in the sunshine would do us all the power of good.' Dale's eyes glitter with mischief.

Evie appraises Dale. Earlier, she'd been shocked by her lesbian stalker saga; now she gets it – the woman lights up a room.

'Sounds dreamy,' Evie says, 'But I can't afford a holiday, I'm not working, am I?'

Susanne leans forward, her face eager. 'No, but you've just inherited. Bet your mum would approve. You've had a terrible year, Evie. You should treat yourself,' she says with conviction.

CHAPTER FIVE

Susanne

It's after nine when Susanne surfaces with a sour taste in her mouth and an insistent buzzing in her head. Listening for signs of life from the guest suite, she hears the shower running and smiles as she remembers how even from a tender age, Dale's capacity for alcohol far exceeded her own.

With a feeble groan, she pulls on sweats and heads for the kitchen.

Dale strides in a few minutes later.

'Ooh, you smell gorgeous,' Susanne says, as she hugs her friend.

'Cheers. That'll be the lemon-and-grapefruit shower gel and body lotion I've just borrowed. You run this place like a hotel, Susie.'

Susanne studies her friend. With damp hair and no make-up, Dale could be a decade younger than her forty-two years.

'I just want you to be comfy, darling. Anyway, why are you so bloody perky? There's a woodpecker in my head.' Susanne massages her temples. 'I wonder how Evie's doing.'

But after wholemeal toast with honey and two strong cups of tea, Susanne is back on form and remembering the conversation from the night before.

'Okay, so you know we talked about getting away this summer, somewhere warm and glamorous,' she begins.

Dale's eyes widen. 'Are you serious? That was just my prosecco-speak.'

'Well, maybe it was, but why can't we? My son's away, you're about to start the school hols and Evie's between jobs while she gets her life sorted. I mean, *hell-oo*? Could there be a better time?'

'Well, put like that… but I can't afford to just swan off, Susie.'

'Ah, but what if we could stay somewhere seriously gorgeous for mates' rates?'

'Interesting. Go on.'

'My neighbours who live next door-but-one have a villa in Tuscany – Veronica and Eddie, they're called. Ronnie can come across as a bit brusque but she's a complete sweetheart once you get to know her. Anyway, I know they're not there themselves because I've seen them around town and—'

'And you think they might lend us their house?' Dale has beaten her to the punch, her eyes sparkling.

Susanne shrugs. 'Maybe. Surely it's worth an ask?' she says, scrolling through her mobile for Ronnie's number.

*

An hour later, resplendent in a canary yellow cotton shift and Jackie O sunglasses, Veronica sips espresso in Susanne's sun-filled orangery.

'And this,' she says, angling her tablet towards Dale and Susanne, 'is the view from the sun terrace. Look, you see those towers in the distance? That's San Gimignano – which is soo charming and less than half an hour away by car. There are other, closer villages, of course – but we love San Gimi,' she sighs, pronouncing it like the boy's name.

Susanne's gaze is wistful. 'Can't believe you're not there yourself, Ronnie. If I owned a villa in Tuscany, I'd be there half the year.'

'Darling, you say that, but it rarely works out that way. Eddie is having surgery in ten days' time – otherwise we might have spent the summer there ourselves.'

'May I?' Susanne takes the tablet from Ronnie and swipes through a dozen or so images. 'Are you sure you wouldn't mind lending us the house for a month or so? We'd pay, of course,' she goes on, unable to tear her eyes from the screen.

Ronnie smooths her dress over tennis-honed thighs and pushes her sunglasses up onto her head. 'Oh, I wouldn't charge you; you'd be doing me a favour.'

'Really? How do you work that one out?' Dale's expression is quizzical.

Veronica's smile is indulgent. 'My godson, Harry, is staying there for the summer. He's been travelling around Europe for a few weeks. Bless him, he's at a bit of a crossroads. He has a business degree from Cambridge, but now he's not sure he can hack a career in the City – and he's already had one false start as an intern. Anyway, his parents agreed to fund his travels as long as he learned a language along the way. So, now he's supposed to be learning Italian.' Veronica's laugh is affectionate. 'Harry's a good kid really – and smart, too – he should be, considering what his father spent on his education. Regardless, boys will be boys and I'd be somewhat reassured by a steadying adult influence.'

'Oh, I see.' Crestfallen, Susanne chooses her words carefully. The idea of babysitting someone else's son when her own is far away and much missed holds little appeal.

'Er, well… do you think Harry would mind sharing with three ladies?' she says eventually, adding, 'I mean, we wouldn't be very exciting company for him – would we, Dale?'

Dale flashes Susanne a desperate look, unsure how to answer.

Veronica crosses her legs and leans forward. 'Of course, the villa's huge so you wouldn't be under each other's feet. Even the pool's a decent size.' She stands and looks from Susanne to Dale. 'Why don't you think it over and let me know in a day or two?'

*

'Look, I get it, Susie. Cody's at his dad's all summer and you're wondering why the hell you should look after someone else's son. But I can't believe you'd turn down a month in Tuscany, in that fabulous villa for the price of a flight. I think we should go. You heard what she said: he's been privately educated and he's having a last fling... he's not some gormless teenager who'll be looking for mummy substitutes, is he?' Dale cackles with laughter. 'Because good luck with that! I bloody hate kids.'

Susanne rolls her eyes. 'You always say that. You're a teacher, for god's sake – I see right through you, Dale Morgan.'

Dale ignores her. 'Oh, please, Susie,' she whines, 'we *need* a holiday. Tell you what, let's put it to the vote – give Evie a call.'

'I'm not sure Evie's a real contender, is she? I think last night the prosecco was to blame.'

Dale's eyebrows shoot up into her floppy fringe. 'Oh really? I think she was pretty keen. Anyway, Evie's a sweetheart... I like her. She should come with us.'

Susanne nods. 'I'm glad. She's been through a lot. Nursing her mum at the end and everything; anyone would need a break after that.'

*

After she's waved Dale off, and as the evening yawns ahead of her, Susanne telephones Colin. 'Hello, it's me. How's my boy?'

'Cody's fine. He's been firing arrows this afternoon,' Colin says, mischief in his tone.

Susanne is horrified. 'He's been doing what?'

'He had a go at archery. All properly supervised. He loved it, the boy's a crack shot.'

'Oh my god! Col, are you insane? I don't want him doing danger sports while I'm not there!'

Colin is laughing now. 'Hardly a danger sport. There were children there as young as nine. Susie, cut him some slack. Melissa and I are taking good care of him.'

Ouch. It's a slap across the line. 'I wondered when you'd admit she was on the scene,' Susanne says, her tone as light as she can manage.

'Admit? Susanne, it's not a secret. You'd like her. Cody does, although I think her dog, Banjo, is the main attraction to be honest. Don't be surprised if he wants a mutt when he gets home.'

Susanne grimaces. 'I'll cross that bridge when I come to it.' Satisfied that her son is safe and happy, she moots the Tuscan trip.

'Go for it. That's a brilliant idea – you always have fun with Dale, and it'll stop you getting depressed while I've got Cody. You haven't mentioned Evie before though. Is she a new friend?'

'We met at the gym. She's had a tough year… she lost her mum recently,' Susanne says simply, wondering what the hell business it is of her ex-husband's.

'Okay, well, sounds like just what the doctor ordered. Book it up – and the sooner the better, most flights are full at this time of year.'

Susanne hangs up and steps out into the street where the late sun sits low in the sky like a big red penny. Then, heels clacking on the still-warm pavement, she trots next door but one and rings the doorbell.

'Veronica, thank you for your extremely kind offer,' she says, flashing her neighbour a winning smile, 'we'd love to stay at your beautiful house this summer – if you'll have us?'

CHAPTER SIX

Dale

'Three G and Ts, please. Oh, and make them all doubles,' Dale says in a clear voice, flashing white, even teeth at the air stewardess.

Susanne and Evie exchange worried looks.

'What?' Dale says, her blue eyes wide. 'My holiday started when school broke up. Let's start as we mean to go on, shall we?'

Evie shakes her head and appeals directly to the flight attendant. 'I'd like a diet Coke, please,' she whispers.

'Me too,' Susanne mouths, adding, 'So, this is going well – we can't even agree about in-flight drinks.'

The women sit three abreast: Evie strapped into the aisle seat, rigid with anxiety, Susanne in the middle, wrapped in fine cashmere layers, ready to savour the latest issues of *Vogue* and *Red* magazine, and Dale, long legs folded into the window seat, a brand-new thriller on her lap, the spine as yet unbroken.

Her thoughts turn to Helena. Only that morning, another text had arrived, imploring Dale to meet for coffee to sort things out. Dale had thumbed a reply: *Nothing to sort*. She had been about to press send when Susanne's words came back to her, so instead she'd deleted the text and blocked Helena's number. Why hadn't she thought of it sooner?

This trip was exactly what she needed, and the timing perfect. A clean break; from school, from London, and from hysterical, crazy would-be lovers. Their Tuscan adventure couldn't start soon enough.

Dale steals a glance at Susanne, who smiles and returns to her magazine. She drains the last of her gin and longs for another but is reluctant to drink alone and anyway, there's no point in peaking too soon, she muses, as she looks out of the window and tries to penetrate the clouds to the view below. Soon she falls into a light doze, waking only when the captain announces their imminent descent and the *fasten seatbelt* sign comes on.

It's early evening by the time they land, but despite the hour, the horizon shimmers mirage-like before them.

Susanne beams. 'Don't you just love that *woooph* of heat as you step down from the plane? And there's that smell, too. Unmistake-able… sort of lemons mixed with jet fuel,' she says, as they file across the tarmac at Pisa International Airport and straggle into lines at passport control.

'Makes me feel a bit sick to be honest, the smell I mean. I'll be glad when we get to the villa,' Evie says, a greenish tinge to her skin.

*

In the car rental bay, Dale's eyes roam the sleek lines of the scarlet SUV with its luxe leather interior and unmistakeable new-car smell. 'Bloody hell, Susanne! Can we afford this?'

Susanne smiles. 'Fab, isn't it? It's my treat, and to be honest I got a very good deal online.'

The women start to protest but Susanne waves their objections away. 'Anyway, I thought that three ladies away for more than a month would need a big boot,' she says as they begin to pile in suitcases and holdalls.

Evie hesitates. 'You don't mind, do you? About me not driving? It's just, I'm a bit nervous about being on the wrong side of the road in a strange car.'

'No, of course not. We've got this, haven't we, Susie?' Dale swaggers, itching to get behind the wheel.

Susanne nods. 'It's fine, Evie, love. I'll drive this time. Dale, you'll need to navigate, but we've got a built-in satnav so we should be fine.'

With the city of Pisa behind them, the women travel south-east, climbing high into the Tuscan hills as the light begins to fade and the sky becomes a violet canvas, streaked with fuchsia and apricot.

Dale feels a rush of excitement as they pull into a lay-by to take in the view.

'So beautiful,' Evie breathes as she surveys the undulating landscape. 'What are those tall, skinny trees called? They're exactly as I'd imagined.'

'Cypress trees,' Dale says, 'they're everywhere in Tuscany.'

Susanne sighs with pleasure. 'Yes, and according to Veronica, there are olive trees in our garden – and a fig tree, too.'

'Don't think I've ever eaten a fig,' Evie says.

'Stick with me, kid; you might be doing a lot of things on this holiday that you've never done before,' Dale says, a huge grin lighting her eyes.

*

It's dark by the time the women arrive at Villa Giardino – a dense, rural blackness pierced only by a smattering of stars and a sliver of opal moon. No lights are visible inside and it takes the women several attempts to find the entrance as they stumble around in the shadows.

'Note to self; buy a torch,' Susanne says when they finally locate an imposing front door using mobile phones to light their way. Bunch of keys in hand, Susanne tries each one before a resounding clunk allows them entry.

'Hello-oo?' Dale calls out, groping for the light switch and casting the stone-floored hallway in a pale golden light.

'Wow, it's quite grand,' Susanne says, 'look at all the paintings – these landscapes are beautiful.'

Bags left by the entrance, the women bypass a narrow passage that spurs off to the left and move through the main hallway towards the rear of the villa, putting on lights as they go. They peer into a comfortable-looking sitting room, its tan leather sofas clustered around a low glass table. Against one wall, a TV screen sits atop a heavy antique sideboard while bookshelves groaning with paperbacks, old copies of Italian *Vogue* and a generous supply of DVDs occupy the wall opposite.

Dale nods her approval. 'Wow, Ronnie doesn't do things by halves, does she? This place feels more like a proper home than a holiday house.'

They pass through a narrow arch and into a spacious modern kitchen, noticing at once the elegant French windows that open onto the garden.

Susanne beams. 'This all looks practically new,' she says, surveying the cream marble topped island and the traditional oak cabinets painted in an elegant shade of ivory.

'I wonder where the bedrooms are?' Evie says, stifling a yawn and adding 'Ooh, sorry. The journey has made me sleepy.'

Dale grins. 'Better find you a comfy bed then, hon,' she says, retreating along the hallway and into the separate passage with Susanne and Evie at her heels.

The layout is simple: three similar-sized rooms, each with en suite facilities and a window overlooking the hillside, line up in a row. But the final room they come to has a dual aspect with French windows overlooking the garden.

'This room has got your name on it, Susie,' Dale says, pulling back the curtain and trying to penetrate the darkness beyond. 'Ronnie's your neighbour, so it's only fair.'

Susanne starts to protest but Evie jumps in and echoes Dale. 'Yes, you should, Susanne,' she agrees, adding, 'I'll take the room next door – the wardrobe's a bit smaller, which is fine for me.'

'Cheers, Evie – we're all sorted then,' Dale says, adding, 'I wonder where Harry sleeps. There are a couple of rooms at the front we haven't looked in yet.'

Evie lowers her voice. 'He might be in bed already.'

Dale snorts, 'If he is, he's a lightweight – it's only ten thirty. He's probably gone out.'

They head back towards the kitchen, Dale pausing to listen outside two closed doors. Satisfied that the rooms are unoccupied, she peeps in and finds an unmade bed in one and a desk, chair and shelving in what appears to be a small study.

Having explored the villa's entire layout, Dale's thoughts return to her stomach. 'I'm starving,' she says, 'wonder if there's any grub in this joint. I think we can assume the shops are shut.'

Susanne nods and paces to the outsized fridge, emitting a little cry of delight. Inside there's a block of pecorino, two types of salami, some cooked chicken and a tub of olives. Two bottles of pinot grigio and several litres of water wink at them from the fridge door. On the island a hand-written note nestles beside two boxes of crackers, a paper bag bursting with ripe, scented tomatoes and a large ciabatta.

Welcome, ladies – Have gone into town for the evening. Please help yourselves to the food. See you all tomorrow. H x.

Evie eyes the fridge contents and claps her hands. 'Oh, how thoughtful. Bless Harry – that's so nice of him,' she says.

'Yes, isn't it?' Susanne agrees, finding a stash of glasses and wasting no time in opening the wine. 'At least we know he's got nice manners. Cheers. To Harry.'

Dale raises her glass. 'To Harry – and to adventure! I can't wait to explore tomorrow when it's light.'

CHAPTER SEVEN

Tuscany, July 2019

Susanne

Susanne wakes with a start, her heart racing, her hairline damp with sweat. There are sounds in the house – footsteps, a clatter of crockery and glass. Disorientated in the blackness, she gropes the nightstand for her mobile phone and swipes the screen: two fifteen.

As her breath begins to steady, the events of the last twenty-four hours judder into place. She's in Tuscany, at Veronica's villa with Dale and Evie. And Harry. Harry must have returned. Where has he been until this hour?

Parched from the wine, Susanne swigs water from the plastic bottle beside her. She lays still and listens for a while, but soon the house is silent again and she falls into a dreamless sleep.

*

'Good morning, Susie. How did you sleep?' Evie looks soft and pale in a pink sundress and flip-flops, her fine brown hair twisted into a clip at the nape of her neck.

Susanne beams. 'Great, thank you. Well, mostly. I woke up at around two, but I soon went back to sleep. Is that coffee you're drinking?' She heaps the strong aromatic blend into the still-warm stovetop pot before going to the open French windows and gazing out at the rustic garden beyond. 'Isn't it a glorious day?' she says, stepping barefoot out onto the warm ivory stone with Evie at her heels.

It's barely nine o'clock but already the sun burns high in a cobalt sky.

The women look at each other, joy shining in their eyes.

Susanne sighs. 'Can you believe we've got this place for the next five weeks? It's so beautiful.' She leans on a stone balustrade and gazes at the tiered garden below, her eyes roaming the scarlet geraniums clustered in terracotta pots, the vibrant pink pom-poms of the bougainvillea trees and hydrangea bushes. In the borders, a sweep of quivering lavender vies with blue-flowered rosemary and dusty sage, while tiny white jasmine stars cling to a wall below. Inhaling their delicate scent, Susanne takes the half dozen steps down to the tiled terrace where the pool glitters hypnotically.

Evie follows. 'Do you think it's deep? I can't swim properly,' she says, pausing at the pool's edge.

'Maybe you can practise while we're here. I used to do a master class at the gym – I can help you if you like?' Susanne volunteers.

Evie hesitates, her smile sheepish. 'Maybe.'

'Hey!' Dale waves and strides towards them looking the epitome of cool in denim shorts, a Nirvana vest and huge retro sunglasses. 'Morning, lovelies. God, it's like waking up in paradise after grey London.' She inclines her head towards the pool and nudges Susanne. 'Are we going in then?'

Susanne shakes her head. 'Not me, I need my breakfast first. We all do, surely? Why don't we drive into the village and stock up? I'll feel better when there's more food in the house and we've got our bearings.'

Dale nods. 'Good idea. Hey, any sign of Harry yet?'

'Not exactly, although I think he got home around two this morning. I heard someone moving about,' Susanne says.

Dale thrusts her hands into her pockets. 'Sounds about right. We used to stay up all night at his age, eh, Susie?'

'You probably still do, but I need my beauty sleep,' Susanne says with a ruffle of her friend's hair.

*

After a trawl through a ring binder stuffed with restaurant menus, maps and leaflets for castles, museums and markets – all curated with great care by Veronica herself, and complete with handwritten post-it notes – the women set out for the nearest *supermercato* less than three kilometres away.

'Let me drive this time, go on, Susie,' Dale pleads, as she slides into the driver's seat with the enthusiasm of a teenage boy getting into his first car.

Susanne laughs. 'I don't know why it's so exciting to you – driving can be such a bore.'

Dale rolls her eyes. 'Says the woman who drives a brand-new Range Rover. Sweetie, I haven't got a car, have I? It's nice for me to have a blast, especially on these roads,' she says, putting her foot down and creating a swirl of dust as they hare off down the hillside.

Susanne looks back at Evie strapped tight to the back seat. 'You okay?' she mouths, sensing her friend's discomfort.

Evie's smile is brave but hesitant, the whiteness of her knuckles giving her away as she clutches the central arm rest.

Ten minutes later, Dale swings into the shop's small car park and lopes towards the store.

Susanne winks at Evie. 'How to make an entrance!'

'Well, come on! I'm hungry,' Dale says over her shoulder as Susanne and Evie step from the SUV.

'What's new?' Susanne mutters.

Once inside the shop, Susanne sniffs the air like a terrier, enticed by the aroma of delicious Tuscan produce. In no time, she has filled a small trolley with fruit and salad, bread, pastries, cheese and several varieties of Italian sausage.

'Pick whatever you want, ladies. I'll get these,' she says, dismissing any arguments with an impatient wave. 'We can sort the money out later, but let me buy these bits, please?'

Dale disappears into the wine aisle and returns with several bottles and a packet of potato crisps the size of a pillow.

'Ooh, now you're talking; we are on holiday after all,' Susanne says, adding Dale's stash to the trolley.

'Evie? Anything you particularly want?' Susanne asks.

Evie shakes her head. 'No, thanks, I'm easy. We do need to split the bill though, Susie. We all need to pay our way.'

'Yeah, whatevs,' Dale says, grabbing a Toblerone the size of her forearm and tossing it into the trolley.

*

Susanne gasps and pauses mid-stride. At the edge of the pool, half leaning up on his side, a bronzed young man is reading a paperback. He sets the book down and runs a hand through the floppy fringe of closely cut espresso-coloured hair.

Feeling voyeuristic but unwilling to break the spell, Susanne watches from the shadows.

'Susie? Where shall I put the—' Dale is beside her now. 'Oh! Is that Harry?' she whispers, pushing her sunglasses up onto her head.

'Who else?' Susanne mouths.

'Shit the bed!' Dale lets out a throaty laugh.

The man–boy gets up and stretches muscled arms above toned, broad shoulders, before climbing the steps towards the house, his movements languid, fluid.

'He totally did that for effect!' Dale says out of the corner of her mouth.

Susanne stifles a giggle. 'Yes, he did, didn't he?'

He's walking towards them now, an indolent grin on his handsome face.

'Oh gosh,' Evie says, emerging from the kitchen, her mouth settling in a silent 'O'.

'Hello! I'm Harry. Sorry I wasn't here to welcome you all,' he says a practised smoothness to his tone.

Dale thrusts out her hand, first to introduce herself.

Susanne's smile is warm. 'Hi Harry. I'm Susanne and this is Evie. Your godmother's my neighbour – so lovely of Ronnie to let us stay. Hope we won't be disturbing your peace while you're studying.'

Harry raises an eyebrow.

'Italian? Ronnie said you were learning?'

'Oh, of course,' he nods, 'no, not at all. I'm more interested in the practical side. Nothing beats hanging out with Italians. Such a beautiful language; *molto romantico*, don't you think?'

Harry's accent is warm toffee sauce poured over ice cream. Everything about his demeanour drips wealth, privilege and confidence, as he stands tall, shirtless and unabashed before three women he has never met before. Susanne wonders what relation he is to punctilious Veronica.

Evie, who hasn't said a word since Harry introduced himself, is growing pinker by the second. 'I'll just finish unpacking,' she mumbles, diving back into the sanctuary of the shady kitchen.

Seconds tick by before Susanne breaks the silence. 'Harry, thank you for leaving us a snack last night. It was very thoughtful of you. We've just bought food in the village. Why don't I knock up some lunch for all of us? We can drag the table into the shade and eat out here.'

Harry smiles on cue. 'If you're sure, that would be lovely,' he says. 'Can I help with anything?'

'Cheers, but we've got this,' Dale says before she follows Evie inside.

Susanne and Harry are left alone, gazing at each other until she looks away.

Ronnie had said her godson was clever, but she'd neglected to mention his model looks. There's a pricking sensation under her arms and beads of sweat begin to pool between her breasts.

'It's so hot,' she says, to break the silence. 'Is it like this every day?'

'Yes, most days. But then it is the end of July, so…' Harry shrugs. There's a pause, before he releases them both. 'Well, thank you for the offer of lunch. If you're sure there's nothing I can do…'

CHAPTER EIGHT

Evie

The lizard's smile is benign. Little longer than Evie's thumb, its pewter-and-emerald scales gleam in the morning sun. Evie sits hugging her knees, paralysed by a blend of fascination and revulsion until with a flick of its tail the creature vanishes back into the lavender.

All her life Evie has been afraid of reptiles. Now she considers the possibility that they are all around her. She pulls her cardigan around her shoulders, despite the intense heat.

No doubt Dale would laugh at her, ridicule her timidity; perhaps she'd have picked the lizard up, just to demonstrate Evie's silliness.

Bold, beautiful, no-nonsense Dale. Evie imagines her at the tough south London school where she works, holding the rapt attention of her class. Twenty-odd hormonally charged fourteen-year-olds under her spell, the boys damp with adolescent desire, the girls in awe of her strength and urban style.

Evie has never met a lesbian before – well, not that she knows of – and is a little intimidated. Then again, the sensations of wrong-footedness and embarrassment are as familiar to Evie as hunger and thirst.

She has been watching the playful, easy, almost sisterly interaction between Susanne and Dale with a stab of envy. Susanne is always so thoughtful and quick to include her, but Evie cannot compete with a shared history that's been decades in the making.

She pinches white pudgy knees, wishing her legs would tan like Susanne and Dale's. She'd barely got to grips with being around the two of them – always feeling like a stout little pigeon in a lagoon of flamingos. But then Harry had burst into their trio and changed the dynamic again, just as Evie was beginning to lower her guard.

It isn't her fault that she is so different to them: that her dad had died of lung disease when she was little, or that her mum had been a dinner lady at the local primary school and a part-time cleaner, yet somehow people always seemed ready to judge her for it.

Well, Evie reasons, at least no one can accuse her of not having nice manners; her mum had made sure of that. Not like some of Harry's type. Boys like him have always made her miserable and she's seen enough of them to last her a lifetime.

At the solicitors' where she'd worked, half the law interns (including some who didn't need to earn a living) had talked down to her, making her feel small and common. It had always amazed Evie that a fine education, backed by wealth and privilege, seemed no guarantee of decency. Quite the reverse: she'd seen the firm's partners on corporate away-days; the men, stumble-drunk and wet-lipped, preying on secretaries and junior solicitors, then closing ranks against anyone who dared to speak up.

Evie offers a silent plea: please don't let Harry get in the way of her new friendships.

Tears well in her blue eyes. Sometimes a wave of grief can catch her off guard. At least this morning she is alone, hiding behind period pain – which, thanks to two ibuprofen, isn't so bad now.

Susanne had made a valiant effort to persuade her to go with them to San Gimignano, where they planned to shop in the market, wander around the antiques fair they'd seen advertised online, then have lunch at a family restaurant that Harry recommended. Overwhelmed by the day's agenda, Evie had cried off and confided in the girls that her tummy ached.

So after a breakfast of toast, honey and figs picked fresh from the garden (which Evie had spat into a tissue when no one was looking – the sweet grittiness had made her shudder), they'd gone out in two cars; Susanne driving the SUV, while Harry had roared off ahead in his black jeep, as he'd 'people to see' in the afternoon.

Evie wonders how Harry can possibly have friends in San Gimignano; like the women, he's only come on holiday. On the other hand, he is self-possessed, good-looking and speaks a smattering of Italian. It's easy to see how people could be charmed by him and sucked into his orbit. Like her friends seem to be.

Especially Susanne. Evie has seen the way Harry and Susanne look at each other. It's unseemly, what with him being only twenty-four and Susanne forty-two. She'd overheard Dale teasing Susanne about it, too, and in quite a coarse way. Susanne had denied it – said that Harry reminded her of Cody and that he was a 'sweet kid' doing his best to be helpful and polite. Evie could tell at once that Dale hadn't bought into that excuse any more than she had.

By one o'clock, the garden is veiled in a shimmering heat-haze. Evie has seen the lizard again and has named it Linford to stop herself feeling afraid (although she concedes that there may be hundreds of 'Linfords' in Veronica's lush garden).

She shifts on her sunbed; her black swimsuit is cutting in now and sweat has pooled beneath her, dampening the towel she's lying on. To her dismay, she realises that her shoulders, arms and chest have reddened.

The water tempts her with its sparkle. Nobody can see her now. No one is home to judge or laugh at her flawed body or meagre attempts to swim. With her sarong clutched about her, Evie walks to the pool and bends to run her hand below its surface.

Then using the steps, she lowers herself in, her breath catching as the water reaches first her waist, then her chest. For a nanosecond, panic rises; what if she slips and drowns, and the others return to find her bobbing like a bloated porpoise, her skin puce and blistered by the sun?

'Oh, for goodness' sake, Evie, get a grip!' she hisses, bending her knees so that she is in up to her neck. She turns her face to the sky, takes a deep breath and allows a wave of pleasure to wash over her for the first time since arriving two days ago.

CHAPTER NINE

Dale

She'd blocked Helena from her smartphone, and it had seemed like an inspired idea at the time. But now Dale finds herself wondering if somewhere in the ether hundreds of messages have built up, each one more vitriolic than the last.

'But, Dale, why do you even care?' Susanne says, keeping her eyes on the road ahead, adding, 'God, I wish Harry would slow down a bit. I can't keep up and this car is no slouch.'

'Good question. I suppose it's a karma thing, you know. I don't want her to feel hurt. I think I might be done with women. It's not the first time this has happened to me.'

Up ahead, Harry's brake lights come on as they hurtle downhill and into a hairpin bend before the jeep slows to a crawl and waits for them.

Susanne flashes her headlights in thanks. 'Dale, sweetheart, please try and forget about it. Look around you. The scenery is incredible – breath-taking. I don't know how you can even think about what's going on in London.'

Dale arches an eyebrow. 'So, you haven't thought once about Cody, then?'

'Of course, he's on my mind the whole time, but that's different – he's my son. Anyway, what do you mean, you might give up women – for what, men?'

Dale lets out a bark of laughter. 'Christ, no! I meant I might swerve off relationships, period. Speaking of which, do you believe Evie?'

'What, that she has a stomach ache? Yes, of course. Why else would she say so, and stay at home on her own?'

Dale chews her bottom lip. 'Don't know… just a feeling. Do you think she's scared of me? You know, sees me as some big scary lesbian?' Ahead, Dale spots the crumbling remains of a church and interrupts herself. 'Oh, wow, look at that! Do you think it was a monastery once?'

'Maybe. It looks medieval, and beautiful, in a creepy kind of way,' Susanne says as she refocuses on the road. 'Look, Evie's fine. I know she's incredibly straight and she's not like us, but she's such a loyal little thing and so thoughtful.'

Dale shakes her head, aghast. 'Oh my god, Susanne. Have you any idea how patronising you sound? She's not a puppy. Oh, just ignore me… it's good to have different kinds of friends – and you know what they say: opposites attract.'

Susanne slows down and pulls up to Harry's bumper as he joins a line of traffic outside the city walls. 'Hey, this is it,' her eyes shine with happiness, 'and it looks stunning.'

*

Heady with the scent of citrus and tobacco, San Gimignano throbs with life. The cacophony of sounds from every direction and the riotous rainbow of colour in the market square makes Dale's senses swim.

'God, I love Italy!' She tucks Susanne's arm into hers. 'You glad we came?'

Susanne nods. 'Yes, I love it here. It feels like we're on a film set.'

Harry flashes them a wide smile, his dark eyes hidden by designer sunglasses. 'You two belong here. Look around you – most of the English tourists couldn't look more obvious if they were carrying a banner.'

Dale snorts. 'Not the best-looking country, are we?' she says, eyeing a rotund couple in their fifties, faces reddened by sun, sweat stains visible on their clothes.

Susanne affects disapproval. 'Don't be mean, you two. Anyway, Harry – you can talk, you look more Italian than half the Italians.'

'I'll take that as a compliment,' Harry says, changing direction to avoid a bottleneck in the crowd.

Dale pauses in front of a stall piled with citrus fruits. 'Ooh, look – lemons as big as rugby balls, and he's selling limoncello. I love that stuff; I could drink it for breakfast. Let's get a couple of bottles. Harry, you can practise your Italian, help us to get a good deal.'

Harry laughs. 'I'm not sure I'm up to haggling, but I'll have a go.'

Susanne's smile is indulgent. 'Aww, he's so sweet,' she whispers to Dale, her head to one side.

Dale makes a face. 'He just likes showing off,' she says, keeping her voice low.

After some lively banter with the stallholder, Harry turns to the women. 'He'll cut us a deal; if we buy two bottles, the second is half price,' he says looking pleased with himself.

Dale's eyes widen. 'Well done – not bad for a beginner,' she says, producing her debit card and inserting it into the machine. 'Hey, Harry, ask him how much three bottles would be,' she adds as an afterthought.

Susanne rolls her eyes and tugs at Dale's forearm. 'What are you like? Come on, let's pace ourselves, shall we?'

Dale allows herself to be pulled away from the market square and into narrow streets that teem with tourists.

Harry strides uphill. 'Shall we have lunch? There's this really cool place I'm dying to show you. You watch, it'll be quiet except for a few locals – that's why I like it.'

Dale nods her approval. 'I'm in, just lead the way.'

*

Nestled in a small courtyard with an overpriced novelties' shop to one side, and a fancy handmade chocolate store to the other, they find Bar Montebello.

'How on earth do you know this place?' Susanne asks as she ducks under a low arch and into a cool, tiled café where a dozen or so people are already eating lunch at gingham-clad tables.

Harry's response is vague. 'I've been here with friends a couple of times,' he says, greeting the owner with a handshake. 'Ladies, this is Enzo. It's his family's bar.' Harry ushers them towards a corner table.

Susanne studies the menu and sighs. 'I know I shouldn't, but I can't resist fresh pasta,' she says.

'And why the bloody hell not? Look at you – you're built like a mop!' Dale answers, impatience in her voice.

'You're both gorgeous for your—' Harry stops mid-sentence.

'For our ages…? Not cool, Harry. Believe me, that's never a compliment,' Dale says.

Embarrassed, Harry studies the menu, just in time for a young man who looks remarkably like Enzo to take their orders.

By the time their food arrives, Dale is practically salivating. '*Buon appetito*,' she says, using the only Italian she's learned – other than *saluti*, the Italian word for cheers. Grinning, she digs into the mound of *paglia e fieno* in front of her, savouring its rich creamy sauce speckled with peas and prosciutto and laced with parsley and parmesan.

'So, how are you related to Veronica?' Susanne asks, dabbing tomato sauce from her lips with a napkin.

Harry takes a sip of water. 'My mum and Veronica are cousins,' he says.

'Ah, I see – so Ronnie's your aunt, as well as your godmother?' Susanne says.

'I think the technical term is "first cousin once removed" or something. Anyway, she's just Veronica to me. How long have you two been friends?' Harry asks.

'Forever. We grew up in the same street in south London, but we became best friends at grammar school,' Dale says, before cramming a huge swirl of tagliatelle into her mouth, her expression one of utter bliss.

'Cool. I can't imagine I'll know anyone that long,' Harry says, mopping up the last morsel of arrabiata sauce.

'That's because you're a baby, but it'll happen, and before you know it,' Susanne smiles.

Dale nods. 'She's right. Anyway, Harry, don't feel you have to hang out with us old birds. I mean, it's sweet of you to show us the route here, and this place of course, but if you've got stuff to do and people to see, go for it,' she says.

Harry places a hand over his mobile phone; it has already buzzed twice during lunch. 'Well, if you're sure you're okay getting back to the villa, I was planning to meet someone this afternoon.'

'You go, have a lovely time, Harry. We'll get this, won't we, Dale?' Susanne says, her lips curving into a smile.

'Of course. Have fun, Harry – see you later,' Dale says, as she turns her attention to the dessert menu.

CHAPTER TEN

Susanne

As July melds into August, the women fall into a gentle routine, adapting their natural roles and habits to accommodate each other. To their collective delight, they discover that Veronica has laid on a weekly visit from Rosa, a cleaner from the next village, tasked with replacing bedding and towels as well as blitzing the bathrooms and vacuuming the house throughout.

But far from feeling relaxed and blissed out by the Tuscan sunshine, Susanne is restless and discombobulated. Why hasn't Cody returned her texts or calls? It's too much; he knows she gets anxious.

She pictures her son playing happy families with Colin and Melissa, doing regular ordinary, companionable stuff together – a life that seems beyond her grasp.

After two days of radio silence, she's relieved when a text arrives from Colin telling her that they've taken a cabin in a forest resort for a few days and that Cody is loving his adventure. Three photographs ping through in quick succession: Cody in walking boots, a backpack on his shoulders, with Banjo at his heels; Cody beside a campfire he's presumably helped build, a faraway expression in his eyes. The last photo is a close-up of Colin and Cody; all goofy grins and thumbs-up to camera. With a pang of sadness, she realises that Melissa must have played photographer.

It's seven o'clock and outside there's a volley of laughter followed by the throb of familiar dance music. Susanne puts down her smartphone and steels herself to return to the others. She'd excused herself to read and shower, but she's done neither; instead she's checked Cody's social media feeds and re-read old text messages.

It shouldn't matter to her that Col has met someone else. They've been divorced for three years and Melissa is certainly not the first. But is she the last? Is she *The One*? Because that hurts. A lot. She, Susanne, was supposed to be The One – the envy of all her friends and living the dream, until one day, something unseen and stealthy had crept up and eroded Susanne and Colin's love. Maybe it would hurt less if she'd met someone herself. But apart from two brief (and in hindsight, totally unsuitable) flings, there's been no one. And it hadn't mattered because Cody had always been enough. Now, Susanne feels the cold shadow of his burgeoning independence fall across her, as adolescence gallops towards adulthood, to a time when he won't need her anymore.

An excited, happy shriek from the garden jolts her back to the present. It's a relief that Evie and Dale are on easy terms after a cagey start. Not that Evie has spoken against Dale (she is far too timid for that), but Susanne has seen Evie's crushed expression whenever Dale insists on banging on about their past antics at school. Stories often wildly embellished and which make the pair of them sound like extras from a St. Trinian's film.

And then there's the Harry Factor. Susanne had expected a naïve boy, but instead she'd been confronted with an urbane, attractive man, mature for his years, as well as clever, well-mannered and accommodating. After all, he'd been there first, had expected to be alone all summer, and to come and go as the mood took him. Then, bam! Three older women rock up to cramp his style. Under the circumstances, it is a mark of his considerable maturity that he hasn't spent the last week sulking. Instead Harry seems relaxed in the women's company, choosing to sunbathe poolside with them during the daytime, sporadically putting down his paperback or removing his headphones and joining in their conversation. And on the nights when Harry stays in rather than seeking the company of his mysterious friends (as Susanne thinks of them), he is content to drink wine in the kitchen, and even to help with dinner preparations which the women share equally.

To everyone's delight, they've discovered a rustic pizzeria nearby. Gino, the owner, is happy for them to order a nominal amount of food and copious amounts of wine. They'd spent a giggly evening getting drunk on Frascati and limoncello shots, before Harry had driven them home, having consumed only a beer. And yet, for all his acts of chivalry and friendship, something about him disconcerts Susanne.

It doesn't help that Harry creeps into her dreams; dreams so real that she wakes up confused as to whether the events have actually taken place or not. In one – on the night of the pizzeria visit – Susanne had woken with a start, slick with sweat, confused and dehydrated, to find Harry at the foot of her bed. Then he'd gone to the window, pulled back the drapes and whispered, 'Come skinny-dipping with me, the water is perfect.'

In the morning, she'd been woken much too early by sunshine falling across her face. Surely she'd closed the curtains, even in her drunken state? Then in a fuzzy, surreal gush, the vision had come back to her, leaving her rattled for most of the day.

Even before the dream, Dale had called her out, asked her if she fancied Harry – and in front of Evie, too. Susanne had denied it of course, and told Dale not to be so bloody silly, claiming that any feelings she had for Harry were strictly maternal, given that her own son was only nine years younger.

A soft knock at the door interrupts Susanne's thoughts.

'Just a minute,' she calls.

She is surprised to see Harry, dressed in an open shirt, ripped blue jeans and flip-flops.

'Hi. I thought you were Dale.' Her voice catches and she clears her throat. 'Everything okay? Sounds like you're having fun in the garden.' Susanne attempts a smile, but it feels stiff and mask-like.

'We'd have a better time if you joined us. Susanne, are you all right? You seem a bit sad today. What can I do to help?' Harry's voice is soft and low.

'Thanks, but I'm fine. I'm missing my son – he's not brilliant at keeping in touch. Anyway, I've just heard from his dad, and they're having a great time, so panic over,' Susanne says with a nervous, wobbly-headed laugh.

'I'm sorry. It must be a wrench, being away from someone you love so much. If I were Cody, I wouldn't want to leave you for a moment.' Harry's voice is a whisper. He takes a step towards her and is so close now that Susanne can see the slight sheen of sweat on his brow, smell his green, woody fragrance. She feels her heartbeat quicken as their eyes lock; any closer and Harry's face will brush hers…

'Hello-oo?' Dale's voice. 'Oh, has the party moved in here?' Her tone is suspicious.

'Hi! No, I'm on my way. Thank goodness Harry came looking for me, I'd fallen asleep,' Susanne lies, wondering if Dale can tell how flustered she is.

Dale hesitates, opens her mouth to speak, then wordlessly turns on her heel and stalks off down the corridor.

Harry smiles but without warmth; a strange, wonky grin that Susanne has never seen before.

'See you on the terrace then,' he calls over his shoulder as he walks away, laughing softly.

Susanne shuts her bedroom door and tries to compose herself. What the hell was *that*? Had Harry been about to kiss her? Heart pounding, she goes into the bathroom and splashes cool water on her hot cheeks.

CHAPTER ELEVEN

Evie

After ten days of relentless cobalt skies and golden sunshine, Evie feels a surge of energy and a lightness she hardly recognises.

Her skin has lost its usual pallor and is lightly tanned. Freckles decorate the bridge of her nose, giving her a youthful glow, and her hair has gained natural highlights that sparkle in the sun. Adamant not to let the pounds pile back on, Evie has taken to power-walking before breakfast, picking a stony path down to the local village and winding back up through vineyards beaded with golden grapes.

Dale is first to comment on her modest transformation. 'Bloody hell, Evie, Tuscan life suits you. You look disgustingly healthy,' she says, slathering on sun cream, ready to top up her tan.

'Thank you, Dale. I'll never be as slim or as brown as the two of you, but I—'

'Hey, stop it! Enough with the self-deprecation. Learn to take a compliment, woman. You look fab – doesn't she, Susie?'

Susanne puts down her paperback. 'Yes, you do look very well, Evie.' She stretches like a cat. 'We need to find you a lovely man now, to go with your hot new image.'

Evie shakes her head. 'Oh, I don't think that's on the cards. I've never had much luck with blokes.'

Dale sniggers. 'You and me both, hon. But you've had boy-friends, right?'

Evie chews her lip and considers, 'Well…'

Dale shoots upright, a look of incredulity on her face. 'Oh my god. Evie, you have had relationships, haven't you? What are you – forty next birthday? Please tell me that you're not a virgin.'

Evie studies the pattern of her sarong. 'No, I'm not… one of those…' She squirms on her lounger. 'Actually, there have been two… men, I mean. One was Paul, a mechanic from Orpington. He had a nice smile and he was kind, you know? Thoughtful. We were together for seven years. My mum always liked Paul; she thought we'd get married. So did I, I suppose… but in the end, we just fizzled out.'

Susanne rolls her eyes. 'Well, *he* doesn't sound very exciting. What about the other guy?'

'Um, he was a mistake.' Evie says in a small voice, a deep furrow appearing in her brow.

And she is back there – in the bland, stale-smelling hotel room in Maidstone, with its cheap, standardised MDF furniture and its big bed with a too-thin duvet, a chorus of goodbyes and shouts of 'Merry Christmas' rising from the car park below, as friends and colleagues pile into taxis. Wishing she were one of them, Evie eyes her green party dress, reduced to a crumpled rag beside rolled-up tights on the burgundy carpet.

There's a flushing sound, then a minor crash as Roland Pincott, lips puffy and wet, shirt open and flies undone, stumbles into the room where Evie waits in bed, a sheet clutched around her quivering body.

'Yum-yum, pig's bum,' Roland mutters, falling against Evie, his winey breath hot against her cheek. With a revolting slurping sound, he kisses her, then pushes her against the bed and lollops on top, forcing her arms above her head with his own. His breath is ragged, he's repeating her name, thrashing and groaning, before he stops abruptly and levers himself off with a protracted sigh.

'You're a cracking girl, Evie; I've always fancied you,' Roland growls. *'Discreet, too,'* he adds, before turning over and snoring like a wart-hog.

'Evie?' Susanne's voice is gentle.

'I'm fine. It's just… such a cliché,' she looks from Susanne to Dale knowing they are waiting for her to go on. She puffs out hot cheeks. 'The solicitors' where I used to work… One year, there was a big Christmas party at a hotel and quite a few people had rooms. Anyway, one of the partners… we'd been dancing and chatting for most of the evening and then at the end, he invited me up to his room for another drink. I knew what he meant really, but I was drunk by then, too, and it just seemed—'

'Like a good idea at the time? Yeah, alcohol does that.' Dale nods kindly. 'Evie, don't feel bad, we've all been there. Everyone's got a few drunken one-night stands in their closet. It's nothing.'

Susanne agrees. 'She's right. We all have to kiss a few frogs before the Prince comes along.'

'Or Princess,' Dale says with a wink.

*

That evening, drying her hair after a long, hot shower, Evie reflects on her confession. She'd been embarrassed to tell the girls her story – even remembering it had made her feel cheap and sordid. But they'd been lovely about it, made it sound normal and as though she was part of their club now. Not that Evie could imagine either of them in that situation. Susanne was simply too flawless and untouchable to let such a sleazy thing happen. As for Dale, she was so assertive, it was impossible to imagine her being coerced into anything she wasn't wholly invested in.

And yet, neither were in a relationship of any description. What chance did she have of meeting anyone, ever again? She'd always hoped – expected, even – that eventually, she'd date someone kind and sincere, fall in love, get married and have children, preferably one of each. But the closer Evie gets to forty, the more remote her fairy-tale ending seems.

The future scares her.

Orphan.

Her auntie Cath had been the first person to use the word after Jean died.

After the funeral, she'd hugged Evie, then pulled away with a defiant expression in her kind brown eyes. 'You might be an orphan, darlin', but while there's breath in my body, you've still got me – and your uncle Ken and your cousins, of course. I told my big sister I'd look after you, and I meant it. Okay, lovey? Fair enough?'

But Auntie Cath lives in Bromley; an hour's drive away in Jean's old blue Nissan Micra and a painful journey by public transport. Hardly conducive to spontaneous visits whenever Evie feels at a low ebb.

She swallows the fear and mounting anxiety that can suddenly overwhelm her. There is nothing for it but to put make-up on her newly sun-kissed face, pull on her favourite jeans, paste on a bright smile and join the others for dinner and drinks.

She wonders whether Harry will join them. Her stomach lurches with a mixture of dread and anticipation. His youthful demeanour, his energy and beauty make Evie feel clumsy and stolid around him. Sometimes, she can feel his eyes upon her, staring from behind the sunglasses he habitually wears; judging her, pitying her – and not in a kind way.

Worse still is that Harry makes Evie feel things she doesn't want to. Butterflies swirl in her stomach when he smiles, walks into a room or levers himself out of the pool, muscles taut, droplets of water glistening on his deeply tanned skin, tendrils of hair framing his face.

If Harry only knew the things that went on in Evie's head; the way she imagined him kissing her, completely naked and hard for her – his dark, lean body pressed against hers. It was embarrassing to have such ridiculous thoughts – as if someone with Harry's looks would even notice – let alone fancy her – at any age, never mind that he was fifteen years her junior. God, how he'd laugh at her if he had any inkling… and so would her friends!

Evie takes a deep and steadying breath, spritzes scent on her wrists, slides her feet into wedge-heeled sandals and goes to find the others.

CHAPTER TWELVE

Dale

Stir-crazy after two days of torrential rain, Dale paces like a caged tiger. The appeal of thrashing the others at Scrabble and watching back-to-back black-and-white movies from Veronica's vintage DVD collection has paled, and with the gardens and the pool temporarily out-of-bounds, the villa seems to shrink around her, making her waspish with the other women.

'Girls, I'm sorry. I love you both to bits but I need to get out of here. I'm taking the car; everyone okay with that?' she announces, shoving her wallet, keys and a paperback into her big slouchy bag.

Susanne's eyebrows shoot up. 'Of course. But where are you going? Shall I come with?'

'Thanks, Susie, but I fancy a few hours alone. Think I might be a bit hormonal. You don't mind, do you? I'll just head off and see where I end up.'

'Ooh, you are brave, Dale. Aren't you afraid you'll get lost, or run out of fuel?' Evie says.

'No, of course not,' Dale barks. 'There's a satnav in the car and I've got a purse full of plastic; there are petrol stations in Italy, you know. Ciao.'

Outside, Dale takes a deep breath. The air is heavy with the earthy scent of jasmine, rain and dust. Who knew it could pour so hard (and for so long) in Tuscany in August? She turns the collar of her denim jacket up and climbs into the SUV, before tearing off down hills bathed in grey-green light, stopping outside the pizzeria to programme the satnav.

Shit. She hadn't meant to cut Susanne and Evie short and leave in such a rush. But god, she really did need her own space. Evie, bless her, had no confidence – nor much in the way of street smarts, that was for sure. And as for Susanne, between mooning about Cody, spending half her time checking her phone for messages from Scotland *and* surreptitiously watching Harry when she thought no one was looking, Dale hardly recognises her oldest friend.

Sitting in the bar in Tunbridge Wells when they'd first talked of getting away, Dale had pictured the three of them on a giddy whirl-wind of cocktails, culture and countryside; discovering glamorous bars full of chic Italians, taking in museums and galleries, and driving through beautiful vineyards, stopping for impromptu picnics. Instead, Susanne and Evie seem content to spend their days at Villa Giardino.

She reaches across to the glove compartment for an Italian guidebook bought in London, and scans the pages, stopping at a chapter on Siena. All those magical images of the medieval city she knows so well from books and movies – it would be a crime not to visit. Using the satnav, she plots a route; only fifty-five minutes. She can have lunch in Piazza del Campo, home of the biannual Palio horse-race; shop for shoes in Via di Città and visit the cathedral, with its liquorice-striped columns and exquisite art. *This* is what she came to Tuscany for!

As if offering a sign, the rain slows to a light drizzle and the sun peeks through silvery clouds.

Dale finds a radio station playing rock music and puts her foot down.

*

The rain has stopped, the sky is a delicate wash of azure and steam rises from the sun-warmed cobbles. Sipping caffè macchiato in Piazzo del Campo, the view of its terracotta-hued palazzo and bell tower in front of her, Dale messages Susanne: *Siena lovely, wish you were here. Sorry for being a grumpy cow.* She attaches a selfie and presses send – and is relieved to get her friend's text by return.

Have a fab time – love you. X

Bless Susanne and her sweet, fragile heart. Other friends may be taken in, but not Dale. She's simply known her for too long. She's seen the way people make catty assumptions based on Susanne's looks and trappings of prosperity: as if money were a magic bullet against heartbreak.

Dale purses her lips. That's what happens when you let kids (or *a* kid, in Susanne's case) rule your life. Cody needs to stop acting like a selfish little shit. How dare he leave his mother out in the cold – after all she's done for him? A thought occurs: is missing Cody the real reason for Susanne's peculiar interest in Harry? Some misplaced and inappropriate maternal sense that is confusing her? Well, not on Dale's watch! She's seen the way Harry looks at Susanne when he thinks there's no one around, and it's not filial. Like the time she'd caught him hanging around Susanne's bedroom. What the hell was that? She'd felt distinctly as though she were interrupting something.

Pushing the thought firmly from her mind, Dale gestures for the bill, pays and starts to walk away. On impulse she looks back at the Piazza which is bathed in sunshine and bursting with life. Aiming her smartphone camera, she shoots – just as a dozen cooing, pecking pigeons startle into the air, their fanned wings blurred by motion. It's a classic photograph. Laughing with joy at her lucky strike, Dale texts it to Susanne.

*

'You should get them. They look ah-may-zing.' The voice is American, cultured – East Coast perhaps.

'You think?' Dale answers, taking in the woman's chic, relaxed style. 'I don't know… I'd never pay that much for shoes at home.'

'All the more reason to treat yourself. First time in Siena?' The woman's grey-green eyes crinkle as she smiles.

'First time in Tuscany,' Dale admits. 'Always wanted to visit though.' She gazes in the mirror, turning her foot this way and that, admiring the black-and-tan faux-python ankle straps from every angle and grins. 'Maybe you're right. They do look pretty special, don't they?'

'You know you want to,' the woman drawls, her eyes sparkling with mischief.

Dale mimes her arm being twisted up her back. 'Okay, you talked me into it. Just hope I can find an excuse to wear them.'

'Well, here's an idea: how about you join us for cocktails this evening. There's a terrific bar a couple of blocks away.'

Dale pauses. So many issues raised in one throwaway invitation – and all under one overarching question: is the woman hitting on her?

'I'm afraid I won't be here this evening,' Dale says, before she can overthink things. 'Thanks for the thought, er—'

'Amanda. Amanda Blake.'

'I'm Dale,' she says, shaking the woman's tanned, beringed hand.

'Well, that's a shame. Enjoy the shoes, Dale. Hey look, the register's free – it's your turn now.' And with that, Amanda Blake is gone.

*

Everywhere Dale looks, something dazzles, glitters or gleams with opulence. Duomo di Siena is the most magnificent cathedral she has ever seen. Tucked behind a crocodile of animated French children, she struggles to take in the beauty of it all.

After half an hour, weary and overwhelmed by a vague sense of vertigo, Dale slides into a pew and bows her head to rest for a moment.

'Gets you that way, doesn't it?' The voice is warm, familiar. Dale raises her eyes and looks straight into those of Amanda Blake who now sits beside her.

'Hello, again. Yes. It's so beautiful, my head is throbbing.'

Concern on her face, Amanda begins rifling her handbag. 'Oh, that's not good. I have some Advil in my purse, if you—'

'I don't *literally* have a headache. I'm fine, but thanks anyway,' Dale replies, unsure whether or not she's comfortable with the woman sitting so close that she can smell her perfume; something delicate, floral – tea-rose, perhaps. 'I was just going,' she says, getting to her feet.

'Yes, me too. There's only so much Catholic iconography one can take on board,' Amanda says, as they file towards the exit. 'Care for that drink now?' she adds as they step out into the searing light and the thronging crowd.

Dale nods, realising that a) her throat is parched and b) she's intrigued by this friendly, stylish American. 'Good idea. I'll follow you. Are you alone?'

'Right now, yes. I'm travelling with my brother, Trey; he's back at the hotel. How about you?' Amanda says as they weave through narrow streets heaving with visitors.

'I'm near San Gimignano with a couple of friends.' Dale checks her watch; it is set to local time. 'Oh! It's gone five o'clock – I had no idea it was so late. I need to head off soon, or the girls will be worried,' she says, lining up her exit.

CHAPTER THIRTEEN

Susanne

Taken aback, Susanne gazes into the vacuum left by Dale moments earlier and wonders if she and Evie have let her down in some way. It wasn't *their* fault that it had been raining for two days straight. Neither is it their fault that Dale has the attention span of a flea at a funfair.

She's always been easily bored, even at school – especially at school. Charismatic from a tender age, and as a result, popular; it was one of Dale's few unattractive personality traits. Dale's ability to pick people up and then drop them so fast and from such a great height that they'd get motion sickness was legendary. Yet somehow their friendship had survived three decades' worth of drama as they'd clocked up life stages and milestones together.

Flashbacks of shared triumphs, failures and heartbreaks scud through Susanne's memory: Double-dating twins in sixth form and losing their virginity within a week of each other; both losing grandparents the year they turned twenty-one; a misspent holiday in Ibiza where they'd taken ecstasy for the first, last and only time, then danced all night and dozed all the next day.

Dale in jade-coloured silk as Susanne's only bridesmaid – gauche but giddy with happiness the day she'd married Colin Campbell at their local parish church; scroll forward to Dale, eyes moist with tears, as a tiny, warm terry-cloth bundle was placed in her arms the day Cody was born.

And then the bomb – which hadn't really been a bomb at all, but which Susanne felt under pressure to diffuse with as much skill as she could muster.

Dale, crouched on Susanne's cream carpet, hugs her knees, eyes downcast, guarding a secret. An empty bottle of merlot, two finger-printed glasses and a bowl of crisp crumbs sit between them on a low glass table. Susanne hears a shriek of laughter from six-year-old Cody, watching cartoons in the next room.

'What? Dale, just tell me. Nothing can be that bad,' Susanne says, becoming impatient.

When Dale finally speaks, her voice is thick with emotion and something else... fear?

'Yeah... it is. It's bad. Well, not exactly bad. But it's big and I don't know how you'll react.'

'Dale, you're my best friend. Please – just say it!'

'I'm gay.'

Finally.

Susanne nods her encouragement. 'Okay. Are you sure? I mean, I doubt Leo Boyle would say that, or Tony Marsh, or—'

'Trust me. I'm a lesbian. I fancy women. All those guys? Disasters! And you know what? The worst thing is that deep down, I've known for absolutely years and I just kept trying to make things fit, with blokes who I had absolutely no chance of ever falling in love with.'

'Jesus, Dale. You poor love.' Susanne quickly corrects herself, 'Sorry, that came out all wrong. I didn't mean "poor you, you're gay". I meant, poor you for feeling you had to hide it.'

'Susie, I know what you meant. Anyway, I'm done with hiding anything – from anyone. I've told Mum and Dad, which was horrible. They looked so... bewildered, and then when the penny dropped, the light completely went out of their eyes as they mentally kissed off having grandkids.'

'Oh, god. Bless them. They'll come around – give them time.'

'And other clichés,' Dale says, a note of bitterness in her voice, adding, 'What if they don't?'

'Darling, they will – you've always been so close. They won't stop loving their clever, beautiful daughter now, just because she prefers girls to boys, will they? That doesn't make sense.'

'I hope you're right.' Dale rakes a hand through her hair, nibbles her thumbnail.

Susanne nods, covers Dale's hand with hers. 'I know I am. And love, all I wish for you is that you meet someone amazing who makes you happy. It's what you deserve.'

And once it had all been said, it made total sense. There was no need to bang on or keep raking over it all. Dale preferred women. End of. It was just another facet of their friendship.

'Penny for them?' came Evie's voice.

Susanne starts. 'What, darling?'

'You were miles away, Susie.'

'Oh, I was just thinking about Dale. Look, I'm sorry she was a bit sharp. It's just her way, she doesn't mean to be rude,' Susanne says, compelled to make excuses for her friend.

'I hadn't noticed,' Evie says, her smile tight. 'Anyway, I hope she has a lovely day out – wherever she ends up. Hey, look, it's brightening up. Perhaps we can have lunch in the garden today.'

'Mind if I join you?' Harry appears freshly showered, his hair in damp tufts, book in one hand and empty coffee mug in the other.

Susanne is momentarily thrown off-kilter. 'Harry. I didn't know you were here. Where's your car?'

'Oh, I left it in the village last night. I had a few drinks at Gino's and walked home. You never know when the *polizia* might show up unannounced.'

'Gosh, you must have practically *swum* home – it was like a monsoon last night. You should have called, one of us could have picked you up,' Susanne says.

Harry smiles. 'Thanks, but it's only water; anyway, it was pretty late. I didn't want to disturb anyone.'

An awkward silence descends. It's almost noon; Susanne has spent an entire morning pottering around the villa with Evie, making breakfast, showering, dressing, tidying up and folding laundry – small, domestic tasks carried out on autopilot, and at no stage had she been aware of Harry's presence.

Susanne's thoughts turn to Cody. There is no mistaking when her son is around. His heavy footfall echoes from room to room as he thumps up and down the stairs; the indie guitar bands he listens to jangle from his bedroom; and he still shouts at the television – something he's done since he was three years old; a life-affirming, reassuring soundtrack that makes Susanne smile and banishes feelings of loneliness. By contrast, Harry, only nine years older, trails around the house silent as a shadow.

Something has subtly changed. Harry's friendly, open demeanour has been replaced by a cool stealth. She can feel him looking at her, as he holds the used coffee cup but makes no attempt to go past and into the kitchen. Under the heat of his gaze, her heart beats faster.

'Well, the rain's done nothing to cool the temperature, that's for sure,' Susanne says, fanning a hand in front of her face and wishing she could escape Harry's scrutiny.

'Here's an idea,' Evie says, 'why don't we all walk down to the village and get Harry's car together? We can buy a few bits for lunch – and something for dinner tonight.'

'Sure. Good plan, Evie,' Harry says, his eyes still fixed on Susanne.

'In fact, how about I make lasagne tonight?' Evie presses on, unaware of the strained atmosphere.

Susanne's smile is forced. 'Thanks, Evie, that would be lovely if you're sure. I'll just nip to my room and get a jacket... it's still spitting out there.' She moves towards the lobby area, conscious she must pass Harry to get to her room. 'Excuse me, Harry,' she says pointedly when he fails to stand aside.

Once on the road, the humidity makes the short walk to the village more arduous than usual and there's little talk other than deciding what to buy from the supermarket. Susanne steals a look at Harry, dressed today in low-slung jeans and his beloved aviator sunglasses. With a pang of discomfort, she realises that with their matching height and colouring, they could be taken for mother and son.

'Where did Dale say she was going?' Harry asks, as if feeling her eyes upon him.

Susanne shrugs. 'She didn't. I think she just fancied a change of scene. Dale's not one to sit about too long.' She smiles, adding, 'She has a lot more energy than me. Here we are. Harry, do you want to sit in the car while Evie and I nip into the supermarket?'

'Sure, take your time,' Harry answers, striding towards the jeep.

Once inside the store, Evie touches Susanne's arm. 'Are you all right, Susie? You seem a bit flat. Have I done something to annoy you?'

'Of course not, Evie – why do you say that?'

Evie tries again. 'Are you cross with Dale for going off on her own?'

'No, really. I'm fine. To be honest, I was just thinking about Harry – how he seems different. He was so sweet and smiley to begin with but now he seems... I don't know, withdrawn, or something.' Susanne bites her lip, conscious she's already said too much.

Evie nods slowly. 'I suppose the thing is, Harry's his own boss, isn't he? He never asked for us to turn up – maybe in his eyes we're like his parents!'

No one speaks much on the way back to the villa but by the time they've unpacked the shopping, the sun has broken through the blanket of cloud, instantly warming the terrace.

Days of heavy rain have showered the pool with debris and have clogged the surface with leaves, petals and seeds.

'We'd better call the pool man. There's a contact number in Ronnie's folder,' Susanne suggests, going inside to find the ring binder.

'I'll call him if you like.' Harry's voice, behind her, so close she can feel his breath on the back of her neck. Wordlessly, he slides an arm around her waist and pulls her tight against him.

'My god, Susanne, you're driving me crazy,' he breathes into her hair.

Shocked, a soft cry escapes Susanne before she can spin around to face him. Their eyes lock briefly before Susanne's gaze shifts beyond Harry and through the French windows to where Evie is at work wiping dust-speckled rainwater from the table and chairs.

'Harry! Please, don't—' Susanne begins, before he silences her with his lips and his tongue finds hers.

She pulls away, her heart thumping in her chest. 'Harry. Stop. We can't. We just…' She hesitates, opens her mouth to speak, then changes her mind and escapes to her room.

CHAPTER FOURTEEN

Dale

'As you Americans say, "Houston, we have a problem",' Dale dissolves into giggles.

Unruffled, Amanda regards her across the glass table between them. 'Let me guess; too many cocktails?'

'In one. These Cosmopolitans are stronger than I realised. I suspect I'm already over the limit to drive, my phone has run out of battery – and not a soul in the world knows exactly where I am.' Dale scans the minimalist bar, its all-white space filled with stylish Italians and tourists. The smell of money is intoxicating.

'Oh, and as if things aren't bad enough,' Dale adds, trying to make light of the situation, 'I may be a tiny bit underdressed.' Conscious of her crumpled street clothes, she straightens her spine and takes a gulp of her third Cosmo – or is it her fourth?

'It's a distinct possibility,' Amanda drawls, 'but at least you've got great shoes.'

'Oh, yes!' Dale feels under the table for the beribboned carrier bag, then flips off her grubby trainers and slides her feet into the elegant faux-python sandals. The result is an instant upgrade.

But her glee is short-lived. What the hell is she doing here with this stranger? This American of indeterminate age, who accosted her – not once, but twice – but who has yet to make a move on her.

Not for the first time, Dale pictures Susanne, frantic with worry. She picks up her phone and switches on, willing the handset back to life after a brief rest, but the screen remains resolutely black.

Amanda's stare is impassive. 'Are you okay?'

Dale nods. 'I'm fine – just figuring out what to do. A taxi home is out of the question – way too expensive from here.' She shrugs. 'Anyway, Amanda, tell me what else I should see before I leave Tuscany,' she asks, sliding her phone back into her bag, a sinking feeling in the pit of her stomach.

*

The cocktail-fuelled walk is an ungainly stumble – a shambolic dance of plaited feet and bumping hips.

'Ta da!' Amanda pauses outside a grand five-star international hotel; a trio of porters scurry forward before the women are even inside.

The receptionist's smile is serene. '*Buonasera*, signora Blake, your key?'

'Yes, thank you, Maria. Hey, am I too late for room service?'

'Not at all, it will be my pleasure. Please, just phone with your order.'

Dale's eyes widen. 'Wow, very swanky. How does she know your name? There must be a thousand guests here,' she says as they step into the lift.

'Because Trey and I have already been here for a week and I tip well,' Amanda answers, pressing a button marked 'Penthouse'.

From the moment the doors close, Dale feels trapped and edgy. She looks across at Amanda whose eyes are threaded with red now; her tan – a healthy golden glow in the afternoon sun – has waned to a sickly pallor in the harsh overhead light.

'This is us.' Amanda's feet falter as they pass along a thickly carpeted landing.

Panic swirls in Dale's gut. She has made a terrible mistake. She no more wants to sleep with Amanda than with her brother, Trey. What was she *thinking*? An impromptu and wholly inappropriate drinking session with a total stranger – and one who, justifiably, now has expectations – was a spectacular faux pas, even by *her* standards.

The what-ifs begin to pile up: what if the hire car gets impounded for being illegally parked overnight? What if it gets stolen? What if Susanne is so worried that she calls the police and Dale winds up on an Interpol database. And most scary of all, what if Amanda is some crazy millionaire who plans on keeping Dale captive as a sex slave?

Keep it together, Dale.

'Amanda. Look, I'm so sorry… I've really enjoyed this evening – too much, in fact. I don't normally drink so much,' the lie tumbles out before Dale can think of a better one, 'and I'm feeling nauseous.'

'That'll be hunger, I feel a little queasy myself. How about we order a couple of juicy burgers and some coffee – that should help,' Amanda says.

'That's sweet of you, but I…' Dale clams up, suddenly exhausted.

'Oh. I see what's going on here,' Amanda says, a bitter edge to her voice. 'You've just realised that you're not that into me, and that if we walk through that door,' she gestures ahead, 'you'll have to put out. Well, forget it.'

'No, I didn't mean—' Dale grimaces.

'You did, and it's fine. Good night, Dale – I'm sure the receptionist can help you with something,' Amanda swipes her key card, and bangs the door shut.

'Oh, for fuck's sake,' Dale says aloud as she marches back towards the lift, stumbling in her new heels.

Within five minutes, she has located the ladies' and has scraped together an emergency repair kit of spearmint gum, concealer, lipstick and hairbrush from her capacious handbag.

The wild-eyed woman looking back at her is beyond dishevelled. 'Hmm. Bag lady chic,' Dale mouths to the mirror. 'Well, just act like you own the place.' Then, head held high, she strides over to the reception desk.

'Good evening – again,' she says with what she hopes is a radiant smile.

'May I help, Madam?' Maria's expression is one of barely concealed amusement.

'Thanks, do you have a pay phone here?'

'Of course, take this corridor, Madam – walk past the restaurant and then turn left.' Dale is saved from making any further conversation as Maria's phone begins to trill.

Once inside one of the five old-fashioned telephone booths, Dale collapses onto the padded high stool and weighs up her options. Without access to her mobile, she cannot get into her contacts book; ergo she cannot call Susanne – the one person who can help her. The only telephone number Dale knows by heart is her parents' landline, etched on her memory since childhood.

Dale offers a silent prayer: *Please, please be at home, and please don't be in bed yet.* She is rewarded when her mother's smart 'telephone' voice pipes over the line.

'Mum, it's me, Dale. Can you hear me, Mum?' She swallows hard, suddenly emotional.

'Oh, hi darling. How are you? It's rather late… it's nearly ten o'clock. Is everything all right? Are you still in Italy?'

'Yes, sorry it's a bit late. I'm an hour ahead of you, too. Look, are you and Dad in bed? No? That's good. Mum, I need your help with something. You know that old-fashioned address book you use? The one with kittens on the cover that I always make fun of? Well, I need you to look up Susanne's mobile number for me, please…'

CHAPTER FIFTEEN

Susanne

Susanne can still taste Harry's kiss: his mouth pressed against hers, fresh and minty but muddled with something strange and earthy.

Had she kissed him back? She hadn't meant to, but Harry had caught her off guard and her body had responded without the slightest input from her brain.

It would not happen again. It *could* not happen again – she'd been crystal clear about that by marching off to her room.

Concealed by the drapes, she peers through her window to find Harry on the terrace, helping Evie to dry the table and chairs ready for lunch.

She can hear Evie's laughter now, a loud hooting as though Harry has said something hilarious. Are they talking about her? Evie looks towards Susanne's window. Oh god. Surely Harry wouldn't tell Evie about their kiss?

Deciding there's nothing to be done except to style it out, Susanne changes into a clean T-shirt, adds a slick of lip gloss and joins Harry and Evie in the garden.

'Here she is,' Evie says. 'How did you get on?'

Susanne's mind is a blank. 'Er… with what?'

'The pool man – will he come out to us? It's a terrible mess, although if we had a net, we could do it ourselves,' Evie says, wiping down the last chair and wringing the cloth into one of the flower beds.

With a knowing grin, Harry turns away and paces towards the pool.

Susanne hesitates. 'I… I couldn't find the number and then I needed the loo. I'll look again after lunch.'

*

'That was delicious, thank you, ladies. You'll both make wonderful wives,' Harry says, nursing an empty Peroni bottle, a mischievous grin on his face.

Pink spots appear on Evie's cheeks. 'Oh, that's all right. All we did was open a few jars and packets, isn't that right, Susie?'

Susanne's smile is glacial. 'He knows that, Evie. He's being facetious,' she turns to Harry, 'just as he knows it's 2019 and not the sixties.'

Harry grimaces. 'Sorry. It was just a joke and a lame one at that.'

Evie changes the subject. 'Wonder what Dale's doing right now?' She pops a last olive into her mouth.

'If I know Dale, she'll be in some fabulous café somewhere, chatting to the locals in shouty English and made-up Italian. Either that or shopping for clothes.' Susanne turns her gaze on Harry. 'What are *your* plans for the rest of the day?'

'None at all. I'm more than happy to hang here. It'll be nice to catch a few rays after the wet weather we've had.'

Evie's expression is wistful. 'You're both so brown already, you've no need to sunbathe – you are lucky.'

An image of Harry's lean, bronzed body against cool white sheets crashes into Susanne's mind; she hastily pushes it away.

'Susanne and I are a similar colour,' Harry says, brushing his arm against Susanne's to compare. 'See… we're the same.' A jolt of electricity sparks in Susanne as Harry deliberately grazes her thigh with the back of his hand.

Harry gets up. 'Tell you what, I'll clear the pool… it's only plant debris and I'm sure I can improvise.'

Evie claps her hands. 'Yay! It's funny, I've never been into swimming – too self-conscious, I suppose – but I've got used to having a little dip while we've been here.'

As the temperature climbs, a languid calm descends while the three of them read and doze by the pool.

Harry's efforts to clear the surface debris have paid off and one at a time, they each revel in the coolness of the water, swimming gentle laps.

Susanne treads water in the deep end, her face turned to the sun. She watches as Harry saunters over and prepares to get in beside her. 'I was just getting out,' she says, her tone brittle.

But Harry's smile is bold, confident. 'No need, there's plenty of room for both of us,' he lowers his voice, 'and don't worry about Evie, she's snoring her head off.'

Sure enough, Evie is lying with eyes closed and mouth open, her paperback collapsed on her chest, her left foot twitching.

Harry glides through the water with barely a ripple, and cups Susanne's face in his hands. 'I'm sorry, but you're just too fucking beautiful for words,' he breathes, tracing her lips with his index finger.

'Harry. Don't. I—' Susanne begins to object before allowing herself to be silenced by a long, deep kiss.

*

Nerves shredded, Susanne paces the living room. For the third time, she calls Dale's mobile. It goes straight to voicemail.

'Why is her phone off? I thought she'd be back by now. "A few hours alone", she said. That was before noon and it's nine fifteen.' Susanne rakes her hand through hair knotted by anxiety. She looks from Evie to Harry. 'Where the hell *is* she? Anything could have happened… she could have had an accident, or she could—'

'Be having the time of her life in some swanky bar, dancing the night away,' Harry offers, placing his hands on Susanne's forearms and forcing her to stop.

'Harry's right, Susie. She's probably lost track of time and hasn't noticed her phone is switched off,' Evie says, looking worried, nevertheless.

Susanne scowls. 'Yeah, maybe. Just wait until I see her!'

'Look, let's open a bottle and try to calm down, shall we?' Harry says.

'No. I need to keep a clear head in case…' Susanne stops, her words hanging in the air like smoke.

Evie's homemade lasagne languishes untouched in the kitchen. No one is hungry, because despite their buoyant words, Susanne suspects that Evie and Harry are as worried by Dale's absence as she is.

As the hours tick by, Susanne becomes more agitated. 'If we haven't heard from her by midnight, I'm going to the police,' she announces.

Evie nods, pale beneath her light tan. 'I agree… it's been too long.'

At ten minutes past eleven, Susanne's mobile lights up with 'Unknown Caller'. She grasps the handset.

'Hello? Dale! Where the hell are you? We've been worried sick.'

'Susie. Look, I'm really, really sorry – and please don't be cross with me – but I need you to come and get me,' Dale says, a pleading note in her voice.

*

She'd pretended to be angry, but now, strapped into the passenger seat of the jeep, with Harry at the wheel, his profile sharp against the moonlight, Susanne feels a rush unlike anything she's felt for years.

The swaggering man–boy has disappeared and has been replaced by someone heroic, strong, responsible; a combination that makes him achingly desirable in Susanne's eyes. Because to Harry's credit, without heel-dragging or judgement, he'd got straight on with

'Operation Rescue Dale', keying the Siena hotel's postcode into the satnav and manoeuvring the jeep with speed and alacrity, mindful of Dale being alone with only a dead phone for company.

'Thank you,' Susanne says, touching Harry's arm lightly. 'You don't need to do this; Dale's not your responsibility and I'm really grateful.'

Harry shrugs off her praise. 'It's fine. Did she say what happened? I didn't get the whole story.'

Susanne scoffs. 'I doubt either of us will get that. All Dale said was that she went for a drink with a woman she met and accidentally went over the drink-drive limit. She can be so irresponsible at times.'

'She has a wild streak, eh?' Harry grins, keeping his eyes on the winding road ahead. 'Well, we've all been there.'

'I haven't. I mean, if I'm driving, I'm not drinking. That's it. But Dale's always been reckless.'

'Maybe you should try it sometime,' Harry says, laughing out loud and groping for Susanne's hand in the darkness. It feels smooth – like Cody's hand. A piece of her recoils and she finds an excuse to release it, fishing through her handbag for some imagined necessary item.

'Harry, can we… can you not say anything please, about us kissing today.'

'I wasn't going to. Look, I get it. I know it must be weird for you. Your friends won't buy us at all, will they? They see me as a kid. Well, maybe I'm not as young as you think.'

Susanne tries to read Harry's expression, but his face is in shadow. *Us? Not as young as you think?*

'What does that mean?' she asks.

'Nothing… I guess I've always been mature for my age and I prefer the company of people a little older than me.'

'A little?' Susanne giggles, 'Well, ten out of ten for diplomacy.'

*

Love, annoyance, relief: Susanne floods with emotion to see Dale, dishevelled and dirty, as she droops on a stone wall outside the Grand Hotel.

'I'm so sorry. Thank you – both of you.' Pink-eyed, Dale looks from Susanne to Harry as she stifles a yawn. 'I feel such an idiot.'

Susanne hugs her friend. 'It doesn't matter. You'd do the same for me. In fact, you have done; remember when I'd just started seeing Col, and I was sick after too many margaritas at that posh restaurant he took me to?'

Dale gives her a weak smile. 'Yeah, you snuck out the back way and phoned me to pick you up.'

Susanne grimaces. 'I had to throw that dress away.'

Harry groans. 'Oh, please, ladies – TMI. Look, much as I'm enjoying this trip down memory lane, we need to get back, or Evie will think we've all gone AWOL.'

'Well, who made the twenty-four-year-old the voice of reason? Now I know we're in trouble,' Dale says, linking arms with Susanne as they walk back to Harry's jeep. Then following Dale's foggy directions to the now-deserted car park, Harry waits until the women are ensconced in the SUV before taking off in the direction of home.

'Sorry,' Dale murmurs, her eyelids beginning to flicker.

'Don't say it again. I'm just glad you're okay. You can give me all the grisly details in the morning,' Susanne says, her eyes trained on Harry's rear lights as they fly through the deserted Tuscan hills.

CHAPTER SIXTEEN

Evie

Energised by her morning power walk and a brisk shower, Evie runs the flat of her palms over her torso and hopes to feel a difference: a narrowing of her hips, or new definition on her stomach perhaps, but the soft rolls of her belly stubbornly remain.

It's just not fair. She eats less than Susanne, drinks far less than Dale and lately, seems to exercise more than both. And yet, they remain resolutely thin and beautiful in their different but somehow complementary way. Which would be really bloody annoying, Evie muses, sliding a canvas skirt and cotton tee over her underwear, if she wasn't so fond of them both. She pulls her hair back and snaps it into a claw. Not that either of them is without fault.

Three days ago, on the evening of Dale's jaunt, Evie had been genuinely concerned. She'd pictured her, broken and bloodied in a tangled wreckage at the foot of one of the endless steep hills they'd driven through, or slumped in an alley after being set upon by pickpockets. But then the truth had emerged, and it was just Dale being Dale: daring and reckless, drinking too much without a thought for how she was going to get home, because from what Evie had overheard her tell Susanne in hushed tones, she hadn't planned to get home at all. Perhaps she was being old-fashioned and maybe gay people did things differently, but it was utterly unimaginable to Evie that Dale could meet a woman in a foreign city, get chatting over a couple of drinks and fancy her enough to even consider sleeping with her only hours after they'd met. And then – the irony of it – Dale deciding that she didn't like the woman after all and expecting her best friend to drive cross-country to bail her out.

Not that Susanne had minded. Instead she'd enjoyed the intrigue and excitement of speeding off into the night with Harry. Evie saw the way they looked at each other when they thought no one was watching, like feral teenagers at a disco. It was odd the way Harry had brought out a whole new side to Susanne, who was usually so sensible. Evie winces; well, hold that thought, because judging by the sounds coming from Susanne's room the night she and Harry had returned from Siena, things have gone far beyond furtive looks and flirting. Evie is ninety-nine per cent sure that Susanne and Harry have crossed a line and are now having sex!

There'd been too many tell-tale signs to ignore: the scurry of feet and muffled, low voices in the hallway. Susanne's room was past her own and right next door, while Harry's room spurred off another hall entirely, so there'd be no excuse for him to be anywhere near their rooms. Then she'd heard crying out – small sighs and louder, deeper groans. Unless, of course, Susanne was alone.

She knew that women masturbated, too. She'd seen a programme about it on Channel 4 once, about a school in California where women learned how to have orgasms. She'd watched in fascination as a roomful of women of all shapes and sizes lay in a ring on the floor, their heads almost touching, their feet straight out ahead of them like the numbers on a clock. Then they'd each been given sex toys to make themselves climax and one by one, the women had writhed around, sighed and moaned as they'd orgasmed – in full view of each other. The film had shocked and excited Evie, leaving her eager to experiment. So, improvising with a roll-on deodorant bottle, she'd laid on her bed and waited to feel something, anything. But as twenty minutes had ticked by and

Evie's only sensations had been boredom and embarrassment, it was to be her first, last and only attempt at having sex on her own.

On reflection, it seemed unlikely that Susanne would have made such a song and dance if she'd been alone that night. In Evie's view, the more probable scenario was that Harry and Susanne had returned from their adventure in a state of arousal, then waited until they believed she and Dale were asleep before piling into Susanne's bed.

Well, trust some arrogant young lad to stir up a hornet's nest and drive a wedge between them all. What had happened to the relaxing, civilised ladies' holiday they'd planned? From where Evie stands it is taking a different turn all together.

Evie stiffens as the sound of soft footfall twinned with low, tuneless humming passes her room, followed by a clatter of crockery from the kitchen. Somebody – probably Susanne – is up and about, starting the day.

Pushing her concern to one side, Evie pastes on a smile and pads to the sun-filled kitchen.

*

'Morning, Evie,' Susanne raises her arms in a languid stretch, 'did you sleep well, love?'

Evie busies herself making coffee. 'Yes, thank you.'

'Did you manage your usual walk? You are good, Evie. You look as though you're still losing weight. Stick with it, you're doing great.'

'Oh, I don't think so – my clothes feel the same,' Evie says primly, buttering crispbreads on a board.

'Are you okay, Evie?'

'I'm fine. Just wondering what to do today, that's all,' Evie answers, keeping her back turned.

'Well, how about a trip out – to San Gimignano, or even Siena. It's not far – I found that out the other night.'

I bet you found out a lot of things the other night, Evie thinks pushing away the image of Susanne and Harry in bed together.

'That sounds nice… but are you sure you wouldn't rather go with Dale? Or Harry?'

'No, of course not. Evie, are you sure you're okay? You're in a funny mood this morning.'

'I'm fine,' Evie says, taking a steaming mug of coffee and a plate of crackers laced with butter and jam out onto the sun-dappled terrace.

'Hey,' Dale appears, damp hair twisted into a towel. 'How's you, Evie?'

'I'm fine, thank you,' Evie chews slowly, avoids Dale's gaze.

'Er… right. But not chatty, apparently,' Dale says, going back inside. Evie can hear muttered conversation. She pictures Dale and Susanne speculating as to the cause of her sour mood and wonders whether Dale knows or cares about Susanne and Harry.

Aware that she's on course to make herself unpopular, Evie takes a deep breath and goes into the kitchen. Her smile is sheepish. 'Sorry if I seem a bit off, but sometimes it hits me… about Mum, I mean.'

At once the women move forward, arms outstretched. 'Group hug,' Dale says, rubbing Evie's back.

'Bless you, it's still so new,' Susanne says.

'I know, and just when I think I'm on top of things and the pain seems bearable, some small memory comes back to haunt me.' To Evie's surprise, real tears have sprung into her eyes.

'Right, that settles it. We deffo need a day out and a good lunch somewhere. Diets be damned,' Dale says, a note of defiance in her voice.

*

With breakfast a swift affair, within forty-five minutes, Susanne, Dale and Evie are ready to set off for San Gimignano.

'My turn to go in the back,' Dale says, much to Evie's surprise and pleasure.

Evie beams. 'Great, thank you,' she says, wondering if the girls are pointedly making more of an effort after her outburst.

San Gimignano had been her pick. 'I missed out last time, when I had a tummy ache – and you made it sound so beautiful. I might even treat myself to a new handbag if I see something I like,' Evie says, warming to the idea at once.

Susanne and Dale are agog, firing Evie with questions about the colour, brand and style of her intended purchase. Suddenly, she is elevated from being stodgy old Evie – the frumpy friend – to being one of the girls. Basking in the warmth of their attention, Evie falls into a trance-like reverie as they glide through the countryside.

*

On her third lap of the town's main car park, Susanne steams into a newly vacated space with a sigh of relief.

'Phew. For a minute there, I thought we'd have to turn around and go home,' she says as they unwind themselves from the SUV.

As they shuffle through the hordes of visitors, Evie stops to survey the tableau before her, a beatific smile on her face. 'Oh, this is heavenly,' she breathes. 'It looks just like you see in the movies.'

'Pretty, eh?' Dale says, adding, 'Okay, where are we going for lunch?'

Susanne giggles. 'All right, hollow legs – we've only just had breakfast. Can't we just wander for a bit and enjoy the atmosphere?'

'Ooh, yes please – this is so exciting,' Evie says, her face pink with pleasure as she takes in the sounds, sights and smells of market day.

Weaving through steep cobbled lanes, they soon arrive at Piazza della Cisterna, its ancient well, cafés and gelateria draped with tourists, like washing hung out to dry.

'Photo call!' Dale says, herding Susanne and Evie to the well, where they smile and pose happily.

'Your turn, Dale. Here, let me,' Evie says, attempting to take Dale's phone from her.

'Please. *Permettimi*,' a punctilious-looking Italian in his forties bows slightly and motions for Evie to join Susanne and Dale for a group shot.

Evie claps her hands in delight. '*Grazie mille*,' she says, surprising herself.

'*Prego, bella signorina*' the man says, aiming Dale's phone in their direction.

'Thank you, that's so kind,' Susanne says, 'good to have one of all of us.'

But the man is gazing at Evie and murmuring endearments in Italian.

'Dale, what's he saying – you did Latin at school,' Susanne says, a look of amusement on her face.

'Yeah, not that kind!' Dale sniggers. 'Suffice to say, Evie – you've pulled!'

CHAPTER SEVENTEEN

Dale

The day had got off to an unpromising start. Everyone seemed fractious, especially Evie. Dale had heard how women's menstrual cycles could fall in sync after a spell of living together. Maybe it had happened to the three of them – or had they simply tired of each other's company and conversation?

But then the morning had taken a happier turn with an unplanned trip into town that had lifted all their spirits. Especially Evie's. Her expression when the Italian guy had taken their photograph and then proceeded to flirt with her had been priceless. Well, at least it had made her smile – a relief after her watery outburst at breakfast.

Then to cap it off, Evie had bought a drop-dead gorgeous handbag; oxblood in colour, butter soft and with a ladylike clasp that looked like a polished pebble; the effect was elegant and sophisticated. The salesman had pretended to give her a discount, but Dale suspected it had already been in the sale. Nevertheless, Evie had been delighted with her bargain, so overall, a great day for Team Evie.

But then something odd had happened.

They'd gone in search of Harry's hidden restaurant – not because the food was exceptional; the standard was consistently fab wherever they ate – but because everywhere they walked the cafés and bars were crammed with tourists and they'd remembered it as a hidden gem. Somehow, Susanne had led them straight to it.

'Dale, I think it's round here… look, I recognise the chocolate shop,' Susanne says, her pace quickening as the faded, hand-painted sign for Bar Montebello comes into view.

'Oh, well done, Susie. I wonder if the owner will remember us,' Dale says, as she stoops beneath the arch and scouts for a table.

'So, this is where the locals eat,' Evie says, nodding her approval, enjoying herself immensely.

Dale's mouth waters. 'I'm going to have spaghetti al pomodoro; Susanne's looked so good last time. Everything tastes so different to what we have at home, don't you think?'

Evie nods. 'Yes, keener and fresher somehow. Think I'll opt for pizza today.'

Moments later, after a cursory glance at the salad menu, Susanne caves into temptation and joins Dale in ordering spaghetti al pomodoro again.

Chilled and happy, the women reflect on a successful morning's shopping, while devouring every scrap of food on the table.

Dale dabs her lips with a napkin. 'I'm absolutely stuffed,' she says, stifling a hiccup.

Susanne pats her midriff. 'Me too.'

With an effusive smile, Enzo hovers beside them. 'Ladies, did you enjoy?' he asks, as he signals to a young waitress who begins to clear the table around them.

'Yes, thank you. Delicious. But you're making us fat,' Susanne says.

'No, *siete tutte perfette*.' A cheeky smile plays on Enzo's lips.

Dale stops short of rolling her eyes and changes the subject. 'Evie, this is Enzo – his family own the place.'

'Ah! You eat here before?' Enzo says, his eyebrows jumping towards his receding hairline.

'Yes, don't you remember? We came with Harry a couple of weeks ago.'

Enzo purses his lips and considers the possibility before Dale presses on. 'Harry? You know, tall, good-looking… English guy.'

Enzo's expression is mournful. 'I know nobody called Harry. I'm sorry, *bella*, my memory… so many people in my restaurant, you understand?' His smile is apologetic as he returns to the kitchen.

Susanne frowns. 'Why would he say that? They seemed really friendly when we were here before.'

'Perhaps Harry was showing off,' Evie says, 'and he just pretended to know the owner; you know what young lads are like.'

Dale shrugs. 'Yeah, maybe, but I saw them shake hands like old friends. Weird. Anyway, three coffees before we hit the road?'

*

Feeling grubby after their trip into town, Dale puts on a bikini, grabs a beach towel and goes out to the terrace. It's almost five o'clock but the pool remains bathed in sunshine.

'Fancy a dip? Come in with me,' Dale says, absently stroking Susanne's forearm.

'All right, I will. Give me five minutes to change. Where's Evie?'

'Taking a nap, I think. Harry's car's not here either, so it's just us. Hurry up!' Dale makes a beeline for the pool and jumps in with a shriek. She begins to swim, revelling in the coolness of the water against her skin.

It isn't long before Susanne returns, looking fresh in a daffodil yellow swimsuit; she lowers herself into the pool and glides into breaststroke.

Enjoying the tautness and power in her limbs, Dale falls in sync with Susanne before the two of them speed up, propelling themselves through the water with long, lean strokes.

'I make that twenty lengths,' Susanne gasps, her eyes pink from chlorine.

Dale's breath is ragged. 'Yeah, me too.'

Side by side, with the low sun on their faces, they tread water for a while, basking in the peace.

'You like him, don't you?' Dale asks.

'Who?'

Dale groans. 'Susanne, credit me some intelligence. Are you fucking him?'

Susanne hesitates. 'What? Who are you talking about?'

'Hon, it's me, remember – and anyway, your poker face is shit. I know something's happened between you and Harry. I heard you, so don't bother to deny it.'

Susanne bites her lip and looks away as colour creeps into her cheeks. When she speaks her voice is a whisper. 'It just happened. I don't know what came over me… I didn't intend to—'

'No shit!' Dale cuts in, her tone harsh, 'Oh my god. Well, that's just brilliant, isn't it? He's, like, a child, Susanne.'

'Hey! That's not fair. Harry's not a kid… he's twenty-four years old – think back to when we were that age.'

'Yeah, you were married to Col by then and I was pretending to be straight! So we *really* made good choices.' Sarcasm drips from Dale's words.

Susanne puffs out her cheeks. 'Do you think Evie knows? I'd rather she didn't.'

Dale shrugs and wades to the side of the pool. 'I've no idea but considering the racket you two made the other night, plus Evie's room is next door to yours… sooo, you know…' Dale gets out of the water and grabs her towel.

Susanne follows her out and they dry off in awkward silence. Collapsing onto a sun lounger, Susanne finally murmurs, 'I don't know why you're so upset.'

'Well, for one thing, we don't know anything about him – oh, apart from the fact that he's eighteen years younger than you!'

'That's not strictly true, is it? He's my neighbour's godson, for goodness' sake. He's been privately educated; he's got a business degree and he's having a last fling in Europe before he starts work in the city in September.'

'Yeah, that's his CV, Susanne. But what's he like? Has he got a girlfriend pining for him somewhere? Who is he, really?' Dale warms to her theme, 'I mean, where does he go? We're here in the middle of bloody nowhere but most days he disappears to see his "mates"? Well, who are they?'

Susanne sighs. 'Does it matter? It was a one-off, and even if I wanted to… keep it going… it's just a holiday romance, isn't it?'

Dale frowns. 'I don't know, is it? Just be careful. There's something about him. He's furtive.'

Susanne stands up, her body language defensive. 'Dale, I appreciate your concern, but I'm not sure you should be lecturing me after you needed rescuing the other night.'

Dale is stung. 'Ouch. Well, cheers for that. Let's drop the whole thing, shall we? Before one of us says something we'll regret.'

'Fine by me.' Susanne's tone is icy as she turns her back on Dale and marches towards the house.

Shit! She's let her big mouth run away with her again. Dale tries to analyse her feelings. Susanne has made a fair point; why exactly is she so upset? Unwilling to dwell on emotions she cannot control, she hurries after her friend.

'I'm sorry. It's none of my beeswax. I just worry about you, that's all,' Dale opens her arms. Susanne hesitates, then steps into her embrace.

'Okay, let's not argue,' she says, hugging Dale back.

CHAPTER EIGHTEEN

Susanne

Susanne pushes her food around her plate; the chicken salad Dale has made as a peace offering turns to cotton wool in her mouth, her appetite stolen by guilt and humiliation.

It's not just the food that is spoiled: the evening seems thick with effort, as Dale's slouchy, sweary familiarity is replaced by a forced heartiness that doesn't suit her. Mindful of the strained atmosphere, Evie creeps around saucer-eyed, clueless to its cause.

Harry had arrived home just as Dale was serving up. He'd joined the women for a glass of Chianti, then had gone to his room, saying he'd already eaten and that he wanted to 'study', whatever that meant, and it reminded Susanne of Cody stomping off to his bedroom when something had embarrassed or irritated him.

But even while he'd stuck around, Harry had barely looked at her, directing his scant conversation towards Dale and Evie, leaving Susanne hurt and confused.

Now, catching Dale scrutinising her expression for at least the third time during dinner, desperate to make eye contact, Susanne makes an excuse.

'I need to speak to Cody,' she says, managing to smile. 'He's got a fishing trip with his dad tomorrow, so he'll be out of range for a bit. Thanks for a lovely dinner, Dale – sorry I only picked at it; I'm just not hungry. Good night, lovelies, sweet dreams.' She pecks Dale on the cheek and blows Evie a kiss before going to her room. She's almost there when she hears the soft slap of Dale's bare feet on the tiles behind her.

'Susanne, wait,' Dale calls.

Sighing inwardly Susanne turns to face her.

'Are we okay?' Dale asks, her expression soft.

'Of course. I just need to speak to Cody... I miss him, you know?'

'And I'm sure he misses you, too – he's still only a kid, really. Look, I'm sorry I got all judgey at the pool today. You were spot on when you said I was the last person who should be lecturing you on your love life.'

'Dale, honestly, I'm fine. See you in the morning. Goodnight.'

*

Cody is brimming with excitement, stumbling over his words in his haste to describe all that he's done in the last forty-eight hours with a degree of enthusiasm only seen in the young. Susanne feels her chest tighten whenever he mentions Melissa – or *Mel* as he calls her – making it clear that he has already formed an attachment.

In the background, she can hear the buzz of conversation, laughter, and a dog barking. And suddenly it is obvious to her that Colin, Melissa and Banjo are in the room with him, doing relaxed, normal family stuff. Wondering if Melissa has yet been taken for Cody's mother gives her a pain that is almost palpable. Feeling her throat constrict, she wraps up the conversation.

'Darling, you take care. Enjoy your fishing trip, won't you? Catch a big one and send me a photo, hey? I love you, Cody. Night night.'

*

It's past midnight. The room is airless and cloaked in shadows. Sleepless, curled up on her side, Susanne remembers the last time she'd lain this way, with Harry spooned behind her, inside her, his hardness making her gasp and cry out.

He'd taken her to places she hadn't been since she and Colin were new, pre-Cody – and it had shocked her how in control of the situation Harry had been.

She'd expected a fumbling awkwardness, a clash of lips and limbs, as they felt their way to each other. Instead, Harry had been matter-of-fact about what he would do to her and had made her wet with longing well before they'd slid between the sheets.

The night of Dale's 'rescue,' as Susanne thought of it now, she'd been amazed by Harry's sudden maturity and gallantry. Something had happened that night, as they'd sped towards Siena – something unspoken but inevitable, and she'd felt all fight deserting her right there in Harry's car.

Then later that night, convinced that Dale and Evie would be fast asleep, they'd drunk almost a bottle of Pinot Grigio in the kitchen; Susanne sitting up on the cool granite worktop, Harry before her, his lean hips within her parted thighs as they'd made out like teenagers until her resistance had trickled away with the wine and she'd ached for him to make love to her.

They'd gone to her room, where without fuss or dialogue, Harry had produced a box of condoms, and despite his lean and youthful body, once they were in bed, their age difference seemed to melt away, and Harry was no longer a boy, but the man she craved.

They'd barely spoken since.

Dale's brutal reaction had only compounded her misery. It was a slap in the face she could do without. It horrified her – made her skin crawl – to think that Dale had overheard them having sex. She'd meant to be quiet, discreet, but emotions had overwhelmed her as Harry had made her come over and over until she became limp and ragged in his arms.

Susanne stiffens when she hears a light tap on her door. At once, she knows it is him.

'I had to see you,' Harry says, pushing past her.

Susanne inhales his scent; it's clean and verdant as usual, but tonight the sweet, musty smell he often carries is stronger than usual. She steps back as he reaches for her.

'It's best we don't, Harry. The others know – at least Dale does, and it won't be long before it slips out in front of Evie.'

Harry shrugs. 'I don't give a flying one. I want you, not them. I bet you haven't slept a wink, have you?'

'Not so far… it's been so hot today and it's still—'

'We're really going to talk about the weather, are we? Susanne, thinking of you just down the hall is driving me insane. Let me take all that tension away. Here, this will help.' He produces a slim, neatly rolled joint. 'Let's share it and then I'll take you to bed and make you feel incredible again.'

Susanne is unbalanced; shock ripples through her. 'Harry, no! I never smoke… I don't do drugs.'

'It'll help you relax, take the edge off. I saw how miserable you were tonight.'

Susanne's eyes blaze; she stands her ground. 'Smoke it if you want, but I don't want that rubbish, nor will I have it in my room.'

Harry's lips curve upwards. 'Wow. You're even more sexy when you're angry,' he says, threading the joint back into a narrow pocket in his jeans. He reaches for her.

'Hmm. Get stoned or make love to the most beautiful woman I know? It's a no-brainer. I choose you, Susanne. Every time.'

'Harry. Stop it. We can't. You're not listening to me. Dale knows and it has really upset her.'

'Well, of course it has. It's obvious why. God, Susanne, for an intelligent woman, you can be terribly naïve.'

Susanne's eyes are dark – willing him not to mention their age gap as the reason for Dale's disapproval.

Harry smirks. 'It's so apparent to everyone but you. Dale wants you for herself. She adores you.'

'Don't be silly,' Susanne snaps coldly. 'She's been my best friend since school – she doesn't see me that way at all.'

Harry's laughter is soft, mocking. 'Oh, I think you'll find she does,' he cups Susanne's face in his hands. 'Open your beautiful amber eyes, Susanne Campbell; your so-called best friend is in love with you.'

CHAPTER NINETEEN

Dale

Eyes hidden by sunglasses, Dale studies Harry.

Lying beside the pool in only swim-shorts and aviators, it's unnerving just how handsome he is. His height, the proportions of his limbs, his cut-glass profile and striking colouring – not to mention the sulky look he often affects – all traits that remind Dale of the male models in *GQ* magazine. Not that she's ever bought it, but she's flipped through the pages in the hairdressers and has seen how they're stuffed with photographs of lithe, intense, otherworldly creatures. Like Harry.

She's seen, too, the way Harry's beauty can be reduced in an instant by a sneer or a mean comment; by a petulance that instantly dilutes his attractiveness, as if suddenly a mask has slipped.

Not that Susanne seems to notice. It's nauseating how smitten she is. How can she lose her head and – oh god – her heart, to a mere boy? A youth. What can they possibly have in common? It's so clearly a mutual shag fest and nothing more. And yet…

Somewhere in the far reaches of Dale's mind, alarm bells are ringing: a sixth sense that makes her flesh crawl to see them together as they act out indifference – a studied nonchalance – while to even the most casual observer, electricity crackles around them like the inside of a novelty plasma ball.

To make things worse, Dale had acted like the jealous bestie, which had embarrassed them both and had put Susanne on the defensive, making her furtive and distant. It wasn't her finest hour. Harry, of course, had lapped up the conflict, smirking and following Susanne with his eyes whenever she passed by, then looking at Dale for her reaction.

Some holiday this was turning out to be. All of them treading on eggshells and trying not to get in each other's way.

As if he can read her thoughts, Harry sits up and turns to her with a knowing smile.

'Fancy a dip, Dale?' he asks, his tone light.

Dale's expression is serene and her excuse spontaneous. 'No, thanks. I've just topped up my sun cream.'

'What time will Susanne and Evie be back, do you think?' Harry asks, shielding his eyes against the midday sun as he moves towards the pool. Once there, he sits on the edge and slides in, reminding Dale of a reptile.

'They shouldn't be long, they've only gone to the village shop,' Dale says, stretching her legs then rearranging them for maximum sun exposure.

'Great, I'm starving.' Harry vanishes below the surface and swims one silent length.

'So feed yourself, you lazy twat,' Dale mutters under her breath, irritation rising. Honestly, such a sense of entitlement! If that's what a private education does for a young man, he can keep it!

And then it comes to her. She is going about this all wrong. The way to scope out Harry is to make friends with him. Spend some time together, exchanging stories and trading secrets. That way, there's a distinct possibility he'll open up (or let something slip!) and betray how he really feels about Susanne. Because right now, it simply doesn't ring true, for as lovely as Susanne is, surely Harry has other fish to fry? Like his so-called friends in San Gimignano, perhaps; why all the mystery? And why has he never invited his mates out to the house? After all, most young guns of his age would be crowing from the rooftops about having a luxurious villa in the family.

Dale watches Harry surface, lever himself from the pool and stride towards her. With rivulets running from his muscular torso, hair in dripping tendrils and thick eyelashes clumped together, he is the epitome of a TV aftershave commercial. No wonder Susanne can't resist him. What straight woman could? The thought of Harry setting her best friend up for hurt and humiliation when he's bored of fucking her curdles Dale's stomach.

With as much warmth as she can muster, she smiles. 'Looking good, Harry. Hard to believe you're single.'

His stare is hard, unflinching.

Shit! Too far, Dale… too bloody far. She lets out a girlish giggle. 'I meant it as a compliment, Harry – take it! I don't give out many, I can assure you.'

Jesus, this isn't going to be as easy as she'd hoped.

A whoosh of gravel signals the arrival of the SUV. 'Great – they're back,' Dale says, tying a sarong around her bikini and heading to the kitchen.

Burdened by groceries, Susanne and Evie call out.

'Hello, lovelies,' Dale says, taking a carrier bag from Susanne. 'Harry and I are starving. What did you get? Here, let me,' she says, starting to load the fridge and exclaiming over their supermarket finds.

Susanne smiles, murmurs something to Evie that Dale cannot hear; Evie's eyes widen.

Dale looks from Susanne to Evie. 'What? What have I missed?'

'Nothing!' Susanne says, turning her back and busying herself with slicing huge beef tomatoes. 'Where's Harry?'

'Sunbathing, we both were – it's glorious today, less sticky. Shall I lay the table outside?'

The three women glide around each other, plating up bread, olives, pecorino and prosciutto, and gathering up crockery.

Outside on the terrace, Harry remains supine. Nobody mentions him giving them a hand; somehow, they have all tacitly assumed the role of mother – or wife, Dale thinks bitterly. She swallows her annoyance. 'Harry, are you eating with us, love?'

She watches him sit up, put on a thin shirt and swagger to the table, making only the briefest eye contact with Susanne, an amused smile playing on his lips.

'Thanks for this, Susanne, Evie. It looks great,' he says, loading his plate.

A silence falls, punctuated only by birdsong and the sound of cutlery scraping.

Dale wants to scream. This is ridiculous! How long can they all suffer the elephant in the room?

She looks at Evie, cutting her food into small neat pieces and chewing carefully, eyes downcast. And then it occurs to her: *Evie knows.* Susanne has used their brief trip to the village to spill the beans.

Ha! She'd like to have been a fly on the wall for *that* conversation. Evie's so prim and proper, she thinks she's being radical if she changes the parting of her hair.

'We're all very quiet and serious today,' Dale remarks, as they near the end of their meal. 'Anyone got any news?'

'I got a text from Cody this morning,' Susanne says, her face softening at the thought of her son. 'He loved his fishing trip with Col; seems he caught a couple of whoppers. Look, he sent me these photos.' She leans across and flashes her phone around the table. 'It's weird, I never had my ex-husband down as the outdoorsy type. When we were married, just going for a walk on the common seemed like a big deal.'

Harry swipes a hand through his hair, scrapes back his chair and gets up. 'Thanks for lunch, ladies. Sorry to eat and run but I'm going out for a couple of hours.'

'Anywhere interesting?' Susanne asks, her voice even.

'Not really. I'm meeting friends in San Gimi.'

Seeing an opportunity, Dale grasps it with both hands. 'Oh, really? Can you give me a lift, please, Harry? I need a few bits and it's not worth taking two cars.'

A furrow appears in Susanne's brow. 'What do you need?'

'Well, for one thing, I'm nearly out of shampoo,' Dale answers, thinking on her feet, 'and I want to buy a couple of books. They've got a decent supply of English paperbacks in the shop next door to the pharmacy.'

Susanne narrows her eyes, opens her mouth to speak, then changes her mind and begins clearing the table.

Harry shrugs, his face a picture of indifference. 'Sure, I'll see you by the car in fifteen minutes.'

'Great, thanks!' Dale claps her hands and hurries off to change, already planning her line of questioning. An hour's round trip trapped in a car together is surely the ideal opportunity to dig for information. Starting with who Harry sees on his secretive little jaunts into town.

CHAPTER TWENTY

Evie

Evie's hand flies to her mouth. She'd had her suspicions but now here Susanne is, admitting it, bold as brass.

'So are you saying that you actually slept with Harry?' she says, her eyes wide.

Susanne grimaces. 'Evie, please don't say it like that. Look, I can tell you disapprove; I can't say I'm proud of myself and it certainly wasn't planned.'

They are still in the supermarket car park; the SUV's windows are down, the boot is full of groceries and Villa Giardino is less than ten minutes away. Other shoppers wheel trollies and chatter in the sunshine. Susanne makes no attempt to start the engine.

'Anyway,' she says, keeping her eyes ahead, 'I wanted to tell you myself because Dale guessed – and believe me, she's not impressed either. But, well, that's what happened, and I wanted to be honest with you.'

'Ah. Okay, well I appreciate you telling me, Susie. As far as I'm concerned, we all make mistakes, but it's over now and there's no real harm done,' Evie folds her arms, 'as long as Harry understands that.'

Susanne hesitates and nibbles her thumbnail. 'That's the problem, Evie, we like each other. I told Dale it was a one-off, that it would never happen again – but it has, and I've realised that I really like Harry and I don't want it to stop. Well, not yet, anyway.'

'Oh!' Evie wrings her hands. 'But Harry's so—'

'Young? Yes, I know, but age is just a number and we've got… a connection.'

'Look, it's none of my business, but how do you know that? You don't know anything about him.'

Susanne sighs and looks away. 'That's exactly what Dale said. The thing is, it's the same at the start of any relationship. No one ever knows, do they?'

Evie's heart sinks. *A relationship?* Susanne is over-egging the pudding now! Evie has never taken her friend for a fool, but this can only be about sex, surely?

'But what do you have in common? Don't you think it's just… a physical thing?' Pink spots appear on Evie's cheeks. 'Harry's very beautiful, like a film star or a model – even I can see that… And Susie, you are too, but—'

'Evie,' Susanne's tone is sharp, 'we're both single adults, so quite honestly, it's up to us, isn't it? We're not hurting anyone and for what it's worth, he's different when it's just the two of us, more mature and sincere. Oh, I don't know…' She starts the engine, revs harder than necessary and they drive home in silence.

'Susanne,' Evie says as they pull up outside Villa Giardino, 'you've been so good to me and your friendship means the world. I'm sorry if you think I'm judging you – I don't mean to, I'm just concerned, that's all.'

Susanne sighs. 'I know, love – I'm sorry. You're a good friend to me, too. But please, don't worry… it's just a bit of fun, that's all.'

Once inside, the women are caught up with unloading the shopping and preparing lunch. Tension vibrates in the air as Dale, her smile too wide, seems overeager to help. Harry is nowhere to be seen.

Not for the first time, Evie is wistful for home. For the peace of her mother's house, with its dowdy walls and naff carpets; with its comfortable, shabby furniture that seems to wrap around her like her mum's arms – a place where she doesn't have to try so hard; where she can wear tracksuit bottoms and watch her soaps on television and eat half a packet of custard creams without anyone judging her for it.

Evie watches Susanne and Dale as they move around the luxurious kitchen, lit by sun streaming through the French windows. The speed of change often catches her unawares. One day she has a mum, the next she does not. One minute she is a legal secretary – the next a full-time carer. She'd rented a home for years, now she owns a property in need of renovation. Sometimes it makes her head spin.

And yet, through all the change and uncertainty of the last eighteen months, Susanne's friendship has been constant; a comforting influence in her shifting world. Kind, positive and hopeful – not to mention glamourous and aspirational – Susanne has been someone to look up to.

It's odd to think back to the night when the three of them had sat plotting in The Gallery in Tunbridge Wells, loaded with laughter and prosecco. She'd seen Susanne as someone entirely savvy – a woman who had it all worked out. Now, thanks to Harry's attentions, it's clear to Evie that Susanne is as capable of making reckless decisions as the next woman, and if anything, she could do with some sensible advice. Evie sighs, knowing she's the last person to be capable of giving it. In her limited experience, other people's opinions rarely go down well, and she's loath to intervene and risk alienating her best friend and ally – especially in a foreign country only halfway through their trip!

In the garden, lunch is a colourful and tasty spread, but nobody says very much until Susanne mentions Cody's fishing trip. Suddenly, as she is halfway through a story, poking gentle fun at Colin's lack of outdoor prowess, Harry gets up abruptly, his face set and sulky, and announces he's going into San Gimignano. Then, to Evie's surprise, Dale scuttles after him, leaving Susanne disgruntled.

Susanne purses her lips. 'So, just you and me sorting the lunch pots as usual then. It's time Dale pulled her weight a bit more.

How come you and I are always left to organise meals and clear up around here, Evie? It's not on – it's our holiday, too.'

'Well, maybe you can suggest it – after all, you've known Dale most of your life so I'm sure she won't take offence.'

Susanne scoffs. 'You don't know Dale.' She frowns and massages her temples. 'After we've cleared away, do you mind if I lie down for a while? I'm developing a headache. Sorry to leave you by yourself, Evie.'

Evie smiles. 'Bless you. I'll sort these – you put your feet up,' she suggests, relieved at the prospect of some time alone.

*

Somewhere, a phone is ringing. Not the rhythmic beep of a mobile, but the old-fashioned jangle of a landline and it takes Evie a moment to realise what it is. After a minute of continuous ringing, she puts down her book, goes inside and wanders through the house where she follows the sound to a small room off the grand hallway. Evie has never been in this room before; none of them have, to her knowledge. Feeling like an intruder, she looks around at racing green walls and neat bookshelves, then leans across a leather-bound desk and lifts the handset.

'Hello?' she says, conscious that the caller is likely to be Italian and wondering what on earth she'll say next.

'Who's that?' The voice is English, clipped, impatient.

'It's Evie… Evie Jones, I'm here on holiday. Can I help you?' she says, going into secretarial mode.

'Hi! This is Veronica – I don't believe we've met. How are things? All well at the house? What's the weather like?'

Evie tries to assimilate the questions and wonders which she should answer first, but before she can say a word, Veronica continues.

'May I speak to Harry? Put him on, please, Evie.'

Evie speaks clearly. 'I'm afraid Harry's out. He's gone to San Gimignano for the afternoon. Can I give him a message?'

'Ha! Sounds like he's got you running around for him – that didn't take long!' Veronica pauses long enough to laugh at her own witticism before adding, 'Okay. Can you ask Harry to give his mother a ring, please? Or he can call me – I'm around this evening. But this radio silence is simply not on. Nobody has heard from him for weeks and people are getting worried. Anyway – say hi to Susanne; must go, bye-ee.'

A click on the line ends the call.

Evie replaces the handset, wondering why posh people need to be quite so abrupt.

CHAPTER TWENTY-ONE

Dale

Harry drives erratically, but if it's to unnerve her, he's on the wrong track. Susanne is always on her case to slow down but driving fast, braking hard and feeling the road rattle beneath her gives Dale a heightened sense of control.

'So, Harry, tell me about these mysterious friends of yours. I mean, how come you even know people in Tuscany?'

'I could say it's none of your damn business,' Harry sneers, 'but that would make it sound as though I have something to hide, wouldn't it?'

Dale lets out a throaty laugh. 'Yeah, maybe.'

'Well, I can assure you the truth is pretty dull. But as you're so fascinated: they're a couple of backpackers I met, Joe and Sander. I met them in Rome a few months ago, and then I just kept bumping into them, which was cool, so we hung out together. It's easy to meet people when you're travelling, at least I find that. Anyway, that's it. That's the story. Sorry to disappoint you, Dale.'

'I'm not disappointed, just interested as to why the hell a hot young guy like you wants to hole up in Tuscany all summer with a bunch of old women.'

Harry smirks. 'Not so old. Look, it's a no-brainer; backpacking's great, but I'd had enough of cheap hotels with itchy linen and bad plumbing, and of moving from place to place. It's good of Veronica to let me stay here all summer, but hey, what are godparents for?'

He laughs, a wolfish leer spreading across his face. 'As for the arrival of three beautiful women… that was just a lucky bonus.'

After parking the jeep, they walk together as far as Piazza della Cisterna – which as usual, is teeming with tourists – and arrange to meet at the spot two hours later.

As they say goodbye, a fleeting thought occurs to Dale: whether she can trust Harry to come back for her. What if he takes off with his so-called backpacking mates and leaves her there? His story made total sense; it's only natural that he craves male company of his own age. Still, she can't help feeling that there is something more to his San Gimignano visits.

*

Dale runs her fingertips over the paper bag on the table in front of her. Inside are three new paperbacks; one is a *Sunday Times* bestseller that she's had her eye on for weeks, the other two attracted her attention on the strength of their covers, each sealing the deal with a compelling blurb on the back. Dale considers her love of books. There's something so solid and reassuring about them – not to mention the unspoken promise of fascinating people and faraway lands that compels her to hungrily tear through the pages. She always has at least one book on the go. Now she has the luxury of three to choose from and is undecided which to read first.

She looks around at the cheerful, bustling café, with its blue-and-white striped umbrellas, hand painted signage and its terracotta pots bursting with scarlet geraniums. Dale swallows the last of her chilled Frascati and considers ordering another. There's almost an hour to kill before she's due to meet Harry back at the fountain, but tempting though it is to get mildly pissed in the afternoon sun, she is keen to explore the lanes and mingle with the other tourists.

Dale turns to follow a hoot of laughter as a gaggle of women walk past. A pang of sadness grips her chest as she remembers her last visit to San Gimignano: the giddy shopping trip followed by a delicious lunch. She pictures Susanne's beautiful, smiling face, but the image turns to one of sourness and disappointment. Things have been tangibly strained between them since she'd called Susanne out about Harry. If only she could learn to filter her thoughts, but tact and diplomacy have never been her strong points.

Perhaps she should buy Susanne a present. An olive branch in the form of some sweet token of friendship to surprise her and make her smile. Pleased with her plan, Dale pays the waitress and heads off into one of the main shopping streets where she's confident that something will catch her eye. And then she sees it: an ornately painted A-board bearing the words *Handmade Artisan Jewellery*.

Hope stirs as she enters the tiny shop rammed with treasures made from silver, crystal and mineral stones in vibrant colours. At one end, a man with a smooth face no older than her own, yet framed by a thatch of white hair, deftly wields a set of tiny tools, mid-creation. She watches him for a moment and is rewarded with a beaming smile.

'May I help you with something special, Madam?' A young woman with copper hair to her waist and a pierced eyebrow smiles encouragement.

'Yes, please. I need a gift for my best friend. Those bangles are pretty, can I see them? How much are they?'

Ten minutes later, clutching a small gift bag containing a carved walnut bracelet embellished with a single crystal, Dale steps out into the light, poorer and happier.

But sometime later, after pondering on where and how she should present Susanne with her gift, she realises she has taken a wrong turn. She pauses and looks around. This is not a part of town she recognises. Shops have made way for offices and the seemingly endless crocodile of tourists has been replaced by Italians going about their daily life. The incessant buzz of laughter, conversation and the drone of scooters is drowned out by a too-loud radio playing Latino music punctuated with shouty Italian commentary, coming from a mechanics' yard where men in overalls work on a battered Alfa Romeo.

A prickle of unease stirs the hairs on the back of Dale's neck as she finds herself in the kind of charmless street unlikely to appear in any holiday brochure. A pungent and familiar smell drifts from a gloomy café attached to a hostel, causing her to peer into its shadowy interior. And there he is: Harry, slouched beside a fragile-looking blonde who looks barely out of her teens. Deep in conversation, with two half-drunk beers on the table in front of them, they appear to be sharing a cigarette – or are they smoking weed?

Spellbound, Dale watches as Harry flips the cover of his phone, makes a face and gulps the last of his drink. Then he embraces the young woman, turning to kiss her cheek.

She can see him patting down his pockets, getting ready to leave the bar – probably to meet Dale as arranged. There is nothing for it but to hide out of sight and then follow him at a safe distance until she is back on familiar turf.

Questions crowd Dale's brain. Why did Harry lie about who he was meeting? Why is he hanging around this drab part of town, so far from the beaten track? Above all, who the hell is he kissing?

Feeling like an amateur sleuth in a low-budget movie, Dale's stride is brisk to keep Harry in her sights as he practically jogs through the narrow lanes, back to their agreed meeting point. Concealed by a stone arch, Dale watches him for a moment, gleeful at his obvious irritation when a busload of garrulous American pensioners crowds him.

Her greeting is cool, unsmiling, before she relents. 'Sorry I'm a bit late. I wanted a present for Susanne and lost track of time.'

'No worries. I've only been here five minutes myself. But Jesus! Some people have personal space issues, don't they?' Harry almost shouts with an indignant toss of his head, edging away from the tourists and looking as though he might shove one of them at any moment.

The suffocating heat inside the jeep hits them as they open the doors. Turning on the air con, they close the doors again and stand beside the car waiting until it cools down, saying little at first.

'How were they?' Dale asks eventually.

'What?'

'Your friends, Jack and Sander?'

'It's Joe, actually – Joe and Sander.' Harry's tone is petulant. 'They're fine, thinking of moving on soon. We had a beer together, which was nice. But just the one as I'm driving, obviously. Shall we give it a try now?' Harry gets into the jeep and starts the engine.

One beer? With Joe and Sander? What a crock. I've just seen you smoking a joint with a young woman, you lying bastard, Dale wants to scream.

Wondering how stoned he is, somehow she manages to keep it together, grateful that at least he is driving at a sedate speed. She stares out at the endless rows of cypress trees, the effort of not confronting him rendering her morose.

Harry slices through the silence. 'So, what did you get her?'

'Oh, a bracelet. It's hand-carved from walnut – I hope she likes it.'

'Sounds expensive. Is it her birthday soon?'

'No, I just wanted to treat her. We had an argument and I wanted to apologise.' Another pause looms as Dale stares out of the window.

'Well, it can't have been serious. What did you row about?'

'Actually, Harry, it was about you.' Dale's brow is furrowed. Why the hell is she telling him this? Are they really about to have the *Susanne* conversation? Well, bring it on.

He feigns surprise. 'About *me?*'

'Yes. Harry, I hate all this cloak and dagger crap. I know you're sleeping with her and I won't pretend I approve. It's not personal, but Susanne's my best friend and I care about her. The thing is, she might look all shiny and in control but she's fragile, and I don't want her to get hurt.'

She can sense the cogs whirring when Harry answers carefully. 'Dale, I totally get why you're worried. You think I'm just using Susanne for sex, don't you? I admit that I'm very attracted to her – who wouldn't be? She's gorgeous. But it's more than that. I really like her. We've got a connection.'

Dale's tone is cynical. 'Funny, that's the kind of word Susanne would use. Look, I just don't want any drama, Harry. She's my oldest friend – and more than that, she's a really good person.'

'So, you're implying that I'm not? Dale, you're preaching to the congregation,' Harry says, his eyes fixed on the undulating road ahead. 'I understand your concern, but what's the worst that can happen?'

'I don't know… you could break her heart, humiliate her in some way.' It's a lame response, designed to mask Dale's real and much darker fears. Fears that had started the day as little more than instincts but are now gaining traction. Because at the very least, Harry is a liar, caught red-handed hanging out with some skank in a sleazy bar, smoking dope. Now the thought of him putting his filthy hands all over Susanne turns Dale's stomach.

Unfazed, Harry answers. 'Why would I do either of those things? She's more likely to break *mine*. I can't bear the thought that you'll all go home in a fortnight and I'll never see her again. Dale, I'm falling for her. I'll be the one who's humiliated when Susanne gets on the plane without a backward glance.'

Dale shrugs, suddenly weary. 'I guess we'll just have to agree to differ on this one, Harry. Let's talk about something else. Are you looking forward to starting your new job in London?'

'Resigned rather than excited. I've loved travelling, but now I've got to knuckle down. All good things come to an end,' Harry says, sounding genuinely regretful.

Dale nods. 'I can't say I'm looking forward to going back to school, either. What financial institution did you say you'll be working for?'

'I didn't. It's a small family firm – you won't have heard of them. They're disgustingly wealthy… contacts of my dad's actually.'

'Yeah, well, the old adage is true, it's who you know. You're so lucky to have had a private education. It's given you so many advantages. You could have gone to a school like the one where I teach in south London. It's a different world.'

'Oh, I'm sure it is,' Harry says, his face set.

CHAPTER TWENTY-TWO

Dale

It's late afternoon by the time Dale and Harry arrive at Villa Giardino. There's a stillness to the place and no sign of Susanne or Evie.

'They must be around somewhere, the car's here,' Harry says, heading out to the terrace before finding it unoccupied and going straight to the fridge. 'Drink, Dale?'

Dale shrugs. 'Sure, why not. Shall we open some wine?'

Susanne wanders into the kitchen, her face sleepy and unfocussed, her hair mussed. 'Sounds like a great idea. I fell asleep,' she yawns, 'my head was throbbing but it's fine now. Did you have a good time in San Gimi?'

Harry nods. 'We did, thanks – and actually, it gave Dale and I chance to talk.'

Dale shoots Harry a warning look.

'Oh, really? What about?' Susanne takes the unopened wine bottle from Harry and starts casting around for a corkscrew.

'Oh, nothing we need to go into now,' Dale says, her voice strained.

'I'm fed up with pretending,' Harry flounces. 'Let's just get everything out in the open, shall we?'

'Oh, I'm all for *that*,' Dale snaps.

But Harry pays no attention. 'The thing is, Susanne, I've told Dale that I'm crazy about you, and that I couldn't care less about the age gap or about what other people think. I'm sick of creeping around and wasting time.'

Susanne raises her eyebrows. 'Crazy about me, eh?' she says, her lips curving into a smile as Harry moves closer and places a protective arm around her shoulders, staking his claim on her.

Is he for real? Un-fucking-believable!

Nauseated, Dale's response sounds forced, even to her own ears. 'Well. What can I say except cheers to the happy couple! You're both adults, who am I to judge?'

Evie appears then, fragrant and damp-haired. Her eyes widen when she sees Susanne and Harry openly snuggled up to each other.

'You look pretty, Evie. Nice bath?' Susanne says, her expression sheepish. 'Oh, the faces on you two! Lighten up. Look, you both know – and we *know* you know, so let's all just get over ourselves, shall we?'

There is a shift in atmosphere as Susanne goes into hostess mode, steering everyone out onto the terrace before refilling glasses and putting on music. Dale watches as she goes off to collect dozens of thick cream candles, and pretty tealights in jars from the stash they'd found in Ronnie's antique sideboard the week they'd arrived; soon the terrace twinkles magically, thanks to Susanne's handiwork.

When a familiar classic dance track comes on, Susanne closes her eyes and begins waving her arms above her head.

'Aww, Dale, remember this? It reminds me of us in Ibiza,' she says, her hips swaying to the beat.

Dale snorts. 'Yeah. We were practically kids... god, I feel old.'

Suddenly, Dale remembers the bracelet. It doesn't seem important now that Harry and Susanne have outed themselves. Every fibre in her body is crying out to warn her best friend about the girl in the bar. Even Harry would struggle to tap-dance his way out of that conversation.

'I have something for you,' Dale says, before going off to get the carved bangle and returning moments later.

Susanne's eyebrows shoot up as she opens the bag. 'Oh, wow. For me? But why? Dale, it's absolutely beautiful, but you shouldn't have,' she says, posing and showing it off to Evie, who gushes her approval and insists on trying it on.

Harry shoots Dale a look laced with smugness and leans in. 'You heard Susanne. As she said, it's time everyone got over themselves,' he whispers, while Susanne is distracted by her gift. 'Why can't you just be happy for us?'

Their eyes lock for a moment before Evie pipes up.

'Shall I make us a snack? There's all sorts in the fridge,' she says, absently rubbing her stomach.

'That sounds lovely, Evie – good idea,' Susanne beams, whilst making no attempt to assist her.

Fuming silently, Dale follows Evie into the kitchen, relieved to let her face slip. She grabs a wooden chopping board and a sharp knife. 'Here, let me help. Evie, what do you think, for Christ's sake?'

'Honestly? I'm a bit worried. I'm sure Harry's a nice lad, but that's the thing isn't it? He's just a boy. Oh,' she cries, 'I've just remembered something: Ronnie called this afternoon. She wants Harry to ring home. Apparently, nobody has heard from him in weeks.'

'Selfish prick,' Dale hisses.

*

By sunset, after an hour spent grazing on Evie's improvised supper and chatting around the table, the familiar rustle and chirp of the night critters is drowned out by the throb of dance music as Susanne, inhibitions lowered by the wine, cranks up the volume and gets up to dance.

At once, Harry is on his feet, pulling her into his arms, twirling and dipping her so that she laughs giddily.

As the song finishes and morphs into the next track, Susanne breaks away from him, her eyes dancing with happiness.

'Wait here, I'll open some more wine,' she says, diving back into the kitchen and beaming at Dale as she passes. A moment later, Susanne returns and refreshes all four glasses. 'Whoops. Well, that didn't last long.' She laughs, steadying herself against Harry, who looks amused.

'That's the third bottle tonight, isn't it?' Dale says, her tone prim. 'Be careful you don't bring on another headache.' A thought suddenly occurs to her. 'Evie – don't you have a message for Harry?'

Evie raises her voice over the music. 'Yes. Harry, while you were out this afternoon, your godmother rang. She wants you to give her a call… or your mum – either, as long as you phone home.'

Harry makes a face. 'Really? What did she say?'

'That nobody has heard from you in weeks and that people are getting worried,' Evie says with a little shrug.

'God, she exaggerates! It's been like two days. Thanks, Evie. I'll speak to my mother in the morning.'

If Harry feels emasculated by his female relatives checking up on him, he doesn't show it, Dale muses, watching him dance and cuddle with Susanne, who looks distinctly like the cat that got the canary.

Evie looks on, her face pensive. 'Dale, perhaps we're being cynical, and they really do like each other.'

'Yeah, maybe. But something's not right,' Dale says, pursing her lips and keeping her eyes on Harry as he whispers something that makes Susanne throw back her head and laugh.

Suddenly, Susanne stops twirling and gyrating. 'Where's my St Christopher?' she cries, feeling for the chain at her throat. 'My necklace… it must have come off. Oh no! Please, help me look for it.'

At once, all four of them drop to the ground and begin feeling around the cool and dusty paving stones.

'Got it!' Harry's smile is victorious as he holds the necklace between his thumb and forefinger where it glints in the candlelight.

Susanne throws her arms around him, her face a picture of gratitude. 'Oh, thank god. I couldn't bear losing it… it's the only thing I have left from Grandma Amy and I'd be lost without it. Bless you, Harry – you're amazing.'

'You're amazing,' Dale mimics sourly, turning away.

CHAPTER TWENTY-THREE

Susanne

Susanne watches as Harry sleeps, marvelling at the length of his eyelashes, the curve of his cheekbones, the straightness of his nose. She strokes his hair, lying dark as a raven's wing against his forehead. He reminds her of a god from a school textbook on Greek mythology that she'd loved. For now, at least, Harry is her living, breathing, personal Adonis.

Telling the others had been unplanned but a huge relief. Dale and Evie seemed to accept, if not exactly welcome, her relationship with Harry. There seemed no point in pretending now, by going off to separate rooms, only for Harry to sneak along the hallway and tap on her door later; a delicious inevitability as the sex was incredible – truly mind-blowing, especially given Harry's youth and relative inexperience.

At first it had seemed fantastical that Harry could be so besotted – not to mention turned-on – by a woman in her forties, but he'd brushed aside the gap in their ages as meaningless and trifling and now Susanne found herself doing the same. In the car with Evie, she'd trotted out the 'age is just a number' cliché but the closer she and Harry became, the more it rang true. And anyway, the whole holiday was a fantasy – there'd be plenty of time to face reality at home. Susanne pushes the future firmly to the back of her mind. One day at a time.

If only Dale would take a chill pill and embrace the moment. She'd caught her watching them drinking and dancing together, her face closed and unreadable.

Bless Dale, always so loyal and protective, even at school when Susanne had suffered a term of bullying at the hands of Debbie and Karen Mitchell, twins from another class who'd become obsessed with Susanne's good looks, waging a hate campaign against her for months.

Once, after a netball match in which Susanne's team had thrashed them, Debbie and Karen had waited until Susanne was alone in the showers, naked and shivering, before commencing their pincer attack. While Debbie taunted Susanne about her burgeoning breasts, calling her a 'fat slapper', Karen had been at work ripping pages from Susanne's exercise book, casting them into the stream of soapy water pooling at her feet.

'Oh, please don't,' Susanne had begged, 'that's my history homework. I'll get detention now.'

Hearing the Mitchells' shrieks of laughter and Susanne's indignant yelps, Dale had charged into the shower zone, grabbed the shredded textbook from Karen and shoved Debbie hard against a wall, putting an abrupt end to their volley of insults.

'Leave her alone. Go on, get out now, or you'll have my brother to deal with – and he's in the army, you losers!' Dale had stood her ground with such authority that the girls had sloped off, eyes narrowed, tutting and cursing as they went.

Then Dale had waited for Susanne to dry and dress herself, before escorting her to geography, their final class of the day.

Susanne had been meek with gratitude. 'Thank you, Dale. But you shouldn't tell lies, you know. You haven't even got a brother, let alone some hard nut in the army.'

Dale had only grinned mischievously. 'They don't know that, do they? And I won't tell if you don't.'

The Mitchell twins had kept their distance from then on, and Dale had gained a new respect in her year group.

Bless Dale. Protective is good. Suffocating… not so much.

What if Harry has a valid point, and Dale's feelings run deeper than friendship, deeper even than the sisterly bond that Susanne has always treasured?

'What time is it?' Harry stirs, his voice thick with sleep. He pushes himself up against the pillows, rubbing his eyes.

'About eight thirty. We should get up. Go for a swim… or for a walk in this beautiful sunshine. Make the most of it all.'

Unsaid words hang in the air between them: *before we have to leave and return to real life.*

'How do you do it?' Harry says, leaning up on one elbow and studying her.

'What?'

'How do you wake up even more beautiful than when you went to sleep?' he says, moving a stray lock of hair from Susanne's face, then adding, 'Does he look like you?'

'Who?'

'Cody, of course.'

Surprised by the mention of her son, Susanne looks away and fiddles with the sheet.

'It changes. At the moment, he looks more like his dad, but when he was younger, he looked just like me. I'm getting up,' she adds decisively, going to the bathroom and locking the door. Right now, she simply can't think about Cody and Harry in a shared context.

*

Dale and Evie are outside, drinking coffee and nibbling crackers. Their conversation dries up abruptly.

'Good morning, Susie, sleep well?' Evie asks.

'I did, thanks. We were quite late last night, and we drank a fair bit, too, judging by the empties in the kitchen. I feel okay though.'

Dale laughs softly. 'Is the boy wonder up and about or have you worn him out?'

'Dale!' Evie looks shocked.

'She's only joking, aren't you, darling?' Susanne smiles. Let Dale have her little dig – the novelty will soon wear off.

'I've been thinking,' Susanne says, pulling out a chair next to Dale and taking a sip of coffee. 'We'll be going home in two weeks; it'd be criminal to leave Tuscany without visiting the Uffizi in Florence.'

Evie looks wistful. 'I'd love to see the *Birth of Venus.*'

Dale nods. 'Yeah, that would be cool. We'd need a whole day there, though – and we might have to queue for hours at this time of year.'

'Well, we could get up really early, or…' Susanne is thinking aloud, 'we could spend a night in Florence, get there the evening before and then make a day of it. What do you think?'

'Yes! Sounds great to me. When are we going?' Dale is on her feet, excited by the idea of a mini adventure in Florence.

Harry slouches over in ripped jeans and an open shirt. He scans the faces of all three women, his expression wary.

'Morning, Harry. We're just planning a trip to Florence. Girls only,' Dale says, holding his gaze.

Harry shrugs. 'Don't worry, Dale – I wouldn't *dream* of gatecrashing your little road trip,' he says, an unpleasant sneer darkening his face.

Susanne is shocked. 'Come on, Harry – Dale didn't mean it like that.'

'I know, I'm only joking,' he answers, with a smile that does not reach his eyes.

*

After breakfast, Susanne waits until Evie and Harry have gone to their rooms to shower and dress before pulling Dale aside.

'Dale, what's wrong with you? What is it between you and Harry? I honestly can't stand the atmosphere. I thought now it was all out in the open, things would be better.'

'Susanne, I'm sorry – but I don't trust him. He's… secretive. Always mooching around, picking up fag ends of conversations.'

'Dale, that's not fair. He's just a bit gauche, that's all. We were young once. Bloody hell, cut him some slack.'

Dale's eyes darken with hurt. 'You know it can't continue, don't you? When we get home, I mean. Or do you imagine Harry moving in with you and being a big brother to Cody?'

'Now you're being ridiculous!' Susanne starts to walk away but changes her mind. 'Actually, you know what, Dale? You don't need to worry, because you were right. It's just sex. And quite honestly, it's bloody brilliant and it's been a long time coming!'

Dale looks at her feet, puts a hand to her furrowed brow but remains silent.

But Susanne is on a roll. 'Yes, I know Harry's gorgeous, but I'm not deluded and when the three of us get on that plane to Gatwick, it'll be over. Finished. What do you think? That maybe he'd like to live two doors down from Ronnie?'

Dale shrugs. 'Maybe! Look, I don't know, but I just think he's got an agenda.'

'Well, haven't we all!' Exasperated, Susanne turns on her heels and marches to her room.

*

In the garden, a welcome breeze stirs the lavender and sage, releasing their heavenly scent. Revelling in the luxury of a delicious hour alone while Dale and Evie are in the village and Harry catches up with friends, Susanne hunkers down on her sunbed, pushes her altercation with Dale to the back of her mind and focusses on the book she's been meaning to finish all week.

After ten minutes, she stares blankly at the pages, realising she hasn't absorbed a jot of what she's read. With a sigh, she sits up and considers a swim, but realises she hasn't the energy. She catches her breath, a secret smile lighting her face. She and Harry had made love for almost two hours last night; no wonder she's exhausted!

It had been intense; the best she could remember. It delighted her that Harry had boundless energy and a matter-of-fact way of asking exactly what she wanted before delivering it in spades, and with only a passing regard for his own pleasure. No wonder she was becoming addicted to him.

If only Dale could be happy for her and accept their affair for what it was.

It was weird how upset she'd become – obsessing about Harry, banging on and on about how he couldn't be trusted.

It was totally uncalled for. Harry was from a good family.

Oh god, *Ronnie*. To think that she is having the best sex of her life with her neighbour's young godson slash nephew slash second cousin once removed… or whatever it is. She makes a mental note to impress upon Harry that Ronnie must never find out about their fling.

CHAPTER TWENTY-FOUR

Evie

For as long as Evie can remember, a faded print of a naked woman with flowing blonde hair standing on a shell has graced her mum's downstairs loo in its tacky gilt frame. Because although her mum much admired Botticelli's *Birth of Venus*, she'd always deemed it too vulgar to hang elsewhere in the house.

Evie corrects herself: it is *her* downstairs loo now. In *her* house. A shudder of panic rips through her as she remembers. Pushing her anxiety to one side, she reminds herself that tomorrow she will see the *real* Venus in all her naked glory.

She regards the neat pile of clothes on the bed: two tops – one is a T-shirt, the other loose and floaty, two sets of underwear (just in case), a pair of trainers for sightseeing and high wedges for eating out. Then there are her toiletries. Who knew that a one-night stay required so much stuff? Evie crams everything into a modest holdall, sprays perfume on her neck and wrists and goes to join the others, whom she can hear moving around the hallway.

As usual, despite the effort she has made with her appearance, Evie instantly feels like the poor relation beside Susanne and Dale: Susanne in her chic designer jeans, mock-croc belt and crisp white tee; Dale dressed in skinny black jeans and an embellished vest, her sun-lightened hair styled in a high quiff.

Susanne's smile is warm. 'You look great, Evie. Okay, have we got everything? Right then: Florence, here we come!' she says, picking up her handbag and her leather holdall.

Dale nods. 'I've already programmed the satnav and it's only an hour and ten so we should be there by six o'clock.'

'Perfect,' Susanne says, 'just in time for wine o'clock.'

Evie smiles, though she longs for a night off the booze. Her friends' capacity for alcohol far exceeds her own. In her recent experience, drinking can make her feel fat and sluggish, but neither Susanne nor Dale appear to have gained a pound.

They'd said goodbye to Harry an hour earlier, before he'd taken off for San Gimignano. His goodbye had been sweet as he'd embraced Dale and Evie, pecking them both on each cheek before giving Susanne a lingering kiss – complete with embarrassing sucking sounds which had made Evie blush to her roots.

'Have a great time, but *please* be careful,' Harry had implored. 'Stick together and watch out for pickpockets. Ciao!' Then he'd sped off in the jeep, a hail of gravel flying in his wake.

Dale had made a face. 'Well, *he's* in a good mood. Anyone would think he's glad to see the back of us.'

And there it was: an eye roll from Susanne, followed by a small shake of the head.

In the week since she'd first mentioned going to Florence, Susanne had been decidedly cool with Dale, keeping her at arm's length and spending hours holed up in her room with Harry. But Evie was keeping out of it. Taking sides or getting between them seemed like a terrible idea, especially as they were sure to become thick as thieves again, which inevitably would leave her at odds with them both and reduce her to an object of scorn.

At the solicitors where Evie had worked, Kerry, one of the other secretaries whom she'd been friendly with, had pinned a trio of postcards above her desk of popular slogans like 'Keep Calm and

Carry On' and 'Believe You Can', which she'd point to when the department was under pressure and people were running around like headless chickens. But Evie's favourite was 'Sisters Before Misters': Kerry, resolutely and unapologetically single, had sworn by it. Evie wanted to say it to Susanne and Dale now. To remind them that Harry was just an arrogant young man – albeit the most handsome one Evie had ever met – who came across as shallow and selfish, taking what he wanted, without a passing thought for anyone else. Because from where Evie was standing, Harry was at risk of ruining the whole trip.

Evie looks from Susanne to Dale, willing them to set aside their differences. *Forget about Harry. Let's just enjoy beautiful, romantic Florence in all its glory,* she longs to say. Instead she gets into the back of the SUV and gazes from the window, drinking in the scenery as it flashes by.

But the warmth of the car and the undulating hills have a soporific effect, and Evie wakes to Susanne crawling in first gear, looking for a space in the hotel's tiny car park. Sticky and thirsty, she wipes a line of drool from her chin before the others notice.

'Sorry, I must have dozed off. Are we here?' Evie peers out at the signature green wooden shutters clinging to ochre, biscuit and terracotta walls that rise above the narrow streets.

'Wow, even the back streets are romantic; we couldn't be anywhere else but Tuscany,' she breathes.

*

The hotel is small and charming, and only a short walk from Piazza del Duomo and the Uffizi. The women are greeted warmly by two young receptionists who are so alike that they are surely brothers, if not twins.

They'd been lucky to find decent accommodation at a week's notice and had jumped on the first hotel that looked clean and affordable. Now, after checking in, there's a brief and guarded exchange about the room configuration; the upshot being that Susanne and Evie end up sharing a rather grand room, while Dale takes a well-appointed, but smaller one on her own.

'But wouldn't you rather share with Dale?' Evie whispers while Dale rifles through a rack of tourist leaflets in reception.

Susanne shakes her head. 'What with *her* snoring?' she mouths.

Once in the room, with its ornate, dated furniture and heavy silk drapes, Evie tries again. 'Look, it's none of my beeswax, but you and Dale have been friends forever, you're like sisters. I hate to see the two of you falling out and being so awkward with each other.'

'Evie, please don't worry,' Susanne's tone is patient. 'You're right, we are like sisters, and sometimes family argues. But we're fine, honestly. Dale just needs to chill out about Harry and mind her own business. It's up to me who I go out with – I wouldn't dream of interfering with *her* love life.'

Knowing she is on thin ice, Evie lets the subject drop, secretly wishing that they'd never met Harry.

CHAPTER TWENTY-FIVE

Susanne

They'd skipped the long lines that straggled outside the Uffizi's main entrance by buying advance tickets. Then they'd stalked the echoing halls, greedily devouring familiar, iconic works by Michelangelo, Leonardo da Vinci, Titian and Botticelli.

Evie's response had been touching. 'My mum always wanted to see this,' she'd said, her voice cracking with emotion and tears welling in her eyes as she'd gazed in awe at the *Birth of Venus*. 'It's in her downstairs loo – I mean, *my* downstairs loo,' she'd added.

'Well, now you've seen Venus for her,' Susanne had said kindly, 'and isn't she beautiful? Just look at the luminous skin tones and the texture of her hair. Gorgeous.'

Dale had agreed. 'Yes, incredible. Check out the realism of the flowers and foliage. You know, I might even try and work old Venus into my Wednesday night drama club.'

Now, standing inside the Duomo, they are speechless. They'd agreed to spend an hour inside, but nothing could have prepared them for the cathedral's grandeur and opulence and one hour soon becomes two.

'Such skill and devotion,' Evie whispers as the three of them gaze upwards towards the soaring painted dome of Santa Maria del Fiore.

They stare in awe at the stained-glass windows by legendary Italian masters and walk over its grand marbled floor, drinking in the magical atmosphere. Eventually, they step back into reality and the afternoon sun where tourists, workers and pilgrims alike mil in the square like players on a magnificent stage set.

Susanne rubs her neck. 'I ache from looking up so much,' she says, 'and I could do with a drink.'

Dale nods. 'Go for it, hon – it's my turn to drive. Evie? Cheeky glass of wine before we head off?'

A pretty café where flower-filled planters divide one establishment from the next and the dishes are named after Renaissance painters beckons them in. Soon they are ordering wine, mineral water and an array of elegant, bite-sized treats; a delicious blend of sweet and savoury traditional Italian fare that seems to disappear in minutes.

Dale closes her eyes, her expression one of utter bliss. 'Oh my god. I think I prefer Italian afternoon tea to the English kind,' she says. 'The arancini balls were to die for and I'll be dreaming about those tiny lemon cannoli for weeks.'

Evie smiles and takes a sip of wine. 'I might have a go at making cannoli when we get home. Would you both come if I did?'

'Is the Pope Catholic?' Dale laughs, brushing Evie's arm affectionately. 'Like a shot, hey, Susanne? We can toast your new des res.'

Susanne nods. 'Absolutely, I'll bring the champagne. We'll need something to look forward to, once we're home and the summer is over.' She glances at her watch. 'Well, no wonder we were all starving; it's almost five o'clock and we've had nothing since breakfast,' she says, blotting her mouth with a paper napkin and discreetly applying lip-gloss. And then she is alone with Dale, while Evie goes in search of the powder room: no distractions, no audience. They both start to speak at once.

'You go first,' Dale says, her smile lighting her eyes for the first time in days.

'I'm sorry for being such a cow, Dale. You're my oldest friend and I love you. I know you were only looking out for me. But I'm not as daft as you think – you don't need to worry about Harry.'

'No, I'm sorry, for steaming in like the bossy bestie. Of course you can handle yourself, Susie, and I'm the last one who should give advice. Just look at the state of my love life!'

Susanne feigns surprise. 'What love life?'

'All right, don't rub it in!'

Evie returns, drying her hands on a tissue. 'That's better. You two look happy. What have I missed?'

Susanne beams, 'We were just having a moment,' she says, winking at Dale and adding, 'I've loved today. I'll always remember Florence and I'm so glad I got to see it with my two best friends.'

*

At Villa Giardino, Susanne is first through the front door. Spotting the sandals at once, she stops in the hallway and frowns. Soft biscuit leather and with a sparkle trim, they are the kind a teenager would wear. A row of grubby toe prints like tiny pebbles whisper of the petite wearer.

Dale is hot on her heels. 'Oh, whose are those? Have we got company?'

Evie straggles in last. 'They're little – who do they belong to?'

Then, as if searching for some modern-day Cinderella, the women dump their bags and go out to the terrace where Harry's deep voice punctures the gathering dusk.

The tableau that awaits them halts Susanne in her tracks.

'We're back,' she calls, unable to tear her eyes from the young woman who, despite the waning heat, is dressed in a bikini top and denim shorts. Side by side, two loungers littered with tanning cream, sunglasses and magazines hint at an afternoon spent sunbathing. Susanne swallows the bile rising in her throat.

'Susanne! Welcome home. How was the museum? Did you love it?' Harry says, springing to his feet and cupping her face in his hands. Caught off guard, Susanne holds back, trying to process the girl smiling and nervously twisting a lock of long blonde hair.

Who the hell…?

'Susanne, everyone, this is Star,' Harry says. 'She's had a spot of bother so I said she could stay here – just for tonight.'

Susanne is aware of Dale and Evie exchanging glances before they both shoot her a quizzical look.

'Oh, right. Of course… how do you two…?' Susanne says, before abandoning the question, unsure what she is really asking.

The girl smiles. 'Aww, thank you. I hope it's all right. Harry said it would be okay.' Her voice is small and her estuary English a stark contrast to Harry's rounded vowels.

'I told Star that you were all kind and would want to help. She's had a huge fight with her boyfriend, Sander, and they both need space to cool off.'

'Oh, you poor thing. I'm Evie, by the way,' Evie says, her head inclined in sympathy.

Susanne hesitates. 'So, you're Sander's girlfriend? Sorry, I don't think I knew he had one. I mean, Harry talks about Joe and Sander sometimes, but we've never met…'

There's an uncomfortable pause; Harry and Star seem to be waiting for something. Her approval, perhaps?

Susanne smiles. 'Look, do stay. Sorry to hear you've had problems. Men, eh? Well… I'll just go and change.'

Feeling deflated and wrong-footed, she turns back to the house. Evie trots beside her but Dale remains rooted to the spot, staring at Star, her face unsmiling, unreadable.

In the privacy of her room, Susanne peers through a crack in the curtains. Dale is saying something to Star, arms crossed, her right hip jutting. It doesn't take a genius to know that her body language is not that of a welcoming committee. Oh god. Just when she and Dale are back on track.

Susanne had expected Harry to follow her inside and to offer further explanation, perhaps. But apart from a quick *hello* kiss and an introduction to the girl, they'd barely interacted. On the other hand, feeling grubby after her day in Florence and the journey home, she'd only have pushed him away so perhaps he was being considerate.

Unwilling to dwell on Harry's lame greeting any further, Susanne twists up her hair and steps into the shower. At once, the warm needles and scented bodywash have a soothing effect and she emerges feeling brighter.

So what if Harry has female friends? And why on earth would he mention whether his young travelling mates were in relationships or not? He barely spoke about them at all, other than to announce that he was 'going out' to see his 'friends'. It had never occurred to Susanne that the group might include young women. And anyway, the girl poses no threat; seems polite, shy – almost childlike, Susanne muses, rubbing fragrant lotion into her tanned skin and putting on a white cotton dress and bejewelled flip-flops.

A thought occurs: where will Star sleep? All four bedrooms are spoken for with the women occupying one each, plus Harry's room off a separate hallway. The obvious solution is for Harry to move into her room and to give up his bed for Star. Dale and Evie have accepted the situation and having Harry in her bed is hardly a hardship.

A shudder of desire and anticipation ripples through Susanne as she remembers the last time they'd slept together. She bats the feeling away; each time may be physically more intense than the last, but *no way* can she lose her heart to Harry.

She spritzes perfume on her neck and wrists, checks her appearance and is about to join the others when a text arrives.

CHAPTER TWENTY-SIX

Dale

Twenty-four hours in Florence had proved to be a bonding experience as the three of them had shared the city's history, art and culture. Both the Uffizi and the cathedral had dazzled their eyes and blown their minds; everywhere they'd looked, Dale, Susanne and Evie had found something that surprised and delighted them.

And not just the antiquities and the architecture, but the people, too; they'd loved the glamourous style of the locals, especially the women, with their glossy hair, cinched waists and flamboyant accessories.

Dale had somehow managed to push Harry to the back of her mind. Not that her opinion of him had changed, but she'd compartmentalised what she had to admit were feelings of sourness and resentfulness that, yet again, somebody who wasn't her was getting close to Susanne. It was cool, she understood; it had ever been thus.

Nevertheless, Harry was a different situation altogether. All that nonsense about having fallen for Susanne – utter bullshit! The kid had a MILF complex and was being led around by his over-ambitious cock. Well, distasteful as it was to watch Susanne squirming in her knickers and making goo-goo eyes around him, at least it was mutual. *For now.*

Susanne was adamant that it was just sex, but Dale knew her too well and her tender heart was easily fractured. It sickened

Dale to imagine Harry gloating over his conquests: she pictured him, boasting about his sexual antics to Joe and Sander, and god-knows-who-else, as though Susanne were some cheap tart to have fun with and then bin off without consequence.

Then there was her niggling doubt that Harry had targeted Susanne for her obvious wealth. The fact that he had his own family money would be no deterrent to a feckless young man with an aversion to hard work. He'd already admitted that he cared little for the job awaiting him in London. Did he view Susanne's money as a nice little stop gap until he himself inherited? Susanne was generous to a fault and he'd surely clocked that by now. Rich, loving and beautiful: a tempting combination for any young man about town.

Regardless of her own misgivings, Dale had filed the whole scenario away – she'd been determined to distance herself with dignity and decorum, because alienating Susanne by making her feel sordid or stupid was unhelpful. And if – no, *when* – things crashed and burned with Harry, Dale reasoned, Susanne would need her to pick up the pieces and help heal the pain, just as they'd always done for each other. Dale wasn't about to let some arrogant rich kid get in the way of their friendship.

So Dale had driven home, tired but happy after their mini adventure, full of a new resolve to let Susanne and Harry's fling run its course – but then they'd arrived at Villa Giardino and things had turned weird.

*

Star? What the hell kind of hippy-dippy made-up name is *that?* Dale looks from Susanne to Harry, then at Star, who is now standing in some awkward one-legged yoga pose, fiddling with a rope of matted hair swept over one shoulder.

Dale watches as though through a lens: there's a fragility about the girl that is familiar. And then, in a gush, it comes to her. Star is the girl from the hostel in San Gimignano; she'd seen them together the day she'd lost her bearings after buying Susanne the bangle. She'd smelled weed, then had looked for the source and had seen Harry and Star sharing a beer and a joint before he'd kissed her goodbye with what looked like real tenderness.

Harry had lied that day about who he'd seen and how he had spent the afternoon. And Dale knows with utter certainty that Harry is lying now. Star is not Sander's girlfriend (if Sander even exists!), but his own. Harry is two-timing Star with Susanne and vice versa.

It is obvious to Dale that Susanne is clueless about Star. No way would she sleep with a young guy (or *anyone*, for that matter) who was already in a relationship. Star on the other hand, seems accepting of Susanne. Unless of course she really *is* Sander's girlfriend…

'Shame about you and Sander. How long have you been together?' Dale says, digging for information once Susanne and Evie have gone inside to freshen up.

Star hesitates and looks to Harry.

Bingo!

His tone is sharp. 'Star, I don't know why you're being coy. You can tell Dale, she's cool.'

Star squinches her eyes shut for a second, as if forming a picture in her mind.

'We… we've been together almost a year. Then we started travelling around Europe six months ago…'

Harry nods. 'With Joe, Sander's best friend,' he cuts in needlessly.

Star licks her lips and fixes her eyes somewhere over Dale's left shoulder. 'Er, yeah. With Joe. That's sort of what we argued about. I'm sick of being in a threesome… Oh! No, not like that, obviously…' She giggles. 'I mean, we're always together. Me and Sander get no privacy. The three of us have been staying in hostels and cheap hotels and I'm sick of it.'

There's a note of sulkiness in her voice. Dale pictures Star stamping her little size-four foot.

'Yeah, I can see that would piss you off. So, what? You gave him an ultimatum?'

'Oh, nothing like that,' Star says, 'but he really shouted at me and I walked out. I just want him to miss me for a day or two, you know?'

Harry is nodding his approval. 'Good call, Star. Sander's great – I mean, I love the guy, but he can be a dick sometimes. Let him sweat, hey, Dale?'

Clever. Trying to get her onside.

Dale smirks. 'Sure. Most men are. Dicks, I mean.'

CHAPTER TWENTY-SEVEN

Susanne

She'd expected the text to be from Cody and is disappointed when Ronnie's name lights up the screen. With an irritated sigh, she walks to the bedroom window. On the terrace, Harry paces back and forth, swigging beer from a bottle, while Star sits on a sunbed, hugging skinny knees, her face creased with laughter and looking like a little bohemian fairy.

'Very bloody cosy,' Susanne mutters under her breath, clutching her mobile. What does Ronnie want? Contact between them has been perfunctory. Then again, they leave in under a week so there may be logistics to sort: keys to hand over, cleaning arrangements to organise and so on.

With a sigh, Susanne swipes the screen.

Hi Susanne, am increasingly worried about Harry. Please tell him to phone asap. Boys will be boys but not calling home on his birthday is not on! Sorry to involve you but all messages are being ignored. Best, Ronnie.

Birthday?! When had it been Harry's birthday? He didn't seem the type to be shy about it; to let it pass by under the radar. Why hadn't he said anything?

Susanne re-reads the message. Why on earth would Harry blank his family? Evie had already passed on one message. He'd rolled his eyes and accused his family of being dramatic, claiming to have spoken to them only days earlier. He'd also promised to call his mother the following morning – well, clearly *that* hadn't happened. With a mounting sense of unease, and before she can overthink things, Susanne hits the call button.

Ronnie answers at once. 'Susanne! Good of you to call. How's that self-centred godson of mine?'

'Hi, Ronnie,' Susanne says, before pleasantries are exchanged. 'Look, I wanted to set your mind at rest. Harry is absolutely fine – in fact, I'm watching him now. He's having a drink by the pool with a young friend who's staying for a day or two.'

'Well, that's a relief!' Ronnie says, with a squawk of laughter. 'Who's the friend?'

'What?' Susanne stalls for time.

'I'm assuming he's picked up some girl on his travels… there's always a girl where Harry's concerned. I warned his parents, I said—'

'Oh, no… she's just a friend. She's been helping Harry with his Italian,' Susanne says, surprised by the speed and ease with which the lie has come to her.

'So he says!' A cynical bark erupts from Veronica. 'What did he do on his birthday?'

'He didn't mention it. I had no idea, actually. When was it?'

'Oh, for god's sake! Yesterday. His mother's pretty upset that she didn't hear from him, and his dad's fuming… he's paying for his bloody trip, after all.'

'Ronnie, I'm sorry. Look, I have to go. Please don't worry, he's in excellent health, I can assure you…' Susanne grimaces. 'I promise I'll get him to phone you or his mum within the next twenty-four hours. Speak soon, bye!'

Susanne ends the call before Ronnie can object and sits on the edge of the bed, overwhelmed by a sudden desire to speak to her own son. She dials Cody. 'Hey, darling. It's Mum. I just wanted to hear your voice…'

*

In the kitchen, Dale is mixing drinks. 'Did you fall in?' she jokes. 'Susie, you've been ages.'

Susanne smiles absently. 'Have I? Sorry, I took a shower and then I rang Cody. I think he's starting to miss me a bit. Maybe the novelty of Scotland, dad and dogs is finally wearing off.'

'Of course it is. Cody's not daft and he knows where his home is. I bet he can't wait to see you.' Dale squeezes a wedge of lemon into each cocktail. 'These are for me and Evie; the kids have got beer. Do you want one?'

Susanne nods. What she really wants is to talk through her phone call with Ronnie, but she can't bear the thought of Dale turning detective and making a big deal out of Harry's odd behaviour. She can read Dale like a book; it's plain to see that she's unimpressed – no, *suspicious* – of Star's arrival.

She watches Dale half fill a glass with ice and free-pour gin from a jewel-bright bottle. Right on cue, Dale lowers her voice: 'What do you think of Star?'

'She seems sweet… bit naïve, maybe. Why, what do you think of her?'

'Hmm… I'm not sure about the boyfriend saga. Listen to this,' Dale says, before relaying the conversation she's just had with Star and Harry about the row – and the Sander/Star/Joe situation which Dale learned had caused it.

So that's what Dale had been grilling them about. Susanne peers out of the French windows. The sun has slipped low on the horizon and a cloud of tiny insects fizzes where Harry and Star are deep in conversation, oblivious to the bugs.

'I don't know,' she says after a pause, 'Three's a crowd… I'd be pissed off if my boyfriend wanted his mate around the whole time, wouldn't you?'

Dale shakes her head. 'Susie, it's not just that. Don't you think it's funny that his friends have never been here and that he always goes off to San Gimi alone? You two are an item and yet he's never taken you into town to meet them.'

Susanne is defensive. 'We've only just met; I'm not sure you can call us an item, Dale.'

Evie enters the room. She too has showered and changed into a pretty floral dress and flip-flops.

'I made you a G and T, Evie,' Dale says, shooting Susanne a look that says this can keep, 'Here you go, hon. Cheers.'

The women clink glasses and hover in the open door, seemingly enjoying the sunset, but Susanne is watching Harry and Star and she's certain that Dale is, too.

Perhaps sensing he's being observed, Harry turns and beckons the women outside.

'Come on, it's still warm,' he says.

Evie shakes her head. 'No, thanks. Think I'll make a start on dinner. We've still got plenty of pasta, some wild mushrooms and a jar of passata if anyone's interested?'

Dale nods. 'Sounds fab, Evie. I'll give you a hand, shall I?' she says, glancing at Susanne.

Susanne is torn between hanging out in the kitchen with Dale and Evie or wedging herself into the new clique that is Harry and Star.

It's a wake-up call: the realisation that if Harry were to become her lover and partner, however close they might be, around his friends she'd always feel like their mother. The thought alone embarrasses her so she mumbles to Harry about supper being ready in twenty minutes and retreats to the kitchen where Dale and Evie are already at work, chopping, dicing and rattling pans.

She longs to have a private conversation with Dale and Evie, keen to get their take on Veronica's phone call but she's unsure how much can be overheard from the terrace.

Not that Harry is paying any attention; he's far too engrossed in Star. A pang of jealousy grips Susanne. Perhaps Dale's insinuations that Harry and Star are more than friends are accurate. Harry has barely acknowledged her – is his coolness for Star's benefit? Perhaps Harry is the real reason for Star's breakup with Sander? The what ifs begin circling Susanne's brain at an alarming rate, rendering her anxious and queasy and she longs to escape.

'Darlings, do you mind if I skip dinner and have an early night? I feel a bit wobbly and not myself at all,' she says, a note of panic rising in her voice.

Dale is at her side immediately. 'You okay, Susie? You do look a bit pale – are you going to throw up? Shall I come with you?'

'Er, would you, I just feel a bit off.' Susanne motions for Dale to follow her. Once inside her room she sinks onto the bed and asks Dale to close the door.

'Hon, I'm okay, really. To be honest, I'm tired and fed up and I don't know what to think about Star's arrival. I mean, she seems sweet enough, but she's a bit clingy with Harry and it makes me wonder... Oh, for god's sake, I need to get a grip, don't I?'

Dale throws up her hands. 'No, it's not you, Susie. The whole thing's weird, if you ask me,' she says loyally.

'Bless you, Dale. I saw you cross-examining the witness through the window... I wish I could be as direct as you are. Anyway, there's something I wanted to tell you ...' Susanne says, before repeating her conversation with Ronnie.

CHAPTER TWENTY-EIGHT

Evie

Evie massages her sore, distended stomach. She'd thrown together a tasty meal from bits and bobs in the fridge and store cupboard, helped by Dale, which had pleasantly surprised her and given them time to chat about the highlights of their Florence trip. But after Susanne had escaped to her room feeling poorly, keen not to waste the food they'd prepared, she'd eaten more than usual. Now, the mushrooms have given her indigestion and the Chianti has made her head fuzzy.

Unable to sleep, Evie tries to concentrate on her book, but the words won't stick and after re-reading the same page three times, she gets up and pads to the kitchen where she gulps down a glass of mineral water.

The strains of a romantic melody punctuated by girlish dialogue are coming from the sitting room. Evie walks in to find Star watching TV in the dark, her face illuminated by the flickering screen. Feeling like an intruder, but at the same time enticed by the soft-focus image on the television, Evie creeps into the room and sits down.

Star turns to smile at her, her face angelic in the half-light.

'Sorry, Evie – did the TV disturb you?' she asks.

'No, not at all. I just needed some water. I'm feeling a bit bloated, to be honest. Mind if I join you?'

''Course not,' Star says, pulling a throw around her shoulders, despite the humidity. 'I love a romcom, me – anything with Julia Roberts or Meg Ryan in it. I prefer the old ones, don't you?'

'Yes. But my absolute favourite is *Breakfast at Tiffany's*,' Evie answers, a smile lighting her face in the gloom. 'It was my mum's favourite film as well, but she… she passed away recently.'

'Oh, Evie, I'm sorry. How awful,' Star says, 'mine too. Well, not so recently – it's been a few years now.'

'Bless you. You're very young to have lost your mum – was it cancer?'

'No. She… actually, I'd rather not talk about it.'

Evie watches Star's face become pinched and hard. Poor kid can't be more than eighteen or nineteen – no wonder losing her mum is painful to recall. 'Sorry, I shouldn't have asked you,' Evie says, getting up. 'Well, I'll leave you to it. I'm feeling a bit sleepy now. Goodnight, Star.'

Without looking at her, Star murmurs 'night' and Evie goes back to her room. Once inside, she can hear yelps, cries and moans coming from Susanne's room next door.

Oh god, it's going to be a long night. She sighs and pulls the sheet over her head to muffle the sound and focusses her mind on Star.

There is something about her – an innocence, perhaps. She doesn't seem mature enough to even have a boyfriend, let alone a serious one whom she's at loggerheads with. Evie had seen Dale's reaction – watchful, suspicious, even. Then again, that wasn't saying much; Dale could be a prickly pear at the best of times.

Soft moans erupt from the room next door that soon mount in volume, followed by a triumphant shout from Harry. She imagines them, spooning, spent and happy, their long, tanned legs entwined as they whisper endearments into the darkness before falling asleep in each other's arms.

*

Dale is up first, prowling the kitchen in a short kimono wrap and flip-flops, bed-hair askew.

'Morning, Evie,' she says. 'Oh my god, did you hear them at it last night?' she says in a low voice while Evie puts water on to boil.

'Yes, wish I could say I didn't,' Evie says, shaking her head.

Dale shrugs. 'Well, bang goes my theory.'

Evie is all ears. 'About what?'

Dale's eyes dart around, as if someone might overhear them. 'Let's take our coffee outside; we can sit by the pool and chat.'

Evie nods, surprised and flattered to be taken into Dale's confidence.

A tiny silver lizard skitters ahead of them on the terrace, roused by the vibration of their feet. 'Oh, sweet! Look at him go,' Dale squeals.

Evie shudders. She'll never be a fan, although after so many sightings, the shock of seeing small reptiles about the place is wearing off. She holds two steaming mugs while Dale drags a couple of plastic chairs closer to the pool, the water rippling gently under the sun's early morning glare.

'What did you mean, Dale… about your *theory*?' Evie asks when they are seated, nursing fresh hot coffee.

'Honestly? I thought that Star might be Harry's girlfriend, rather than his mysterious mate Sander's. But judging by last night's shag fest, I guess I was wrong.' Dale laughs and shakes her head. 'This has been the weirdest holiday ever. We'll all need another one to get over it. Preferably one without any random blokes!'

Evie's laughter is polite. Unsure how to answer, she changes the subject. 'I think I might swim today – we'll miss this pool when we go home. I'm not sure I'm any better at it, but at least I feel a bit braver in the water now.'

Dale stretches her arms over her head and yawns. 'Evie, love – you can swim well, okay? The only thing you're missing is confidence. In everything,' she adds kindly. 'I know you've had some bad knocks, but, well, haven't we all? Sorry if that sounds harsh, but you just need to grab life by the bollocks and take a few risks.'

Touched by Dale's attention, Evie can feel herself blushing. 'I know. I've always been a jelly. But I've promised myself that I'll start living when we get back. I'm going to look for a job, do Mum's – I mean, *my* – house up and start taking control of my life.' Evie squeezes her soft midriff. 'Starting with this… think I might have put a few pounds back on – it's all the yummy pasta we've been eating.'

'There you go again! Stop with the self-deprecation, you're lovely as you are,' Dale snaps, shaking her head. 'Anyway, lecture over.' She drags her chair closer to Evie's and lowers her voice: 'So, listen to this. I might have been wrong about Star, but young Harry is definitely up to something. Do you know, he still hasn't phoned home?'

Evie's eyes widen. 'How do you know? What's happened?'

Dale's expression is triumphant. 'When we got back yesterday evening, Susanne got a text from Ronnie, basically annoyed that Harry hasn't been in touch for ages. Get this: it was his birthday while we were in Florence, and he didn't even give his mum a call. I mean, I know posh folk do things differently to us, but not phoning the woman who gave birth to him? That's just rude form.'

'And Susanne told you all this last night? When she said she felt ill?'

'Yes, but I think she was just tired and crabby – and not at all impressed by Harry being all over Star like a rash.'

'He was just trying to cheer me up, that's all.' Barefoot, Star has stolen up behind them, and is gazing at the pool, her face still puffy from sleep.

'Star! Sorry,' Evie says at once, 'we were just—'

Dale flashes Evie a warning look. 'We were just wondering why Harry never mentioned his birthday. We could have done something – thrown him a party or taken him out.'

Star's blonde eyebrows shoot up, her face a picture of surprise and amusement. 'Oh, well… I didn't know either. Yeah, why not give him a party tonight? That'll surprise him. Hey, I can help – that's if you don't mind me staying another night. I mean, I wouldn't want to get in anyone's way.' Evie and Dale's eyes meet.

Dale is right. Evie needs to start taking control of her own life, having opinions and sticking to them instead of deferring to everyone else all the time. Star's relationship with her boyfriend is none of their business and the very least the women can do is to provide some sisterly support.

'Star, you're very welcome,' Evie says, sounding decisive. 'As far as I'm concerned, you can stay as long as you want.'

CHAPTER TWENTY-NINE

Susanne

Susanne wakes early and snuggles closer to Harry. *The sleep of the just* – or should that be the sleep of youth? She pictures Cody on school-free days, snoring happily, long after the alarm has gone off.

Oh, for goodness' sake! She must stop comparing the two of them. Harry may be young but he's twenty-four (she corrects herself: twenty-*five*, he's just had a birthday) – ten years older than her son and at a completely different life stage.

Dale's sad, heated words come back to her: *do you imagine Harry moving in with you and being a big brother to Cody?*

Would that be so terrible? Nobody would bat an eyelid if it was the other way around and Harry was seventeen years her senior.

Toy-boy was a term she loathed but that's what people would call him if Harry became part of her life; it would make her a cougar, which was even worse! At least nobody could accuse Harry of being a gold-digger. His family were wealthy, successful, and soon he'd be working for a fund manager in London, climbing his way up in the world – just as Colin had done in his youth. Oh God, *Col* – what on earth would her son's father have to say about it all?

She is doing it again; jumping ahead, giving Harry a significant role in her future, fantasising about a life that could not be. She'd talked a good game, scattering words like holiday romance and fun fling; a shag fest was what Dale had so charmingly called it. And it should have been all those things and certainly nothing more.

And yet.

Something about Harry touches her deeply. The more physically connected they become, the more she sees inside him. Yes, he'd been so full of confidence and given Susanne the ride of her life from their first night together, his moves so practised that they'd bordered on rehearsed. But recently things had changed between them; sometimes, at his most open and vulnerable, the swaggering public schoolboy would seem to vanish, revealing someone gentle and unsure – needy, even – behind that persona.

After coming back from Florence and finding a cuckoo in the nest – for that's what Star's arrival felt like – Susanne had watched them together, chatting, playing and flirting. And it had stirred ugly feelings of jealousy and spite. She'd even imagined that Star was involved with Harry, and it had hurt and embarrassed her to the point where she couldn't face being around the others.

Then the text from Ronnie had arrived and they'd spoken, about Harry's birthday and how he'd failed to call his family even then. How could anyone, even a single young guy, be so bloody selfish?

To Dale's credit, when Susanne had relayed the conversation with Ronnie, she'd made little of it – which was most out of character for Dale.

'Young guys aren't exactly famous for their tact and diplomacy,' was all she'd said, before trying to persuade Susanne to join everyone in the kitchen. Susanne had declined, preferring to read in her room. Later, Harry had come to her, with a renewed tenderness, saying he'd missed her terribly and had wished he'd taken her to Florence himself. Lying in his arms, her heart had soared and she'd snuggled closer, pushing Star from her mind, wanting to savour the intimacy between them.

Carefully, so as not to wake him, Susanne slides out of bed, pulls on a light robe and goes into the bathroom.

*

A welcome breeze stirs the lavender. Susanne catches its delicate scent as she passes by on her way to the pool area, attracted by the laughter that bubbles from it.

'Good morning. Sorry, I overslept a bit.' She sounds sheepish even to her own ears. Raucous laughter erupts through the *hello*s.

Susanne scowls, 'What's so funny?'

'Oh, nothing,' Dale says as her eyes flick to Evie and Star, 'just being childish. Where's Harry? Can he still walk?'

'I'm pretty sure you've used that gag before,' Susanne says, determined to hide her annoyance. 'I left him asleep. Anyone had breakfast yet?'

Dale shakes her head. 'No, just coffee. Susie, I told the girls about it being Harry's birthday while we were in Florence, and we all agree that it would be nice to celebrate. What do you think?'

It's hard to say what annoys Susanne more: the fact that some exclusive club (*the girls* and *we all* indeed – when had everyone got so matey?) has formed without her, or that Dale had betrayed a private conversation. And when had Dale become such a fan of Harry's that she's now championing his birthday?

As if realising her lack of tact too late, Dale shrugs. 'Soz, it's entirely your call, of course – I just wanted to mention it before Harry gets up.'

Susanne's smile belies her irritation. 'Yes, it's fine. Actually, that's a great idea. We could surprise him. Evie, Star, what do you think?'

Star grins. 'Yeah, why not? I'm always up for a party.'

'We can all chip in,' Evie says, 'I'll make canapes, or something tasty anyway – and maybe a cake!'

Dale gets up and starts to pace. 'Susie, how about you and I do a booze run? Star, can you get Harry out of the house for a couple of hours while we get our arses in gear?'

Star hesitates. 'Yes, I suppose so.'

Susanne is warming to the idea. What the hell? They mean to be kind. 'All right. Well, I guess that settles it then. Not a word to

Harry, okay? Meanwhile, I'll tackle him about phoning home. I know boys will be boys, but this is ridiculous.'

*

Harry sits up in bed, a huge grin on his sleepy face. 'Where did you go, gorgeous girl? I missed you.'

'Oh, so you're alive, then,' Susanne climbs on the bed beside him. 'Only I did wonder – everyone else has been up for ages.'

Harry kisses her, and with a playful growl, pins her down.

'Don't!' she giggles, pushing him away. 'I need you to be serious for a minute, Harry.'

Harry groans and mutters that he's woken up in the doghouse.

'Not at all, but last night, I had a phone call. From your godmother. Well, actually, she sent me a text and I rang her back. Harry, Ronnie's worried about you – they all are.'

His expression darkens. 'Why? Everyone knows where I am. What did you say?'

'I said that you were in rude health, thanks very much – but that you were being a selfish idiot.'

Harry's expression is one of incredulity.

Susanne rolls her eyes. 'Of course I didn't say that, but, Harry, it's not very kind, is it? Especially when—' She pauses, careful to avoid the subject of his birthday. 'When you've been away for months and your dad is paying for your trip!' *Phew, well-rescued.*

'Oh, so you think I'm freeloading. Shit, Susanne, you have no idea!'

Harry gets up, marches to the bathroom and slams the door. When he returns, his face is set as he pulls on clothes discarded hurriedly the night before.

'Look, why are you so upset? Harry! Talk to me,' Susanne says, hurt and confused by his reaction.

Dressed, he turns to her, fury in his eyes. 'Firstly, don't treat me like a kid and guilt-trip me. Secondly, you don't know the whole story.' He swipes a hand through his hair crossly.

'Then tell me. I'm sorry, Harry. Look, I'm not getting at you, but it puts me in a weird position with Ronnie. I am her guest, after all. Don't you think I'm already a bit freaked out because of… because of us?'

Harry takes a deep breath. 'One day, I'll explain, but right now, I just need to… Oh, never mind.'

Then Susanne is left hanging as he stalks off down the corridor from where she watches him barge into his old room without knocking, mindless as to whether Star is there or not, before he heads out through the front door. Moments later, Susanne hears an engine start and the tell-tale whoosh of gravel as Harry speeds off down the hill.

What just happened? Susanne sits on the edge of her bed, a sinking feeling in the pit of her stomach.

CHAPTER THIRTY

Dale

She can see Susanne is suffering. Torturing herself about Harry's outburst before he took off in a cloud of dust and temper.

'It was kind of a joke when I called him a selfish idiot, but he took it really badly. I might as well have called him a murderer for how pissed off he was. But, you know… not calling home *is* incredibly selfish. I just keep thinking how I'd feel if Cody went away for a month or two and didn't get in touch.'

Dale snorts, in no mood to mince her words. 'It's not your fault, Susie. You hit a nerve, that's all. Because the truth hurts and he's acting like an egocentric arse. Typical young guy, wants everything his own way, and sod everyone else.'

They are in the booze aisle of the supermarket – or booze shelf, to be more accurate. The modest village store is hardly Sainsbury's, though it has served them well all holiday long, thanks to Susanne and Evie's resourcefulness.

'Peroni or Moretti?' Susanne scrutinises bottled beer brands. 'Actually, screw that! Can't believe we're bloody bothering – there's no guarantee that Harry will even come back this evening. What if he's taken off with Joe and Sander, and he goes AWOL for days?'

'Okay, you're scaring me now, Susanne. Remarks like that sound an awful lot like you're obsessed with him. He's only meant to be a shag fest, remember? We'll be home in a few days, so you need to chill out about Harry. Let's get some beers and mixers; we've already got wine, gin and a bottle of champagne at the house – and if *he* doesn't drink them, *we* will.'

Dale steers the trolley through aisles lined with snacks and fancies, stuffing it with crisps, nuts and chocolate-covered marshmallows.

'It looks like we're shopping for a kid's party,' Susanne says, watching the mound of junk food grow.

'My lips are sealed,' Dale says, giving her friend a playful shove.

*

Evie is red in the face, a smear of flour across her right cheek and a tell-tale glob of chocolate at the corner of her mouth.

She indicates a triple-layer sponge cake topped with cocoa frosting. 'What do you think?'

Dale and Susanne exclaim over Evie's handiwork, marvelling at how she's managed to bake such an extravagant masterpiece in a strange kitchen with odd baking tins and no scales except for a set of measuring spoons with the numbers almost worn away.

'So now we have a shedload of alcohol, a ton of crisps and junk, *and* a gorgeous cake. What we don't have is the birthday boy,' Dale says, mentally adding *the sulky brat*, while managing to keep her face a judgement-free zone.

Evie nods. 'Star rang Harry while you were out. Apparently, he's fine and just needed some time alone. He told Star that he'd have a bite to eat in San Gimignano and that he'd be back in a few hours. Apparently, he's cooled down now and is sorry for going off in a huff.'

Dale watches relief flood Susanne's face. 'Well, at least Star didn't have to make up some cock-and-bull story to get him out of the house. Where is she?'

'Outside somewhere,' Evie says. 'Think she's been in the pool. I might take a dip myself as soon as I've cleared this lot up.'

Happier now, Susanne smiles. 'Evie, you've worked hard on that wonderful cake. Get your cossie on and Dale and I will wash up. I mean it, go on.'

Evie starts to protest, thinks better of it, then with an endearing clap of her hands, she runs off to change.

*

Despite her own misgivings about whether or not Harry deserves a party, Dale finds herself swept up in her friends' enthusiasm and by four o'clock, with preparations out of the way, the women have an hour or so to relax. The temperature has risen, driving all four of them into the pool, two at a time. Star has removed her bikini top in an attempt to fill in her tan lines – Dale watches her from behind large sunglasses, amazed by her total lack of inhibition and by how happy and carefree she seems.

'Star, have you spoken to your boyfriend recently?' she asks, angling herself towards the younger woman.

'What?' Star's eyes are wide.

'Sander. Have you called him? Or are you still making him sweat?'

Star shakes her head. 'Oh, no. I rang him this morning, but he didn't pick up.'

'What a jerk,' Susanne says, pushing herself out of the pool.

'If Sander's being an arse, that's his problem. He should have apologised by now,' Dale says, in an attempt to be friendly and supportive.

Star doesn't reply but rolls onto her stomach and closes her eyes.

Dale and Evie exchange looks, while Susanne makes a business of blotting her hair dry before reaching for her mobile phone.

'Okay, I'm calling Harry. I'll try and get an ETA from him. Everyone keep quiet, please. Remember, the last conversation he and I had was not good,' she says, putting her mobile on speaker mode.

The phone rings once. 'Hello, gorgeous.' Harry's voice. 'I was just about to call you. Susanne, I'm so sorry about earlier, please forgive me. I was being an idiot and you were right of course, as usual. But, darling, there's stuff you don't know – I'll tell you later. I'll be back by six.'

'Apology accepted, of course I forgive you.' Susanne's face softens.

'Anyway, you phoned me. Was there anything specific, Susie?' Harry asks.

'Er… no, just wondered what time you'd be back and if you could get me some chocolate,' Susanne says, wincing at her own poor improvisation.

'Chocolate? Of course. Anything for my Persian Princess – what else are slaves for if not to—'

Susanne stabs a button on her phone; it silences Harry mid-sentence. She turns away and wanders a few metres from the giggling women before concluding the call.

Dale's shoulders shake with laughter. *Persian Princess?*

'It was just a silly game, you know how it is…' Susanne's cheeks redden.

'No, I don't. Still, whatever floats your boat.'

Embarrassed, Susanne mumbles something about getting ready and starts towards the house.

Dale grimaces. 'I was only joking,' she calls out, but Susanne does not look back.

'That was a bit mean,' Evie says, her face puckered with concern.

'I was just teasing. Jesus, I am fed up with walking on eggshells around here,' Dale grumbles before going to the pool and jumping in with an extravagant splash.

She treads water for a moment, luxuriating in its coolness. Why is Susanne being so bloody touchy? There was a time when they could say pretty much anything to each other – and they'd usually laugh it off. Clearly, those days are over. Dale starts to pull long, lean strokes, swimming faster and harder until her shoulders ache.

*

By six o'clock everyone has gathered on the terrace. On the linen-covered table, champagne tantalises from an ice bucket. Beside it, a row of glasses sparkles. Plates of canapés and bowls of snacks are dotted around, and Evie's chocolate cake forms a mouth-watering centrepiece.

In the mellow light, Dale studies the women. Susanne, stylish in a black jersey dress and strappy sandals, glowing with sunshine and anticipation; Evie, pretty in a rose-printed sundress, her hair twisted at the nape of her neck; Star, youthful in distressed blue jeans and halterneck top, beaded earrings peeking through her hair. Everyone has made the effort for Harry, Dale thinks bitterly. She smooths down her denim playsuit, feeling oddly apprehensive as they wait.

'He's here!' Susanne cries, hearing Harry's jeep pull up. She hoists the champagne in a napkin, ready to pop its cork. Evie and Star exchange excited glances. Only Dale remains cool, observing the scene with detachment. Harry may have a bucketload of charisma and have her best friend under his spell, but she remains unconvinced.

Inconsistencies bother her; perhaps her teacher training is to blame. Always having to read between the lines, find the hidden subtext. Star may not be his girlfriend as she'd first thought, but there is something about their interaction that doesn't quite ring true.

Neither does Star's indifference to her recent upset with Sander. A few hours earlier, when asked if she'd spoken to her boyfriend, she'd seemed surprised, as if she'd forgotten all about him and was content to hang out in female company.

Dale looks across at Susanne, watches her return the champagne to its ice bucket. The minutes tick by: five, then ten, and still Harry does not materialise.

Dale frowns. 'Where the bloody hell is he?'

'Loo, probably,' Evie mouths. But when Harry eventually appears, his hair is in damp tufts and he's wearing a crisp, new-looking T-shirt.

He hangs back and surveys the party scene, a look of bewilderment on his face.

Beaming with relief and happiness, Susanne twists open the champagne, fills five glasses and presses one into Harry's hand.

'Happy birthday, babe,' she says, wrapping her arms around his neck and kissing him.

CHAPTER THIRTY-ONE

Susanne

In full view of the others, Susanne kisses Harry with a fervour that surprises her. At once the feel of his lips on hers and the scent of his citrusy shower gel and cedar shampoo makes her tingle. With his arms around her and his fingers resting on the small of her back, all she wants is for everyone else to melt away – and for Harry to take her to bed and make her feel more alive than she'd ever thought possible.

But when they break apart, there's a hesitancy in his eyes. He gulps some champagne and shakes his head, blinking in confusion.

'Busted, I'm afraid, Harry,' Dale says, 'did you think we wouldn't find out?'

Harry's eyes widen; he takes another sip of champagne.

'That it was your birthday, she means. Your godmother told us,' Star says, a forced heartiness in her tone. 'You could have said, Harry.'

Then Dale, Evie and Star gather round, hugging him and wishing him many happy returns.

Susanne sees a look of relief wash over him. 'Well, what can I say? Thank you, that's so sweet of you all. Oh my god, who made the cake? It looks fantastic!'

Evie beams with pride and raises an index finger. 'Hope you like chocolate.'

'Everyone likes chocolate,' Dale says. 'Right, let's get this party started! More champagne, anyone?'

*

By sunset, Star and Evie are dancing, inhibitions loosened by alcohol, but Dale has snuck away and sits hunched by the pool, her legs dangling in its depths.

Concerned, Susanne extracts herself from Harry's arms. 'Oh dear, that's not a good sign. Wait here while I check she's okay,' she whispers, promising to return.

'Hey, love.' She drops to Dale's level, removes her shoes and plunges her toes into the water. She gasps. 'Oof, that's colder than I expected. Are you going to tell me what's wrong, or do I have to guess?' Susanne says, her tone gentle.

'Nothing. I'm fine… Probably had too much gin.' Dale waves her almost-empty glass.

Aware that Dale is drinking quickly, Susanne nods and swishes the water, her feet and ankles beginning to acclimatise. 'Must admit I feel a bit worse for wear, too. Are you sure? Nothing else bothering you?'

Dale's laughter is brittle. 'Nothing you want to hear, trust me.'

Susanne sighs. 'Maybe. But tell me anyway. And then I think we should go and dance with the girls, maybe even get Harry to throw some shapes. It's supposed to be his party, after all.'

Dale drains her glass and sets it down, her eyes suddenly hard. 'All right. If you must know. I don't trust Harry further than I can throw him, and as you ask, I don't trust Star, either – or whatever the bloody hell her real name is. I just don't buy it, Susie. Something's off. With both of them.'

Susanne puffs out her cheeks and exhales, swinging her feet out of the water and getting up awkwardly.

'So, we're here again, are we? You've got a very suspicious mind, Dale – maybe you've been a teacher for too long. Let's not talk about this now; everyone else is having a good time and it's not fair.'

'Susanne, wait.'

Dale paws at her hand, but Susanne ignores it, instead walking back up the shallow steps, carrying her shoes and leaving a trail of wet footprints as she crosses the terrace.

Evie calls out to her and Susanne sees at once that her ladylike dress has been swapped for jeans and a T-shirt. 'Come and dance, Susie. Look, I'm twerking! Star taught me how to do it,' she giggles, her words slurred, her hips jutting back and forth in time to the throbbing base. Star staggers, shrieking with laughter, while Harry watches from the shadows, a bemused grin on his face.

Susanne smiles and gives Evie a thumbs up before joining Harry.

He clasps her hands and pulls her towards him. 'Thank you, Susanne. It's lovely of you to organise this. But that's you all over, isn't it? You're so thoughtful. And beautiful – you look amazing in that dress,' he says, emitting a playful growl.

Susanne smiles. 'You think? It's not the dress I was planning to wear. I've got one just like this in cornflower blue, but I couldn't find it.'

And not for lack of trying. Susanne had searched every corner of her wardrobe and even checked her laundry bag, but there'd been no sign of it.

Just then, Susanne catches sight of Evie weaving towards the kitchen. 'Let's follow her – she looks pretty hammered.'

Once in the kitchen, Evie gulps water from a bottle, leaning unsteadily against the sink, face flushed and eyes gleaming.

Susanne and Harry exchange an amused grimace.

'Evie, I can't think why you would, but have you seen my blue dress anywhere?' Susanne asks, already anticipating the reply.

Evie shakes her head. 'Nope, sorry. Don't mer-rember you wearing anything blue since we got here.'

'Okay, darling. Never mind, it'll turn up.'

Harry is watching Evie intently, a look of consternation on his face. 'Evie, are you all right? Are you going to throw up?'

Evie emits a loud hiccup. 'I'm fine.' A sleepy smile spreads across her face before she teeters outside, slamming her shoulder against the door frame as she goes.

Susanne winces. 'Ouch. That's going to be a nasty bruise.'

Harry shrugs. 'She's drunk, probably didn't feel a thing. Look at her, dancing with Star. Bless her, she's having so much fun.'

Susanne presses herself against Harry and wraps her arms around his neck. 'Are you, though?'

'Am I what?' Harry brushes her lips with his own.

'Having fun? I realise that spending your twenty-fifth birthday with four women, three of them old bags, isn't exactly a dream celebration.'

Harry sniggers. 'Hey, one of those old bags is my girlfriend, if you don't mind.' He smiles and takes her hands. 'Anyway, spending it in a gorgeous Tuscan villa with the woman I love could scarcely be better.'

Susanne's brow furrows as she studies his face, unsure how to answer. Her heart is beating so loudly in her chest, she's sure Harry can hear it. Is he really saying he loves her? Or is the heady cocktail of champagne and gin doing the talking for him?

He makes a face and runs a hand through his hair. 'Sorry. Too much? Susanne, time is short… I just wanted to be honest with you.'

Susanne attempts to silence him with a kiss, but Harry pulls away. 'Wish I hadn't said it now…' He pouts. 'I'm being much too serious, aren't I? Come on, let's go join the girls.'

Susanne resists a sudden urge to tell Harry that she loves him too, and instead leads him outside where Star is still on her feet, but no longer dancing, fatigue having clearly set in.

Dale is plodding up the steps, the black cloud over her head almost visible.

Harry groans. 'Jesus, what's wrong with her? She can be a moody bitch at times. I mean, I've made a real effort to be friends but she's bloody hard work.'

'Talking about me?' Dale smiles sweetly, suddenly eye to eye with Harry.

He shrugs. 'I'm sorry, Dale, but I hate to see you so pissed off. What can we do to cheer you up?'

Dale's eyes widen. '*We?*'

Susanne watches Dale's face harden into a mask of belligerence. Determined to quell the brewing storm, she takes Dale's arm and leads her away, babbling about needing help in the kitchen. It's a ruse, but Harry follows them.

Dale droops, puts her head in her hands. 'Look, I'm sorry. Just ignore me. Mixing my drinks does this sometimes. Think I'll go to bed and leave you to your toy-boy. Night.'

Toy-boy? Susanne flinches and starts to protest, a flush creeping into her cheeks, then decides to let it go as Dale blows her a kiss and lopes off to her room.

Guilt and relief wash over Susanne as Harry pulls her into his arms. At once, her body responds, and she aches to be alone with him.

'I know exactly what I want for my birthday,' he whispers, his breath warm against her ear.

A sigh escapes Susanne's parted lips, but she pushes Harry away as Star and Evie burst through the door.

'Can we cut the cake now?' Star whines.

'Yes, let's,' Harry replies. 'So sweet of you to make one, Evie – must have taken you hours. How on earth did you know that chocolate's my favourite?'

Back outside, a breeze stirs and the candles flicker. The music has stopped, leaving only the background fizz of the night critters.

Evie dishes out huge wonky slabs of cake: there's a satisfied silence as they all take first bites.

'Mmm, delicious. What a shame Dale missed out,' Harry says, licking chocolate from his lips and fingertips.

'I suspect Dale had too much sun,' Susanne says.

Harry rolls his eyes. 'And too much booze, *and* too much of me. I'm afraid your best friend disapproves of us – and nothing anyone says will change her mind.'

Susanne glances in Evie's direction. Unsteady on her feet, she's starting to clear plates and glasses, her expression uneasy.

Susanne warns Harry with a slight shake of her head. But Harry either doesn't notice or doesn't care. 'Dale wants you all to herself. I don't know why you can't see it. Everyone else can, eh, Star?'

Star yawns. 'What? Dunno, it's none of my business, and anyway, my bed is calling. Thank you for a lovely party, everyone. Can't remember the last time I drank so much or danced like that. Na-night, sweet dreams.'

Evie moves into the kitchen, scraping debris into a bin liner and clattering glass and crockery, marking the end of the party.

Suddenly, alone with Harry, Susanne remembers something – a hangover from their phone conversation that afternoon.

'Harry, I'm so sorry – what was it you wanted to tell me?'

His expression is vague. 'What, other than saying that I've fallen in love with you? Yeah, Susanne, about that. I—'

'No, not that – as lovely as it is. It was something you said on the phone today: *there's stuff you don't know, I'll tell you later.* I've only just remembered, but please, tell me now. I'd like to understand.'

Harry cups her face in his hands and kisses her. 'Doesn't matter, Susie… I can't even remember to be honest. Now can I please take you to bed and do what I've wanted to all evening?'

CHAPTER THIRTY-TWO

Rome, May 2019

Brandon

Brandon surveys the bar. It's dead this evening, with almost as many staff as punters. Palazzo Angeli is his second venue of the night; two blocks away, at Hotel Clio, it was the same story. Well, what did he expect, midweek in May?

His knock-off Rolex is saying eight fifteen. One drink. Just one, then he'll call it a night and pick up a takeaway on the way home – maybe get some of that angel hair pasta with the creamy mushrooms that Star likes so much.

He signals to Marco, who nods, goes to the bar and returns with a beer and a small dish of olives.

'It's too quiet in here, Marco – what's going on?' Brandon says, spearing an olive and letting its saltiness burst on his tongue.

The waiter shrugs. 'Is normal. We busy this weekend – you come then, my friend.'

Brandon nods resignedly. 'Maybe, or perhaps I'll go somewhere new.' He pauses as a sleek blonde in a fur-trimmed jacket glides past, straight to a booth near the bar.

Marco's smile is that of a lizard basking on a rock. 'Scusami, I have *real* customer,' he says with a wink and a small click of his heels.

From his vantage point across the lounge, Brandon watches as the woman downs two drinks in quick succession, kicking off with something pink and cloudy in a martini glass – a cosmo-politan? – followed by a glass of white wine, thick and golden in colour – probably chardonnay, he muses.

The timing of his approach has to be right. Move in too soon and he risks the imminent arrival of her date and she'll tell him to get lost; wait too long and at the speed she's tipping back alcohol, she'll be morose and maudlin and will tell him to piss off anyway.

Brandon straightens his jacket and rakes a hand through shoulder-length hair. Most of the women he meets like it long, winding their fingers into it, exclaiming over its thickness – a mark of his youth, a reminder of what was once theirs.

His walk across the room is purposeful. 'Good evening. Mind if I sit here?' he says, taking a seat opposite the woman without waiting for an answer and adding, 'What are you drinking? Chardonnay? Think I'll join you.' He motions to the waiter.

'Hey, Marco, can you add a couple more drinks to my bill, please? Two glasses of chardonnay when you have a moment.'

'Ha! No need to ask if you're a regular. So that's his name.' The woman's voice is low; her accent has the layered intonation of the well-travelled. 'He's been giving me the evils since I got here. People often judge a woman who drinks alone.' Her eyes glitter and her matte scarlet mouth curves into a mischievous smile.

'Yes, I've always thought that rather unfair,' Brandon says. 'Why is it more acceptable for a man to drink alone than for a woman? After all, it's 2019, not 1919. I'm Brandon, by the way.'

'Hello, Brandon.' She extends a slender arm. Emeralds and diamonds sparkle from a hand older than its corresponding face. 'Simone,' she says, holding his gaze.

There's a pause in the conversation while Marco sets down two glasses of wine before retreating with a barely perceptible smirk.

'I have a friend in England called Simone; she's very chic, too. Well, she's not really a friend, exactly,' Brandon says, 'she's my agent.'

'Oh god, spare me from another starving actor,' Simone groans, a look of resignation crossing her carefully made-up face.

'Actually, I'm a model; it'll do for now, until I figure out what's next.' Brandon lifts his chin and shakes back his hair – all the better to be admired.

'So that makes you, what? Seventeen?'

'Not quite,' Brandon says, flashing his most engaging smile. 'It's helpful in my line of work that I look younger than I am, but as you ask, I'm twenty-seven.'

More laughter, a shrug and then the gluttonous draining of one glass, before starting the next.

This woman can drink, Brandon observes, weighing up whether to call it quits; she may as well have *cynic* tattooed on her forehead.

'You sound English, West London, perhaps?' Brandon says, going back to basics.

'Originally. And you?'

'Same, London – but I've moved around a bit. I've been in Rome for three weeks.

I flew out for an audition with a high-profile designer. Unfortunately, I didn't get the gig, but thought I'd stick around anyway. Rome's so beautiful and I love being a tourist.'

'Nice work if you can get it.' She leans forward, with sudden interest. 'Who's the designer?'

'I'm afraid I'm sworn to secrecy. In fact, they made me sign a confidentiality agreement because it was linked to a launch… fragrance, accessories… that sort of thing, I'm sure you understand.'

Simone rakes scarlet nails through expensively highlighted hair and nods. 'Of course.'

Brandon leans closer. 'That's a beautiful ring you're wearing. Your husband is a very generous man and has excellent taste.'

'My *husband*,' Simone enunciates the word with emphasis, 'is a very dead man and had nothing to do with it – although indirectly you could say he paid for it, thanks to his life assurance policy.'

'Oh, I'm sorry to hear that – it must be difficult for you.' Brandon attempts empathy, but Simone's expression registers only boredom.

Wow, what a hard bitch. Brandon takes a sip of the cold wine while he considers his next move. Can he really be bothered to escort this wealthy, bitter widow to her room, and shag her for a few hundred euros, or for a new suit bought hastily on her credit card in Via dei Condotti the following day?

He considers the overdue rent on his cramped and shabby apartment.

Needs must. He attempts a warm smile. 'Being alone can be stressful and exhausting. I can help you to unwind if you like.'

Simone feigns surprise before letting out a throaty laugh. 'Oh, don't worry. You can drop the act. Model, my eye! I had you pegged the moment you came over here, for god's sake. Buy me another drink and I'll think about it.'

*

Simone's hotel is three blocks from the bar. When she takes Brandon's arm, he knows it's for balance and not affection as she's tottering in four-inch heels through the quiet cobbled streets.

'I have a view of the Pantheon from my suite,' she says, making small talk as they arrive outside the smart but anonymous hotel.

The night manager's greeting is brief as he hands Simone her key. Brandon has come to expect this. In his experience, hotel staff are adept at looking the other way and saying little.

On the fourth floor, in a room hushed by luxury and with barely a word exchanged between them, Brandon undresses Simone with a practised hand and enacts his soulless seduction.

Sometimes the women he meets are timid, nervous, even apologetic to begin with, becoming bolder as their confidence and arousal grow. But Simone is savage in her desire, digging her nails into Brandon's back and biting his shoulder as she cries out in ecstasy.

'Hey, easy, tiger,' he admonishes softly, when what he wants is to slap her spiteful face and shove her hard across the room.

Performance over, despite his growing revulsion, Brandon strokes Simone's toned thigh and tells her she is beautiful.

'And so I should be, the amount of time I spend in the gym,' she says with a sardonic laugh, before adding, to his relief, 'I'm tired now and I need my beauty sleep. Stay or go… I couldn't care less which.'

Brandon's smile is benign as he swallows the words, *just pay me so I can get the hell out of here*.

As if reading his mind, Simone reaches for her robe and goes to the safe before peeling large bills from a wad of cash.

'Four hundred euros as agreed,' she says, her voice clipped. 'I'll be leaving Rome in three days so I doubt our paths will cross again.'

Dressing with his back turned, Brandon affects disappointment. 'That's a shame. Where are you headed next?'

'Florence. I have friends there. You should visit – the art is breath-taking.'

Brandon smiles. 'So I've heard. Maybe I will. Take care of yourself, Simone.' He drops a kiss on her forehead and leaves without another word.

*

It's eleven thirty by the time Brandon arrives home laden with takeaway and a bottle of cheap white wine. He climbs two flights of stairs to the cramped apartment above the tacky souvenir shop, closing his eyes to the cracked plaster and peeling paint, and wrinkling his nose at the smell of disinfectant as he approaches his own front door. Jesus, if his rich-bitch clients could only see where he lived!

Star is still awake, watching an ancient romcom on cable. Meg Ryan's face fills the screen, her cornflower-blue eyes blurred by tears. Absently, Brandon dumps his jacket on the back of a chair and sets down a bag bulging with boxed pasta on the cheap laminate counter.

'Don't say I never give you anything.' He opens the wine and takes two glasses from a shelf.

Star yawns and rubs her eyes. 'I ate at the restaurant. What is it?'

'Your favourite. *Shit* – what a waste of money. I got paid though. Fuck, I earned it tonight – the bitch scratched me. Take a look, will you?'

Star visibly sags. 'In a minute… I'm watching this.'

'Nice. So that's the thanks I get for busting my arse.' Brandon scoops the now-congealing food into a bowl and nukes it in the microwave. He scans the room, a sneer blighting his handsome face. 'We need to clean up tomorrow. This place is a tip. Can you wash my shirts for me, too? I can't work if I don't look good.'

Star huffs. 'What did your last slave die of? I'm your sister, not your cleaner.' She stomps to the kitchen area of their cluttered open-plan living-and-kitchen space and grabs one of the glasses of wine Brandon has poured. 'Cheers.' She takes a sip, relaxes and finally relents: 'Ah, go on then. I'll iron you a couple, too. So, was she horrid then?'

'Actually, she looked pretty good, it was her personality that was shitty. I've had it, Star. I can't keep it up.'

Star explodes into giggles. 'Well, that's inconvenient in your line of work.'

Brandon makes a face. 'Very funny. You know what I mean. I can't go on like this. We can't. Bumming around, moving from one city to the next, living hand to mouth. I can't stand the women. Sometimes, I look at them – these spoilt fucking bitches – and I just want to wring their scrawny necks.'

When Star settles back down in front of the film, he crams angel hair pasta into his mouth and reflects on the evening. Simone had dismissed his cover story about being a model. *What the hell?* He'd done plenty of modelling… just not for a while. Eight years earlier, he'd been 'one to watch', the Covent Garden agency had said. But they'd been full of crap, promising regular work and delivering a total of five jobs in eighteen months. When the modelling failed to launch, he'd tried promotional work. But spritzing fragrance in Selfridges and directing footfall at exhibitions had turned out to be boring and poorly paid, and he'd ended up on the books of an escort agency.

The clients were an even split, with about half the women wanting sex, and the other half needing only handsome and charming company on their arm for the evening. He'd stuck with it for a while, until one night, while escorting an octogenarian to the theatre and sitting through a distinctly average performance of Noel Coward's *Private Lives*, his sinuses burned with the unmistakeable smell of urine. Despite an intense urge to throw up, he'd done his best to conceal the dark, spreading stain on the poor woman's dress with his programme as he and his date filed out onto the Charing Cross Road for a taxi. The next day, he'd sent his boss a two-word text: *I quit.*

So now he hustled menopausal women in hotel bars – and what of it? At least both parties knew what they were getting.

Brandon dumps his sticky bowl in the sink and runs the hot tap over it. Tomorrow he'll tidy up a bit, buy some fruit and flowers, try to make it a bit more homely for both their sakes.

'I'm going to jump in the shower and go to bed,' he says to the back of Star's head.

'Okay, na-night, Brandon,' Star says, her eyes still fixed on the movie.

CHAPTER THIRTY-THREE

Tuscany, August 2019

Evie

Evie wakes to an eerie silence. Wondering if it is earlier or later than usual, she opens her right eye; her left remains resolutely shut, sealed by the dried mascara she'd neglected to remove the night before. Sitting up, she offers a silent prayer that the jackhammer in her head will stop, before the sour fuzziness in her mouth reminds her that she'd got up in the night to throw up. Twice. Well, she hopes, at least she'd got *that* indignity over with.

*

Star sits up on the marble worktop, swigging cola from a can. Panda-eyed, she too has slept in her make-up. Her face breaks into a huge grin.

'Oof! You look how I feel, Evie, mate. Have a Coke, that'll sort you out. My mum used to swear by it for a hangover.'

Evie swallows hard and shakes her head. 'Think I'll just make some tea. Do you want one?'

'Go on then,' Star jumps down from the counter and goes outside.

Evie had expected more mess, but there's little clearing up to be done. Through her brain fog, she recalls grabbing a bin bag to get rid of the rubbish and filling the dishwasher, before stumbling off to bed, leaving Harry and Susanne still drinking in the garden.

Yes, it was all coming back to her now. They'd kicked off with proper champagne, which had been fabulous, then they'd gone onto prosecco – also lovely – but then someone (Dale?) had produced a litre of gin and that had disappeared, too.

At around ten o'clock, drunk and cross, Dale had gone to bed. Unlike Evie, who in her deluded, tipsy state had mistaken herself for Beyoncé, and danced her socks off with a girl half her age. Twerking indeed! What had she been thinking?

Then later (although timings are a bit fuzzy at this point), Evie remembers Harry being vociferous about not hitting it off with Dale. Hearing him criticise her had felt disloyal and very uncomfortable indeed. Because recently, Evie had become truly fond of Dale – in ways she'd never imagined possible, loving her no-frills honesty, instead of being a little afraid of it as she was when they first met.

'Cheers, Evie,' Star says, taking the hot tea from her and blowing on it.

Overhead, clouds smother the weak sunlight and a light wind whispers through the garden's once green shrubbery.

Evie's smile is rueful. 'Look at this poor garden – it was so lush when we arrived, now everything looks sad and parched. Can't believe that this time next week, I'll be at home in Tunbridge Wells. Where do you think you'll be?'

Star shrugs. 'Oh, I don't know… no plans, really, just see how things go.'

'Well, do you think you'll patch things up with Sander, keep travelling for a while?' Evie asks, surprised by the younger woman's lack of concern for her future.

'I'm a free spirit like my mum. Maybe it's all over with Sander. We're only young. I mean, I never thought we'd get married or anything. Sorry, Evie, I feel like I really need a shower.'

And then Evie is alone, feeling guilty for pushing Star; she hadn't meant to pry.

'Morning, lovely,' Dale's voice booms behind her, 'hope your head feels better than mine. We were caning it last night. At least you had a good time. Sorry I was in such a foul mood – drinking makes me crabby sometimes. Anyone else up?' Dale folds herself into the seat beside Evie, nursing a pint of water.

Evie smiles. 'I feel a bit rough, too. I was sick in the night,' she admits with a shudder. 'Star's in the shower, no sign of Susanne and Harry yet.'

Susanne and Harry. She says it as if they're any other couple. But they aren't and seeing them around together feels weird and jarring.

'Urgh, Evie… I think I was on Susanne's case about Harry last night.' Dale plunges her head into her hands. 'I can't help it. I've known Susanne since we were in ankle socks and Clarks shoes, and there's something very wrong with all this.'

Evie puts a finger to her lips. 'Shh… if the windows are open, they'll hear us!' she whispers, aware that Dale's voice carries. 'I know what you mean, but Susanne's an adult and our friend and we can't tell her what to do. For what it's worth, I'm worried, too. I haven't known Susanne long, but this whole thing with Harry seems so out of character. I'm amazed she's so smitten; it would be awful if he messes her around and breaks her heart. And,' Evie glances from side to side, 'his relationship with Star seems odd, too. They're so comfortable with each other, as if they've been friends all their lives. Yet they say they met in Rome.' Evie throws up her hands. 'Let's hope it's a holiday fling and nothing more than that.'

Dale shrugs. 'Amen to that. That's what I'm counting on, too.' She gulps water. 'Okay, I need a caffeine fix now. Can I get you anything, love?'

Evie shakes her head and watches Dale trudge towards the house. Headache abating, she begins to wander the garden, inhaling the herbs and shrubs that have become so familiar. Who would have thought that she, Evie Jones, would ever summer in Tuscany, in a smart villa with two beautiful and successful women, and a wealthy young Adonis? What on earth would her mum have thought of it all?

She walks down the stone steps to the pool, and stands on the edge, willing herself to jump in as Dale or Star would do. But it is simply not in her DNA to be impulsive. Always so careful, so cautious. All her life, she's been a spectator – observing others living to the max, while she has merely existed. Well, things have to change. *She* has to change. She'll be forty next birthday; high time, then, to start embracing life and taking a few risks!

With a growing urge to jump, Evie stands poised on the edge, daring herself to strip off and dive in.

'Sod it,' she says aloud, pulling her T-shirt over her head, releasing the clasp of her bra and unbuttoning her shorts before she can change her mind. Then, with a whoop of joy and surprise, she takes the leap. Gasping and spluttering at first, she treads water, before striking out for a full length of the pool.

'I did it!' She cries as Dale returns, a mug of coffee in one hand and a day-old croissant in the other.

Dale beams and stops dead in her tracks. 'What?'

'I swam a whole length without putting my feet down – and I jumped right in! In my knickers and everything!'

Dale is laughing now, approval written all over her face, enjoying Evie's triumph with her. 'Yessss, Evie – way to go!' Dale cheers, coffee and croissant parked as she strips down to her underwear and leaps in after her friend.

'Now that's what I *call* a hangover cure!' she says after thrashing half a dozen lengths in quick succession while Evie continues her careful, determined stroke.

By the time they get out of the water, the heat has intensified and the clouds have become wispy. Dripping, they lie on adjacent sunbeds, letting the sunshine caress their semi-naked bodies.

Suddenly, Evie is self-conscious lying beside Dale's athletic form.

As if reading her mind, Dale says, 'Don't know why you bang on about your weight all the time, Evie – you're perfect as you are. Really feminine, and you've got great boobs. Who knew?'

Evie blushes and is about to bat away the compliment when she thinks better of it. 'Thanks, Dale – that's so nice of you to say.' She settles back, feeling the water evaporate from her skin, basking in the warmth of Dale's admiration.

Then, Dale springs up, suddenly serious. 'Evie, I don't want to ruin the moment, but something really odd happened when I was inside just now…'

CHAPTER THIRTY-FOUR

Dale

After comparing hangovers with Evie, Dale had gone inside to make coffee but before she'd had the chance to run water, clatter crockery or signal her presence in any other way, she'd been aware of an argument coming from the room next door. So she'd listened intently, straining to catch Harry's voice mixed with Star's girlish tones, as they'd bickered about a missing dress belonging to Susanne, before Star had stomped off to her room, leaving Harry alone.

After making coffee and microwaving a day-old croissant, Dale had hurried into the garden, impatient to dissect this new nugget of information with Evie – only to find her in the pool, giddy – and topless! – triumphant at having swum an entire length without putting her feet down. Not wanting to break the spell, Dale had stripped right down and joined her, enjoying her friend's sudden burst of confidence.

Now, lying on the loungers, their skin warming deliciously in the sun, the normal rhythm of Dale's breathing returns – as does the thought of Harry and Star's altercation.

'Evie, I don't want to ruin the moment, but something really odd happened when I was inside just now,' Dale says, her voice low.

Evie leans up, shielding her eyes from the sun's glare. 'Go on... what happened?'

'Well just now, Star must have come out of the shower, because she and Harry were rowing in the sitting room. I don't think they knew I could hear them, but Harry said something strange.'

Evie waits for the punchline.

'He said something like, "Susanne's been looking for the blue dress".'

Evie nods. 'She asked me last night if I'd seen it. I said I hadn't; I didn't even know she had one.'

'Yeah, neither did I,' Dale says, 'but why on earth would Harry mention it to Star? What could possibly be of interest to either of them? When it comes to Susanne's clothes, the only thing Harry cares about is how quickly he can get her out of them.'

Evie winces. 'So, how did Star react?'

Dale frowns. 'Well, she wasn't happy. I think she said, "Get off my case, you know the score. Why do you always blame me?" and then she stomped off. What on earth is that all about?'

Evie nibbles her thumbnail. 'Don't know... it's definitely weird. Maybe we should mention it to Susanne later – tactfully though, we don't want to make a big deal out of it.'

*

Susanne is last to surface, groomed and elegant as ever, but today there are shadows under her eyes and her mouth is set and miserable. Not the expression Dale had expected to see after a night of partying and abandoned lovemaking.

'You look fed up, hon; come and talk to us,' Dale says, taking their chance as Harry and Star have gone into the village on foot and will therefore be out some time.

'I've lost something,' Susanne says, her tone mournful. 'My St Christopher has gone.'

Dale frowns. 'What do you mean, gone? When was the last time you had it?'

Susanne shrugs, muttering that if she knew that, it wouldn't be lost.

'Well, where do you normally keep it?' Evie asks.

'In my room, in the top drawer of the dresser. I haven't worn it for a while, but just now I was going to put it on and it wasn't there.'

'Oh, Susanne, I know how much it means to you. It'll turn up. We'll help you look,' Evie says.

'It fell off the other week; the catch is a bit loose so maybe it just happened again…' Susanne muses. 'At least I know it's got to be here somewhere; I didn't take it to Florence.'

'I remember, you did drop it out here once and we looked for it—' Dale narrows her eyes, her instincts kicking in.

The blue dress, and now the St Christopher, both missing: Dale seizes the opportunity to ask Susanne if the dress has turned up.

'No – why?' Susanne says, clearly picking up on the knowing looks passing between Dale and Evie.

For the second time that morning, Dale repeats the conversation she'd heard between Harry and Star.

Susanne frowns. 'So, let me get this straight. You're implying Star's a thief? Why on earth would a young girl take a frumpy old frock – and a necklace that's worthless to anyone but me? It doesn't make sense.'

Dale sighs with exasperation: the more she thinks about it, the more she feels certain Star is responsible for the lost dress and the missing necklace. 'I agree it sounds daft, but we don't know anything about her. Star just appeared while we were in Florence. And all that bollocks about splitting up with Sander – who might not even exist, by the way; it's not like any of us have even met him. I'm sorry, Susanne, it just doesn't ring true with me.'

'So, what do you suggest then? Put her on the spot and ask her if she's taken them? Yeah, that'll make for friendly relations with Harry – she's his friend, remember?'

Oh, for god's sake! Dale wants to scream. It is as though Susanne has been brainwashed – or lobotomised.

Dale gets up, motioning for Susanne and Evie to follow her. Then she goes to the front door and peers down the lane in the direction of the village; there are no signs of either Star or Harry.

'Evie, keep watch,' Dale orders, seizing the opportunity to search Star's room.

'Dale, don't. Please!' Susanne protests.

But Dale is adamant. 'Try and stop me!' And then, with Evie on lookout duty, she and Susanne are in Star's room – *Harry's* room, which Star has reduced to a pigsty. Clothes are strewn on the unmade bed, shabby flip-flops and sandals lay askew on the floor. A tangle of necklaces, bangles and earrings disgorge from the kind of jewellery box that a teenager would use, and an array of grubby make-up palettes fill an open drawer.

'How can she live like this?' Susanne says.

Dale shrugs. 'People do when they're travelling and living out of a backpack. Okay, no sign. I can't think where else to look – between all their junk, this place is a tip.' She wrinkles her nose in disgust.

And then Dale sees it: on the floor of Harry's wardrobe, nestled between a surprising number of men's shoes (some of them oddly smart). A black tin box. The kind businesses use for petty cash, or lovers keep for hiding letters. A tin made for secrets. Dale gives it a gentle shake; there's a metallic rattle from within.

'Damn! It's locked. Of course it is,' Dale says, a note of triumph in her voice, 'but I'm telling you, Susanne, this is where you'll find your Grandma Amy's necklace. One second, I've got an idea.' Dale dashes to her room, then to the kitchen and back, hoping she's solved the problem.

But annoyingly, it isn't like she's seen in dozens of films; the lock doesn't conveniently release after Dale has jiggled it with first her luggage keys, then her tweezers and lastly, a tiny, sharp kitchen utensil that none of them can identify, and after what seems an age filled with utter frustration, Dale returns the tin to Harry's wardrobe.

'Okay, let's just ask her. If Star has seen either the dress or the pendant her reaction will give her away.'

By now, Evie has deserted her post and all three of them are huddled outside Harry's room. But the conversation is cut short as they hear voices, and Star and Harry spill through the front door, weighed down by several bags of groceries.

'Remind me not to go shopping without the car again,' Harry moans, heading for the kitchen as Star trails after him. 'We bought quite a lot in the end… feels like my hands are bleeding.'

'Yeah, we bought loads,' Star echoes. 'By the way, I'm making dinner tonight. It's definitely my turn.'

But Dale has got the bit between her teeth now and wastes no time in tackling Star head-on. 'Thanks, Star, but we need to ask you something. Susanne has lost a necklace – her St Christopher – and we wondered if you'd borrowed it.'

Star looks nonplussed. 'Why would I?'

Dale shrugs. 'I don't know, you tell me. But it's missing and Susanne hasn't seen it since before Florence.'

'Well, I haven't bloody got it!' Star snaps.

Dale's expression is stern. 'She's lost a dress, too. Do you know anything about that, Star?'

'No, of course not!'

Harry raises a hand. 'Whoa! That sounds an awful lot like an accusation, Dale, and it's really not fair. I can't imagine why Star would borrow *anything* without asking.' He pauses and shoots a look at Susanne. 'But just to be sure, why don't we look in her room, see if she's hiding anything? Or rather, *my* room – to be specific – which I was happy to give up for a few nights. The least I could do was to be a good host, seeing as how it's *my* godmother who owns the place.'

Susanne runs a hand through her hair, eyes downcast, embarrassed by the whole thing. 'She didn't mean it to come out that way, Star. Did you, Dale?'

But Star continues to stare Dale down. 'Go on then. I *insist* you check my room,' she says, her voice laced with sarcasm.

Dale's eyes blaze. So, Star is calling her bluff; clever. Which probably means that the necklace has been stowed elsewhere. Fuming, she pushes past everyone, and into Star's room, making a business of checking shelves and drawers before throwing open the wardrobe and going straight to the black tin.

'What's in here?' she says, holding it aloft.

Harry squares his shoulders and seems to grow taller. 'Not that it's any of your concern, but it's where I keep my passport,' he says icily before digging around inside the bedside drawer and producing a tiny key. Once unlocked, Harry flips the tin's lid and reveals a UK passport and a few coins.

Dale steps back, deflated. 'Sorry, I thought…'

Shit! She'd been so sure. This wily pair, with their well-worn double act: every day she became more convinced that they were working together. But to do what, exactly?

'I'm going out,' Dale says, suddenly desperate to escape. Five minutes later, she's in the SUV, speeding down the hillside.

CHAPTER THIRTY-FIVE

Tuscany, August 2019

Brandon

Sick of slumming it in the hostel she's in, Star is getting antsy and is on Brandon's case.

He gets it, he really does. She's come out of the deal pretty badly, all things considered. But she needs to be patient now that he's on the trail of something; something big, he can feel it.

In the greenish shadows of the hostel's run-down bar, Brandon studies her young face. Pale, blotchy and without any make-up, it tells him all he needs to know. Guilt and pity stir in equal measure. He needs to instil hope – and fast.

'Star, you've got to be patient. Susanne isn't like the others. I'm onto something this time,' he says, clamping a joint between white teeth and taking a stash of euros from his wallet. 'Here, take this and make sure you have dinner at a decent restaurant tonight; eat some steak or something, you look like you need a treat.'

The cash earns him an eye roll and an exasperated sigh. 'Thanks, but you know I hate red meat. Anyway, do you think I care about food? Eating alone is shit. Why can't we have dinner together?' Star whines. 'It's okay for you. Living in some swanky villa with a load of rich bitches.'

'I told you: it's only Susanne who's wealthy. The other two are just normal working women.'

'Brandon, I can't do this much longer; hiding in the shadows while you wait for some spoilt cow to fall in love with you.'

Brandon grits his teeth. 'Star, please. Look, it'll be better in a few days, when Joe and Sander get back from Amalfi. And then… just a couple more weeks – that's all I need. I swear the stupid bitch is falling for me.'

'Yay!' Star's thin arm shoots up in an ironic fist pump. 'Then where does that leave me?' she snaps. 'We should have stayed in Rome – at least there I had a job and we had an apartment together.'

'You can be a waitress anywhere. We lost the apartment, remember? You're not thinking straight. We knew what we were getting into when we took this gig.' Brandon's tone leaks frustration. 'I can't do it anymore. Screwing vile old crones for cash and clothes. You have no idea what it's like for me. Sometimes, I swear I could puke all over their bony bodies. What happened to us… it was *fate*; some weird fucking *golden* opportunity. Well, I am grabbing it with both hands. Here, finish this. I've got to drive soon.'

Brandon passes Star the joint and watches her take a hit, looking over his shoulder, more from habit than concern. Guido, who is polishing and stacking glasses behind the bar, is happy to turn a blind eye when no one else is around.

Star slumps lower on the faux-leather banquette. 'But I don't see how this woman can help us. She'll go back to England soon and you'll be just some fuzzy holiday romance.'

'No, not this time. I haven't figured out the details yet, but I'm working on it and I'll make sure you're okay. You know I'll always look after you.' He moves a strand of blonde hair from her face. 'Look, I've got to go; the schoolteacher hitched a ride at the last minute and I'm taking her back. Jesus, she's painful – she's always watching me and hanging around like a bad smell. Still, I'll sort her. As for the mouse woman… maybe I'll shag her as well, just to keep her quiet.' His laughter is high-pitched, verging on girlish. 'I'm *joking*!' he adds quickly, seeing the look on Star's face.

Star shakes her head, her expression a mixture of disgust and despondency. 'Okay, go. Be careful… See you tomorrow?'

'I'll try and come. Take care, hon.' He pecks Star's cheek and feeling the weed begin to percolate, walks out into the afternoon sun.

*

Trying to ignore how stoned he feels, Brandon jogs across town making it back to Piazza della Cisterna right on time. But when he arrives, breathless and with a sheen of sweat on his nose and forehead, to his immense irritation, there is no sign of Dale. A gaggle of American pensioners begin to crowd him, all talking at once about what they've seen and where they're bound for next. Itching to shove them back, Brandon thrusts his hands in his pockets and waits.

Then Dale is striding towards him, her expression closed, unsmiling. Why the smacked-arse face? He hides his annoyance behind the milling Americans, flouncing about the lack of personal space.

The weed ripples in Brandon's solar plexus, creating a rush of vertigo followed by a pressing desire to be horizontal. Dale is bleating about a present for Susanne, but her voice sounds muffled and far away. Shit. Now he has to get in his car and drive home – and all the while listening to Dale banging on and *on*, bombarding him with her fucking nosy questions. The woman is a rottweiler.

When they arrive at the car it's in full sunshine. Opening the jeep's door, the back draft of heat feels like a physical blow. Knowing he'll puke if he gets inside, Brandon blasts the air con.

Dale is watching him now, sizing him up. She asks about Jack and Sander - like she cares! Brandon arranges his features into what he hopes is a pleasant smile and corrects her. 'It's *Joe*, actually,' he says, before telling Dale that they had a beer together, and that his friends are thinking of moving on. Like it matters. It's a pain having to make small talk, especially when he's trying so hard to keep it together.

The drive back is slow, blurry at first, but then he feels himself coming to and she's telling him about the gift for Susanne again – a bracelet as a peace offering after their argument. *Focus, Brandon: this is interesting.* And then an admission; that she disapproves of him and Susanne together. *No shit!*

So then, acting his balls off, Brandon tells Dale that he and Susanne have really got something – a *connection*. And just for good measure, he lays it on with a trowel, about how he's fallen for her and how he's scared of getting his heart broken, and he can tell she's thinking it through.

Not that Dale has any right to be so fucking high-minded and judgemental. From where Brandon's standing, it looks like they're all freeloading at Susanne's expense – especially Dale – as if some shitty wooden bracelet will redress the fact that Susanne is always the first one with her purse out.

So that evening, he stirs things up a bit, gushing about how he's *crazy* about Susanne in front of her friends. He's taking the calculated risk that Susanne will be flattered and wooed by the idea, rather than cringing with embarrassment and shame. If anything, it goes even better than expected, with Susanne openly making out with him, then they all get wasted and dance together.

But then the mouse woman pipes up that his godmother, Veronica, had phoned that afternoon, complaining that nobody has heard from him in weeks. Thinking on his feet, Brandon denies it, accusing her of exaggerating, and of being overly protective. Luckily, the subject gets dropped.

He even manages to play the hero and score extra points when Susanne's necklace falls off while they're dancing. Judging by the look of panic in her eyes, he can tell it must really matter to her. After all four of them scrabble around in the dust on their knees looking for it, he suddenly spots it. Susanne is over the moon – and so obviously grateful. In fact, just for a moment, even *he* feels good, too.

That night, Susanne begs him to fuck her faster and harder – and it kind of bothers Brandon, reminding him of the women he'd rather forget. But her clawing, cat-like aggression is fleeting and soon turns into the softer, tender passion he's come to recognise, born out of loneliness and frustration from not getting laid enough – which, he has to admit, is pretty amazing, given how good she looks. A woman like Susanne should have been fighting men off with a shitty stick.

CHAPTER THIRTY-SIX

Brandon

When the women decide to spend a night in Florence and visit the Uffizi, just for a moment Brandon feels a stab of disappointment at not being invited.

'Girls only,' Dale states with a smugness that makes him want to slap her. Instead he makes some cutting remark, but it only upsets Susanne and he regrets it at once.

Well, fuck it. He doesn't need to queue in the heat only to go crawling round some overrated museum rammed with tourists and relics from the past. The future is all that matters now.

And anyway, getting the villa to himself will be a total bonus; Star will certainly think so.

So, he happily says a pleasant goodbye to them, as if they were his family, telling them to be careful and to stick together. He kisses Susanne last, like she's his wife, heading off on a business trip or something; it feels weird, but not entirely bad.

*

Star is standing on the cobbles, two backpacks at her feet, a shaft of sunshine slicing through the tall buildings making a halo of her hair. She smiles and flaps small hands, as though he might miss her and drive right by.

'Hey, get in,' he calls, pulling over to the curb while she climbs in, throwing her stuff in the back.

'I'm starving,' she says, putting sandaled feet up on the dashboard.

'Look at you, you're a stick insect – you need to eat more, Star,' Brandon says, revving so hard that his tyres squeal.

'Hey! Don't drive like a wanker when I'm in the car,' Star says, flipping open the glove compartment and rifling through it. 'Haven't you even got any sweets?'

'You're eighteen, not eight. Wait until we get to the villa, you can stuff yourself then. By the way, you can have my room tonight.'

Star's brow puckers. 'Where will you sleep?'

Brandon's grin is wolfish. 'In *her* bed, of course. I'll say I missed her so much I want to fall asleep inhaling her perfume. Clever, eh?'

'Clever. But gross,' Star says, 'Are you sure they won't find out?'

'How will they? They're in Florence until tomorrow night – and you'll be gone by then.'

'Yes, back to that shit-tip hostel. I hate it there, Brandon. It's not fair that I should—'

'Star, we talked about this. You've just got to trust me.'

*

In the car, Star had chattered all the way over, but now she silently stomps into the kitchen and opens the fridge. 'I thought you said there was loads of food. I hate all this stuff. Can we go shopping?'

'Okay, look, stop acting like a brat. You eat chicken – and cheese and olives and fruit – so don't pretend you don't.'

Brandon opens a cupboard, finds a large packet of the cheese puffs Dale is partial to, and tosses them to his sister. 'Here, have some of these, grab a Coke and I'll take you out for dinner later. Let's go to the pizzeria in the village.'

'Good plan, bro,' she says, filling her mouth with a handful of the salty puffs before stepping outside through the French windows.

Brandon watches as Star paces around the garden, now stippled by the late afternoon sunshine. Then she's running towards the pool, her sandals slapping on the stones and for a moment, he pictures her leaping in fully clothed.

Instead she stops, a huge grin lighting her young face. 'I'm going in!' She begins to wriggle out of her jeans and T-shirt, stopping only at small red knickers.

Brandon shakes his head, relieved to see his little sister smiling, nonetheless.

Star sits on the edge of the pool and slides in. Then she's gasping with temporary shock before swimming to the far end and letting out a victorious whoop of delight.

Brandon saunters down to the pool terrace and grins.

'God, I love it here,' Star calls, pulling long strokes through the water. 'Can't believe you've been here all summer – living the life of fucking Riley, while I've had to stay back at that dump.'

Star stops swimming; her small white breasts stencilled from a golden tan sit just below the surface as she treads water and shields her eyes from the low sun. 'Think I'll stay a while,' she says, cocking her head to one side.

'I thought you wanted to eat out.'

'You know what I mean. Go on, Brandon – let me stay here for a couple of days.'

Brandon's laughter is hoarse. 'Yeah, that'll work, Star. How on earth do I explain you away? As far as I'm aware, Harry doesn't have any pain-in-the-butt little sisters.'

'You're a good liar, you'll think of something.' Star crosses her eyes, pinches her nose and ducks beneath the surface. Seconds pass; he knows she's holding her breath, desperate to get a reaction.

Ignoring her game, Brandon goes and sits at the table, which is still adorned by frothy white flowers picked by Susanne and tenderly placed into a jam jar as decoration. The flowers are now beginning to wilt. Brandon sags in sympathy.

Shit. He should have known this would happen. A pang of guilt washes over him. The sad thing is, Star has a point. It isn't fair, the way things have worked out.

She is out of the pool now and walking towards him, shivering. She reaches for a towel left drying on a chair by one of the women.

Brandon is reminded of the two of them, playing on the beach at Camber Sands: a self-conscious, dark-haired boy of thirteen, all ribs, knees and elbows, and a four-year-old girl with white-blonde hair, wearing a pink polka-dot swimsuit, her chubby hands patting sand into a plastic bucket. A few metres away, their mother Ingrid sits smoking, long hair whipped by the wind, tanned legs drawn up as she hugs her knees and gazes out to sea.

'All right. Two nights. We'll work on our story over dinner. Now go and get dressed – and for god's sake, put something decent on.'

*

When Star reappears, shiny-haired and sweet-smelling, she has transformed herself into an adult.

Brandon nods his approval. 'Very nice, sis, you scrub up well. That dress suits you – don't think I've seen it before? Very grown up!'

Star smooths down the cornflower jersey dress and squares her shoulders. 'I can be feminine, you know. You're not the only good-looking one in the family.' She checks her appearance in the hall mirror. 'Anyway, I borrowed it.'

'You *borrowed* it? Star, where did you get that?'

'From the room at the end – the one that smells nice. I was just having a little look around. No one will know, will they? Anyway, I think I look good. I mean, it's a bit long, but other than that…' She continues to preen in the mirror, adding, 'Brandon, I'm only wearing the damn dress to a restaurant, not running a marathon in it. Just chill out, will you?'

'Oh my god, you're a bloody liability. I told you not to touch anything!' Brandon sighs and covers his eyes. 'That's Susanne's room, so it's her dress you're wearing.' He shakes his head, and paces to the front door. 'Let's just go, before I make you take it off. Honestly, you are *such* a pain!'

Star scowls. 'Oh, I'm *such* a pain, am I?' she mimics. 'Brandon, just because you can do the accent – which by the way, you can drop when it's just us – doesn't mean you're better than me. You're not with your affected model mates or those bloody women now.'

*

It had taken fifteen minutes to walk down to the village and Star had complained that her feet hurt for ten of them.

'Well, you should have worn trainers,' Brandon says, greeting the restaurant manager and scanning the room for a table.

'You said to wear something decent. Stop giving me a hard time, Brandon. Ooh, look at that!' Star eyes a bubbling plate of golden lasagne as it goes past them. 'I'm having that,' she says, her mood lifting in an instant.

Brandon takes in the scene: each table is covered by a blue gingham cloth, a red tea-light holder burns and a single gerbera blooms. There's a cheerful buzz of conversation, but not so loud that he can't hear himself think. Ah, the smell: an enticing blend of garlic butter, herbs and lemon suffuses the air, making him salivate.

The atmosphere is welcoming, reassuring, familiar. Better than that, he can be himself tonight. Just plain old Brandon Connor, of no fixed abode, having dinner with his kid sister, Star. For a moment he feels he could cry with relief.

Tomorrow, he'll go back to playing the role of Harry Klein, twenty-four, public school educated and with a Cambridge business degree. The spoilt, over-privileged bastard.

Star is watching him. 'You look pissed-off, bro – you okay?'

'I'm fine. But when I think about what I'm doing here, my brain hurts… I just can't quite—'

A waiter hovers at Brandon's elbow, a stubby pencil raised above a worn notepad.

Brandon changes the subject and focusses on the menu.

CHAPTER THIRTY-SEVEN

Brandon

Seething, Brandon strides several paces ahead of his sister. He'd called her a liability earlier; now she's fast becoming one.

'Wait, don't be like that. It was an accident. I said I'm sorry, didn't I?' Star whines, struggling to keep up with him as he marches uphill towards the warm glow of the villa.

'What good is *sorry*? Susanne's dress is ruined, by not a drip, or a dribble of red wine, but a whole fucking glassful sloshed down the front! Jesus, you're clumsy!'

'Accidents happen! Anyone would think you're really in love with her,' Star pouts.

'Oh, grow up!' Brandon snaps. 'It's not about that and you know it. You'll just have to wash it when we get home, dry it overnight and hope to god the stain comes out.'

'Sorry,' Star says, her voice small.

Brandon remains silent, weighing up the options. There's a distinct possibility that Susanne, with her huge wardrobe, won't even miss the dress. No way can it go back into her closet with an angry stain all down the front.

Neither of them says another word until they arrive back at the villa. Once inside, Star peels the dress off and, still in her underwear, goes to the utility room where she begins attacking the stain before loading the dress into the washing machine.

Realising that there is nothing more to be done, Brandon rolls a joint and takes it outside where a sliver of opal moon lights his way. Lifting his face heavenward, he gazes into an indigo sky studded with stars, and waits for the weed to take effect.

He pictures Susanne, looking up at the same stars, in a new city, before climbing into bed, her long hair fanning across the pillow. He wonders whether she's alone, or whether she's sharing a room with Dale. Spiky, suspicious Dale, who could at this very moment be filling Susanne's head with poison about him. The tension between them is plain to see but if he's going to pull off his master stroke, he'll need to deal with Dale once and for all.

Star shuffles up to him, dressed in her own scruffy combats, a sulky look on her face.

'Any luck getting the wine out?' he asks, passing the joint to her.

Star shakes her head, closing her eyes and inhaling the weed before letting out a plume of smoke. 'Maybe we should dispose of it completely so that she thinks she never packed it?'

A thought occurs to Brandon. 'Not a bad idea, but I might have a better one.'

Taking long, purposeful strides, Brandon passes through the kitchen, out into the entrance hall and along the corridor that leads to Susanne's room. Star trails behind, bombarding him with questions.

Once inside, he switches on the overhead light, startling a gecko in its journey across the ceiling, which makes Star jump in the process.

'It's harmless,' Brandon says, shushing his sister as his eyes dart around the room for inspiration.

'Why are we in here? What are we looking for?' Star says, keeping an eye on the lizard.

Brandon is opening and closing drawers, a determined look on his face. 'Insurance.' He grabs Susanne's St Christopher necklace from a shallow drawer, surprised that it has been left behind, and hands it to Star.

'But it's cheap, worthless crap,' Star says, wrinkling her nose.

'Maybe – but it means a lot to Susanne, her dead nan gave it to her. Right, one more thing… *bingo*!' Brandon plucks a white bikini top from Susanne's bedside table, stopping to inhale her familiar scent.

'Perv.'

Brandon ignores her. 'Where's the dress now?'

'It's on a rack; in this heat, it'll be dry in the morning.'

Brandon's eyes gleam. 'Then I know exactly what I'm going to do with it.'

*

Brandon watches Star cracking eggs into a frying pan, tapping their shells with a knife, the way their mother used to.

People could never get their heads around them being siblings, what with Star being as fair-haired as Brandon is dark, her long pale hair framing her small face from which topaz-blue eyes gaze out. And at barely five foot two inches, she's dwarfed by her big brother in stature, too; even her hands and feet are childlike.

At least their nine-year age gap had spared them the taunts of other kids at school, and by the time Brandon had entered young adulthood, it no longer embarrassed him that he and Star had different fathers.

Different, and yet the same – a case of lightning striking twice. Because neither one had stuck around to love, protect or provide for Brandon, Star or for poor Ingrid herself.

Star jumps back as a bubble of fat bursts with a loud crack.

'Make sure you wash that lot up properly,' Brandon says, surveying the messy kitchen. 'Susanne and Evie are both neat freaks.'

'Ha! Well, that doesn't bode well for you, bro. You'll have to clean your act up when we get back to England.'

'Look, just be careful what you say, okay? And stick to the story, no improvising. I don't want anything to slip out. Which is why I'm taking you back to San Gimi tomorrow.'

Star turns to face him, brows knitted, a spatula poised in mid-air. 'But we agreed last night that I'd stay for a few days,' she protests.

'I said a couple of nights and tonight makes two. You're going back in the morning. Star, I can't afford to fuck this up now. I'm on a major charm offensive here and I don't want you getting friendly with anyone, *especially* Dale. If she starts digging around, you need to clam up, pretend to get upset, whatever; just don't get into conversation with her. Promise me.'

'Oh, shut up! You're not my dad – stop telling me what to do!'

Brandon grabs her roughly, his finger and thumb digging into her chin, and jerks her head back sharply. His voice is icy. 'Then stop acting like a child and just cooperate, will you? You're right. I'm not your dad. Because your father is a worthless piece of shit. Just like mine. And it's because of them that Mum died and it's just us. So I suggest you start listening to me – unless you'd like to go it alone of course.'

Tears spring into Star's eyes and spill onto her cheeks. 'Ow! That really hurt,' she whimpers, setting down the spatula and rubbing her jaw, which is pink with fingerprints. The eggs fizz and pop in the frying pan, brown around their frilly edges. 'Now look: our eggs are ruined.'

Appalled that he has lost his temper with the person he loves most in the world, Brandon pulls his sister into a hug, and strokes her hair.

'Star, I'm sorry. But you've no idea how stressful it is pretending to be someone else all the time. That's no excuse though and I shouldn't take it out on you. Come on, stop crying now,' he says, scraping the burnt eggs into the bin. 'Tell you what, you go sit in the garden with a cup of tea and I'll find us something else for breakfast.'

CHAPTER THIRTY-EIGHT

Susanne

Susanne cups a hand over her mouth as a wave of nausea rises within her. Whether hangover related or pure and utter shock, she cannot be sure, but right now, standing beside Dale's unmade bed, she feels physically sick.

'No. Not Dale. She wouldn't… it doesn't make sense,' she whispers, staring at the crumpled dress, its ugly blood-like stain visible, and her St Christopher pendant, chain knotted, balled up inside it – and randomly, a white bikini top that she hasn't even missed.

'Susanne, I tried to tell you. The woman's obsessed with you. It's why she has such a problem with me – with us being together. And as for the charade of searching Star's room just now? That was a classic case of smoke and mirrors. To be honest, I worry about Dale's mental health, I really do. I mean, if she's capable of this, who knows what she'll do next?'

Susanne shakes her head, blinking back tears. How has this happened? And more importantly… She searches Harry's face. 'How did you know?'

'I didn't. But her reaction to Star when we got back from shopping was so extreme, she acted like a crazy person, and then I started to think, maybe she was projecting her own guilt and shame onto someone else. It's not her fault, Susanne. Clearly, she isn't well.'

'But shoving my stuff under her mattress? Harry – it's so creepy. Look, do me a favour, I know there's no love lost between you and Dale, but we'll be leaving soon and I don't want any more unpleasantness. I'll talk to her, but alone. And if there's a problem, I'll help her.'

'You really are an angel, you know that?' Harry says, taking Susanne into his arms and rubbing her back. 'There's no end to your goodness. It's one of the reasons I love you.'

But Susanne stiffens and pulls away. She needs to think. What if Harry is right and Dale is fixated on her? And somehow, seeing them together has tipped her over some hitherto unseen precipice?

'Look, promise me you won't say anything to Evie or Star.' She can hear them, clearing up the lunch pots, Star's infectious giggle proof that she's already recovered from Dale's bizarre outburst.

Harry nods. 'Okay. Here, take your things. But let's put everything else back the way we found it. For the sake of your friendship with Dale, Susanne, I won't say anything.'

*

Desperate to be alone, Susanne had gone to her room; Harry had attempted to follow her, but she'd been firm.

'Please, I just want to be on my own for a bit, to speak to my son and then have a nap. We didn't exactly get much sleep last night. Go on, seriously, I'll be fine.'

Then she'd phoned Cody, and for the first time, he'd said the words she'd longed to hear since he'd boarded the plane to Edinburgh: that he loved and missed her, and that he was ready to go home.

'Mum, Dad's brilliant and everything, and it's great here… there's so much to do, but I want it to be just us again.'

'I want that, too, darling,' she'd answered, her voice thick with emotion.

Four more days; another ninety-six hours of weirdness and secrets; of bizarre behaviour from her oldest and dearest friend. It was unfathomable to think of Dale rifling her drawers, taking things from her room; and exactly when and how did the opportunity arise? It would take a herculean effort to say nothing, to let it go – until they were home and could discuss it like civilised adults, *without* an audience or entourage.

CHAPTER THIRTY-NINE

Rome, June 2019

Brandon

'Mind if I sit here?' The voice is clipped, English.

Brandon raises his head to find its owner is tall and floppy-haired. Without waiting for an answer, the man pulls out a chair opposite and begins casting around for a waiter.

'The service here is a bit patchy, but the calzone is to *die* for,' he says, removing his sunglasses and setting them down. Undeterred by the fact that neither Brandon nor Star have uttered a single word in reply, the young man presses on.

'So, are you travelling, or on holiday? I'm Harry, by the way.' His smile is confident as he extends a lean, tanned arm. Brandon is momentarily dazzled by the sun glinting off his Rolex; most of the backpackers he meets sport cheap, disposable brands or none at all, given that most people tell the time with their mobile phones.

Brandon shoots a look at Star and judging by the way she has straightened her back and is flicking her hair around, her interest is piqued, too.

'I'm Brandon – this is Star,' he says, shaking Harry's hand, which, despite the fierce June sunshine, is cool and dry.

'Nice to meet you, Harry,' Star beams, her voice breathy as she fixes her eyes on his and offers her hand. Then she's distracted, halfway out of her seat, waving at someone. 'Brandon, look: there's Joe and Sander,' then to Harry, 'love those two. We keep bumping into them – this is the third time in two weeks.' She calls out to them and they turn and wave.

'Well, hello, it's the beautiful people,' says the blonder of the two men as they sidle up to the table. And who is this?' Theatrically, he lowers his sunglasses and gazes in Harry's direction.

Harry smiles and introduces himself, adding, 'And you are?'

'I'm Sander – and this is my boyfriend, Joe. Mind if we join you? I'm gasping in this heat.'

There are more handshakes; a round of drinks arrives, glasses misted with condensation, then another, and somehow, an hour passes by, during which time nobody eats anything – and the pace of drinking accelerates.

'So,' Harry says, on his third beer, eyes flicking between Brandon and Star, 'you didn't answer my question. What's a beautiful couple like you doing in Rome in June? I can tell you're not on holiday, you look far too at home for that.'

Brandon laughs. 'Actually, we're travelling. Around Europe. And Star,' he gives her a gentle poke, 'is my sister, not my girlfriend.'

Harry's eyes glitter with amusement. 'Oh… OH! Things are looking up around here,' he says, 'well, chin-chin to that!' He clinks Star's glass with his own, his eyes holding hers.

*

Slick with sun cream, Star dozes on the roof of their apartment as is her custom on her days off from the restaurant, while Brandon reflects on their impromptu gathering at Café Paolo.

To the casual observer, Harry, Joe and Sander are the same, each bearing the tell-tale signs of middle-class wealth and privilege. Young men on a gap year, funded by doting parents or part-time jobs fitted around uni; their clothes, accessories, manners and accents paint a familiar picture. Would anybody suspect that he,

Brandon, is from a different world? Probably not, he decides, wondering how he can use this to his advantage.

Star sits up. 'Brandon, get me a drink, will you? My head's throbbing. We only went out for a quick Coke, but then ended up having such a good time. I think I had about three beers.'

Brandon huffs but gets up regardless and disappears into the flat below. He returns with a glass of iced water and a packet of crisps. Grinning, Star tears open the packet.

'Thanks, Bran. They were nice, don't you think? I mean, for posh blokes. I love Joe and Sander, they're so sweet and funny.'

'Some might say affected,' Brandon mutters under his breath.

'And Harry... do you think he's good-looking? I can't decide.'

'He obviously thinks so – arrogant twat. Anyway, Star, guys like him don't hang around with people like us. And don't even think about going after him – he's too old for you.'

'He's twenty-four! I asked him. Three years younger than you... how can he be old? Honestly, you treat me like a kid sometimes,' Star pouts, holding the crisp packet to her lips and tipping her head back to receive its salty crumbs.

'I wonder why,' Brandon rolls his eyes. 'The point is, Star, we're not like other people, are we? Think about it. All those fucking Trustafarians on a gap year, or whatever. Then they go back to Mummy and Daddy and it's all on a plate for them. Car, career, flat. You tell me which of those boxes we can tick, huh? Oh, hang on, that's right. None of them.'

Star is on her feet now, beside a vent belching out the stench of fried food. 'All right! It's not *my* fault. Why are you being like this?'

Brandon's head lolls back, he blows out his cheeks. 'It's just... sometimes, when I meet smug bastards like Harry, I get the red mist. Star, I can't stand the injustice of it all. I bet I'm just as clever as him – and I'm *much* better looking. And yet, he's all set, isn't he? He was telling me how much he hated the public school he went to, but that it pretty much guarantees him a career in finance or politics. He actually used that word, *guarantee.* In fact, this trip – which his old man has paid for – is his last fling before he starts a new job in September, working for a fucking fund manager!'

'Brandon, please calm down. Why are you so upset?' Star says, her voice small.

But Brandon is on a roll. 'He's already been through France and Spain and in a week, he's off to Tuscany to stay in his godmother's villa. It's got a pool and everything. Says he's meant to be learning Italian but hasn't picked up a word yet.'

Then Star is on her feet and hugging him tightly. He feels her bird-like frame through the vest she's wearing and picks up the faint tang of sweat from under her ribbon arms.

'You've got me. Brandon, we'll figure something out. All this anger. We already lost Mum because she… she couldn't handle things. I can't lose you as well.'

'I'm sorry. I guess drinking in the afternoon does nothing for my mood.' He pushes Star away. 'I need to cheer up, take a shower and pick out something to wear. I'm meeting some fat, rich American in Piazza Navona tonight.' He shudders. 'The mood I'm in, god knows how I'll get through it.'

*

Given Brandon's expectation, the evening had been okay – pleasant, even. Tandy Taylor – all five foot nine and two hundred pounds of her – had been chatty, amusing and only mildly flirtatious. By the time she'd paid for cocktails and dinner in one of the Piazza's smartest and most expensive restaurants, the evening barely felt like work at all. As they left, arm in arm, Brandon braced himself for the night's usual conclusion to play out. Instead, Tandy had kissed him on both cheeks, and gazed at him for the longest time. 'What in hell's name are you doing this for? Brandon, you can be anything you want. Here, take this for the ride home.' She'd pressed a wad of cash into his right hand, adding 'Thank you, dear.

I've had a lovely evening, best I can remember since my divorce. Now go on… Goodnight.'

Weaving through familiar backstreets, Brandon feels the money, fat in his pocket. He'd counted it as soon as Tandy had been ensconced in a taxi: 250 euros. A decent haul for dinner, drinks and swapping a few funny stories. At least she hadn't wanted sex.

Taking the fire escape up to his apartment, he expects to find Star in front of the television in her PJs, but the place is in darkness. Maybe someone at the restaurant had called in sick and she'd been summoned to cover their shift? Putting on the dull overhead light, Brandon finds a note by the kitchen sink:

Got a text from Harry. Gone for a drink.
P.S. Don't be cross!
P.P.S. Don't wait up!
P.P.P.S. Just don't!
xxx

Cross?! Was she insane? They'd spent less than two hours in the guy's company and somehow, Star had deemed Harry good dating material. And it really wasn't a case of him coming on like the heavy-handed big brother; it was common sense. They were in a strange city, in an alien country – just the two of them – and it was his job, and his alone, to keep her safe.

He pictures Harry, plying Star with alcohol and getting her wasted in some over-priced bar, then luring her back to some seedy apartment. Trying to ignore the vein throbbing in his left temple, Brandon goes to his room, takes off his 'date' suit and carefully hangs it up. Then he hears the apartment door rattle open and bang shut.

'Star? Is that you?'

'No, it's Lady Gaga. Yes, of course it's me, silly.'

Striding into the living room in his underwear, he finds Star, bright-eyed and in a scarlet dress, strappy heels in one hand.

'Where the fuck have you been?' he hisses.

'I left you a note. Didn't you see? Anyway, I had a lovely time, thanks for asking,' Star's tone is facetious and her eyes glitter. 'We went to that place on the corner – the one with the conservatory thing at the back. Quite posh, actually. Then he took me for gelato at that place where all the scooters park up.'

Brandon exhales. 'And that's it. Dinner and ice cream. Nothing else?'

Star rolls her eyes. 'I know what you're thinking but Harry was the perfect gentleman. He's really nice. Brandon, it's not his fault that he's from a rich family, any more than it's ours we're from a poor one. I really like him. You will, too, once you get to know him.'

'Oh, I doubt that somehow,' Brandon says, stalking off to bed and slamming his door.

CHAPTER FORTY

Brandon

Brandon had to hand it to Harry; the guy was a superb networker. In the course of a brief and accidental drinks meeting, he'd snaffled the phone numbers of Star, Joe and Sander and had wasted no time in hooking up.

A few days after Star's date, Harry texts inviting her to dinner: *Bring your gorgeous brother this time. I'm sure he'll only worry if we meet alone.*

Brandon scowls. 'How nauseating. He's right, though – at least if I'm there I can keep an eye on him, make sure he doesn't try anything.'

Star shakes her head. 'No one will ever be good enough for you, will they? Harry's nice. I told you, he didn't even try it on with me. Hey, maybe that's it. Perhaps *I'm* just an excuse and it's *you* he's interested in.'

'Don't be ridiculous,' Brandon snaps.

*

By dusk, almost half the tourists have melted away and they're moving freely through the city's narrow streets, bound for a pop-up restaurant on the banks of the Tiber.

Star wrinkles her nose. 'Yuk, it stinks!'

Brandon nods. 'Rivers tend to. Are you sure this is the place? Looks kind of shitty for a rich mama's boy like Harry. Are Joe and Sander coming? None of this smells right to me – and I don't mean the river.'

And then the unexpected: a gang plank to a shambling single storey building where Star and Brandon are asked for their names and located on a list before their hands are rubber stamped and they're handed a printed card with half a dozen rules on it.

Now Brandon has a swagger in his walk. 'Well, good old Harry. It's a speakeasy. How the hell does he know this place?'

Star beams. 'Because he's posh and he's got connections, maybe? Look, there they are!' She trots across a stone courtyard furnished with rustic tables groaning with fruit, blossoms and seemingly hundreds of tall church candles. The sounds of jazz draw their attention to a small band and three couples in head-to-toe black, sunglasses covering their eyes, shuffle around a minuscule dance floor. Groups of diners shine like extras in a Dolce & Gabbana commercial.

'Cool,' Brandon says, cheering up immensely.

They spot Harry, Joe and Sander already at a table, and walking over to them, Brandon pumps Harry's hand. 'Thanks for the invite. Man, this place is incredible. How on earth did you find it?'

Waving away Brandon's questions, Harry hugs Star before letting out a low whistle. 'Wow, look at you – *trés chic, mademoiselle.*'

Star flushes with pleasure and gives a little wiggle, playing to the gallery.

Joe and Sander stand to greet them, full of smiles and compliments.

'We're drinking martinis,' Joe says, signalling to a waitress.

As drinks and antipasti begin to arrive, Brandon relaxes, lulled by the light-hearted and witty conversation that flitters between them.

'So, Brandon, what's your world?' Harry asks, spearing an olive and popping it between full pink lips.

'Good question. I guess I haven't decided yet. In London I was modelling, but the work was too erratic. I scored a couple of good gigs in Milan, but you know… it's not for me.' Brandon is squirming now, his toes curled inside his good shoes. Escort and gigolo are not job titles he wishes to bandy about in present company.

Sander is triumphant. 'I knew it! I told Joe you were a model. I've seen one of your shoots in *GQ*.'

'Yes, probably.' Brandon nods, knowing that this cannot be the case.

'My handsome big bro!' Star says, giving his shoulder a little rub of sisterly affection.

Harry flashes white teeth. 'Clearly, good looks run in the family. Must say though, don't think I've ever seen siblings less alike. How come?'

'Different dads,' Star says with a shrug. 'Hey, anyone like to dance?' And to Brandon's relief, she tugs at Harry's sleeve and leads him to an area of the floor where two men are dancing together, and a lone woman dressed as a unicorn is performing ballet poses.

'This place is nuts,' Sander says. 'I love it, it's perfect.'

Brandon nods, whilst keeping Star and Harry in his sights.

'I can see that you're very protective of her. Something's happened, hasn't it?' Joe's tone is tender.

'It's just us,' Brandon says, desperate to change the subject. 'Our parents are dead.'

Sander's eyes widen. 'Oh, god! Sorry to hear that,' he says. 'How?'

Brandon hesitates, fixes his eyes on Star while Harry flings her, laughing, around the floor. 'Actually, do you mind if—'

Joe raises a hand. 'Of course. Sorry, didn't mean to upset you. So, where are you two headed next?'

'Wherever the wind blows us, then home to south London when the money runs out,' Brandon admits. 'How about you guys?'

'We'll tour Italy for a while. Rome's wonderful, but there are so many other places to visit. We're off to Tuscany next. Come with us; it's great travelling in a group, means there's always somebody to play with.'

Brandon's laugh is dry. 'You know Harry's headed that way, too? He's spending the rest of the summer at his godmother's villa, he told me last week when we first met.'

Sander raises blond eyebrows. 'Nice work if you can get it. We, on the other hand, will book somewhere cheap and cheerful online, all very seat-of-the-pants, bargain basement.'

'Which is just how we like it,' Joe says, giving Sander's knee an affectionate squeeze.

Feeling like a gooseberry, Brandon picks up the menu and pretends to study the cocktail list. Perhaps it's time to leave Rome. People are beginning to recognise him as he cruises the same handful of bars at night. How long before the rumours begin? None of his female clients would welcome being the subject of gossip. In London, a well-preserved heiress had said something once that had stuck: *the only thing sadder than a man paying for sex, is a woman paying for it.* Brandon replaces the menu and looks up: Star is waving to him, gesturing for him to join her and Harry on the dancefloor. As if! He'd rather stick pins in his eyes.

*

After a fruitless search for a vacant taxi, Star and Brandon walk through the city and are stumble-tired by the time they arrive at the apartment.

'Feels later than midnight,' Star yawns, leaning against her brother for support.

'That's because you mixed your drinks and danced half the night,' Brandon says, jiggling his key in the lock before he hears a satisfying click and they burst through the door with relief.

'I expect you're right. *Ow*, my feet – they're twice their normal size,' Star moans, looking down at them. 'Oh, what's this?' She bends to pick up an envelope addressed to *Signore Brandon*.

Brandon frowns. 'I'm not sure I want to open this tonight… But then again—' He rips at the seam, releasing a single sheet of paper. 'Great, that's all we need,' he says, reading the hand-scrawled note.

Star's eyes widen. 'What? What's wrong?'

Brandon rakes a hand through his hair. 'We're being evicted, Star – with immediate effect.'

*

Harry's grin is tinged with smugness. 'Well, that settles it, then: you're coming with me for the rest of the summer. It's a no-brainer.'

Star is bouncing on the balls of her feet, eyes shining. 'Wow! We'd love that, Harry – wouldn't we, Brandon?'

But Brandon isn't convinced. He's neither ready to reveal himself to this irritating, hyper-confident rich kid – which could mean either a total suspension of income, in which case, how would they live? – nor prepared to live an elaborate deception, while he cruises the medieval towns of Tuscany, looking for wealthy women of a certain age.

'That's very kind of you, Harry – really generous, but we can't impose like that,' he says, his voice measured.

'Impose?' Harry winks at Star. 'Your brother's gone all Victorian on us. Come on, you'd be doing me a favour. I'll be bored shitless rattling round that huge villa and swimming in the pool all by myself.'

Brandon gives a slow shake of his head. 'Harry, thanks – but no thanks. Maybe it's time for Star and me to go home.'

Star pouts. 'Oh, come on, Brandon… please? We've only got two days to get out of the flat!'

Harry feigns indignation. 'Two days? That's outrageous. Or, maybe it's a message from the universe.'

'Actually, it's a message from our landlord's mother; she's arriving in Rome in forty-eight hours – no prizes for guessing where he's planning to put her.'

Harry's grimace and slight shudder is comical. 'Oh, well – that *is* serious. Look, why don't you stay at Veronica's villa while you figure out what to do next.'

'Can we, Brandon? Please?' Star wheedles. 'I've always wanted to go to Tuscany, see if it's like the films.'

Brandon throws up his hands. 'Looks like I've been outvoted. Okay, Harry, if you're sure. Just for a few days.' He turns to Star, who is beaming happily, hands clasped.

'Brilliant!' Harry smiles. 'It's a four-hour drive. I'll sort out a car and pick you up tomorrow at noon.'

'Great. I'll chip in for the car and Star and I will pay for all the food.'

Harry waves his suggestion away. 'Certainly not. You'll be my guests – although technically, we'll all be Ronnie's guests and she's loaded, so please, don't give it a second thought. There is something, though. I promised my folks that I'd learn Italian; it was kind of a condition of bumming around here all summer. You couldn't give me a hand with that, could you, Brandon? I've noticed you speak a little.'

Brandon makes a face. 'Yeah, very little... but, you know, maybe we can practise together?'

Harry nods. 'You're on.'

*

He can hear Star singing as she's packing – throwing brightly coloured, childlike garments into two nylon bags. His brow puckers. Are they doing the right thing? They know nothing about Harry, other than the fact that he's a spoilt rich bastard who likes to ask a lot of nosy questions. And it will mean never letting their guard down and limiting the conversation about their background and how they've been living of late.

On the other hand, business has been brisk all summer and he's managed to save nearly seven thousand euros, meaning he can afford to chill out at the villa and swerve the ladies for a while.

As if reading his mind, Star stomps into his room and squats among the neat piles of clothing on his bed.

'Bran, have we got any money?' she says, straight to the point.

'Enough. I've been saving up. We'll be okay for a couple of weeks. Maybe we can treat this like a proper holiday, you know? Swim, sunbathe…enjoy the scenery.'

Star's eyes shine. 'Oh, that sounds so amazing. I'm sick of working at the restaurant anyway, so good bloody riddance to that!' She chews her lip, hesitates for a moment. 'Do you think Harry fancies me, though? Only, I like him and everything – and obvs I've already snogged him – but I've decided that I could never shag him.' She wrinkles her nose and begins searching her hair for split ends.

Brandon sighs and shakes his head. 'Gross. Well, I'm glad we've cleared that up, but why are you telling me? Has he tried it on with you yet? No? Right, well, if that changes, you just tell me, and I'll kick him into touch.'

Star clambers off the bed, scattering Brandon's clothing to the floor, before throwing her arms around him. He'd complain, except that now he can't speak for the lump in his throat.

CHAPTER FORTY-ONE

Tuscany, July 2019

Brandon

They leave their apartment owing two weeks' rent and without cleaning up, even leaving dishes in the kitchen sink. It was a hovel anyway, Brandon reasons, and their landlord, Signore D'Angelo, had taken quite enough from them already.

But as Harry pulls up in a black open-topped jeep, Star panics. 'Brandon, what if D'Angelo goes to the police?'

'And waste their time? It's much too trivial. Come on, smile for our host.' Brandon waves. 'Ciao, Harry!'

With their bags loaded into the car, they set off and Harry puts his foot down, shaving half an hour off the journey. In the back of the jeep, Star squeals with excitement as they approach every bend or steep hill, exhilarated and unaccustomed to travelling with the top down, her hair whipping about her face.

Finally, Brandon begins to relax. Maybe Harry is okay after all and Brandon has just been unfair. He muses that Harry is certainly generous – having been adamant that Brandon and Star need not contribute.

'The three of us will have a blast and I told Joe and Sander to swing by when they reach San Gimignano in a few days, so we'll be quite the party,' Harry had said.

'Jesus, Harry,' Brandon had replied, 'what will your godmother say when she finds out there are three strange blokes and a teenage girl squatting in her house?'

Harry had smirked and winked. 'Well, I won't tell her if you don't.'

*

At Villa Giardino, Star is running from room to room, her bare feet drumming on the tiles.

'*Wow!* Are we *really* staying here? It's like a film set! Harry, I love it. Your auntie must be minted,' she squeals, eyes shining.

Harry laughs. 'Ronnie's not exactly my aunt, she's a cousin of my mother's. Anyway, I told you, she's my godmother. But I can't fault her taste, this place is rather fabulous, isn't it? Come on, I've saved the best till last.' Harry beckons them into the garden, where the late afternoon sun caresses the ivory stone terrace and the neatly trimmed herbaceous borders create an artists' palette of pastel colours.

Despite his attempts to play it cool, Brandon's face breaks into a huge grin as he spots the swimming pool shimmering in the sun.

'Cheers for this, Harry – so kind of you to let us stay,' Brandon concedes, longing to peel off his shirt and dive into the crystal water.

'Yes, Harry – thank you *soo* much. It's amazing!' Star echoes, kissing Harry on the cheek with a loud *mwah*.

'Well, why don't we unpack, then have a dip before dinner – there's a cracking little pizzeria in the village.'

'Think I've changed my mind,' Star hisses once Harry is out of earshot, 'I might actually *marry* the guy after seeing all this.'

'Yes, well, it's not his, just remember that. Come on, the sooner we unpack, the sooner we can dive into that pool,' Brandon says, striding off to his room.

*

By day three, after an initial burst of activity which had mainly revolved around stocking the house with food and booze, Brandon and Star have fallen into a languid stupor, content to read, swim and sunbathe. But Harry seems restless, keen to explore and sightsee.

'You know Tuscany's got some incredible local wines, don't you? In fact, my father knows someone who owns a vineyard near here – we should check it out.'

Brandon shrugs. 'I'm not really a wine buff, to be honest.'

From the comfort of two loungers placed for maximum sun exposure, Brandon and Star watch as Harry springs up and goes inside, muttering something about Ronnie keeping a good library in the study.

'Why can't he just relax? The guy's got the attention span of a gnat,' Brandon grumbles in a low voice. '*My father knows a vineyard owner*,' he mimics. 'Pretentious arsehole.'

Star wrinkles her brow. 'Brandon, shut up. He's not like us, is he? He's cultured. Anyway, I could get used to this... and drinking fancy wines. Closest we ever get is buying whatever's on special at Tesco.'

Harry returns, holding up a fat volume with a glossy cover.

'Found this on Ronnie's bookshelf. I knew it. There's a place about twelve miles from here where they do tastings and everything. Oh, and there's a disused monastery I'd like to see on the way. It's fifteenth century, or older.'

'Fascinating,' Brandon says, throwing a glance at Star who is also feigning interest.

'How exciting, Harry, I'd *love* to go,' she says, her tone decisive. 'In fact, we should *all* go. Right, Brandon?'

*

It's almost eight o'clock when the call comes. Harry, dressed in ivory-coloured jeans and black T-shirt, is at the hob, sautéing wild mushrooms, garlic and herbs for dinner.

When his mobile phone rings from his pocket, Harry grimaces and hands the spatula to Star. 'It's Veronica. Keep an eye on these, baby – I don't want them to burn.'

Baby? Since when is Harry using pet names for his sister? Nauseated, Brandon glares at Harry's back as he paces out into the hallway, phone pressed tight to his ear.

Star makes a goofy, comical face, revelling in being treated like a grown-up for a change. Then she's telling Brandon something about an Italian recipe she's seen in a magazine, but he puts a finger to his lips, eager to eavesdrop on Harry.

'Three of them? Gosh! Righto… Well, okay. No, of course not, Ronnie… I'm sure it'll be fine, but…' Harry's words trail off.

Star's eyes are round. 'Three what? What's he talking about?'

He frowns. 'No idea, but he doesn't sound very happy… Shh, he's coming back… Everything okay, Harry?' Brandon asks helpfully.

Harry picks up his glass, takes a mouthful of Chianti. 'I'm not sure,' he says, reclaiming the spatula from Star and absently returning to the buttery mushrooms.

Brandon tries again. 'Hope it wasn't bad news. Is there anything we can help with?'

Harry's smile does not reach his eyes. 'No. Thanks, but everything's fine. Oh, look at me hogging the wine… Top up, you two?'

CHAPTER FORTY-TWO

Tuscany, August 2019

Dale

She'd been so sure. Susanne's dress, the necklace. Star had them, she knew it. But where? And why? Susanne was right; they were hardly aspirational must-haves for a young woman – particularly one rocking a boho, festival-chic style, who most of the time looked as though she needed a shower.

Now, hidden in the farthest corner of the pizzeria, sipping her second Americano as the first lunchtime customers begin to arrive, Dale is embarrassed and contrite. Caroline Ditton, headmistress at the school where she teaches, had once accused her of being a hothead; well thank god Mrs D hadn't witnessed today's outburst.

A waitress hovers at her elbow. 'Would you like to see the lunch menu, Madam? I can tell you the specials.'

With a sad smile, Dale shakes her head and waves the woman away. She's not hungry – guilt and shame have killed her appetite. There's nothing for it but to go home and apologise. Throw herself on her sword and spend their last days tiptoeing round everyone and being as polite and meek as she can manage.

Dale pays for her coffee, walks out to the SUV and drives home at a more sedate pace than the one she left in.

*

At Villa Giardino, peace and order appear to have been restored. Susanne and Harry are sunbathing, while Evie sits in the shade, half covered by a sarong.

'Hi,' Dale's greeting is hoarse. She clears her throat. 'Where's Star, I need to say sorry. I don't know what came over me. She must think I'm completely mad… or at least very rude.'

Harry and Susanne look up at her and say nothing. Evie smiles and gives her a little wave of acknowledgement before turning back to her book.

'Okay, well, I'll just…' Christ, are they planning to ignore her for the rest of the day?

As she turns back towards the house, Star emerges in her bikini, holding a magazine, flip-flops slapping the ground beneath her feet.

Dale takes a deep breath. 'Star – may I speak to you, please?' Her tone is polite, formal. *Teacherly*, she realises, as the words leave her unsmiling lips.

Star rolls her eyes. 'Not if you're going to accuse me of nicking something, no.' She struts past Dale and pulls a chair up to where Evie is sitting.

Shit! This is not going to be easy.

'Star, I understand why you're angry but, please, can we just—'

'Whatever you want to say, you can say it here, in front of everyone.' Star says, crossing her legs primly.

'Star, I'm sorry, all right? Really sorry,' Dale has everyone's attention now – and not in a good way. 'I was completely wrong to come down on you like that, but the thing is, Susanne's stuff has only gone missing since you arrived and so I just—'

'Put two and two together and made seventeen! As I said, I never touched her things and I haven't seen them.' Then with her face set, Star angles her chair to the sun, and pretends to be engrossed in her magazine.

Dale clears her throat. 'Star. I'm genuinely sorry. Please accept my apologies,' she says, adding, 'and now I'm going to my room, my head's still fuzzy from last night.'

*

Lying on the bed, listening to the intermittent whine of a mosquito, Dale is surprised when there's a knock on the door. Her heart does a little skip. It's Susanne, surely, wanting to check on her, wanting to offer support, away from the gaze of the others.

She's touched to see Evie, proffering a drink that rattles with ice.

'You are kind, thank you,' Dale says, taking the glass from her. 'I expect you're all talking about me: *poor barmy old Dale – lost the plot*. Evie, I swear I overheard them talking and I don't know what happened to Susanne's stuff, but I honestly think that Star is at the… Oh, shit. I'm doing it again, aren't I?'

'Don't upset yourself,' Evie sits down beside her; Dale can feel the heat emanating from her skin and for a second, she wants to hug Evie for her kindness.

'Dale, nobody is talking about you. Everyone's just bored and hungover. Hey, I reckon you and I had the best start to the day – that little swim we had this morning was lovely.'

Dale regards Evie's gentle round face; the softness in her pale-blue eyes.

'Evie, you're lovely, do you know that? When we first came here, I wasn't very nice to you… I thought you were a bit straight – boring, even.' Dale shakes her head. 'Well, I know better now and I could not have been more wrong. You're a kind, honest, clever woman. And that's worth a lot. I know we're not exactly neighbours, but I hope we can still see each other when we get home.'

Evie smiles shyly. 'Of course. I'd be gutted if we didn't. Dale, don't hide away, it'll all blow over. Star's just a kid and it shows.

She'll be fine by tomorrow. And as for Susanne, she loves you. She's just a bit embarrassed.'

Dale nods. 'I think you're right. Thanks for being such a good mate, Evie, and for the drink as well.'

Relieved, she watches Evie creep from the room, before falling into a light doze.

*

'Hair of the dog: it's the only way,' Harry says, free-pouring gin over ice, before topping up the jug with tonic water and lemon wedges.

A collective shudder ripples around the kitchen.

'Ladies, trust me. It'll be very refreshing,' he says, filling glasses and passing them around.

Dale hangs back, still groggy from her afternoon spent hibernating in her room, and is convinced she'll be missed out. Instead, Harry hands her the first drink, his eyes locking with hers.

'Bottoms up, Dale. Glad to see you're feeling better.' He turns to Star. 'Are you still planning to make dinner? I'll be sous chef if you like.'

Above Dale's head, a cloud lifts. She has been forgiven. Tonight, they'll eat, drink, talk and laugh together, as though no unpleasantness has taken place.

*

'Bloody hell, Star. This pasta is delicious,' Dale gushes. 'Where on earth did you learn to cook like this? I couldn't boil an egg at eighteen,' she says, quick to praise Star's culinary efforts once they're seated before steaming bowls of creamy carbonara.

Star giggles. 'Oh, I can't boil an egg either. Trust me, this is the only thing I can cook. I worked in a trattoria in Rome for a while, waiting tables mostly, but one week I helped in the kitchen and I watched.'

'Ah, is that where you two met?' Evie asks, dabbing her chin.

Star hesitates, chews her food. 'Well, we—'

'We met at another café,' Harry says, talking over her, 'quite near where Star was working. She, Sander and their friend Joe were having a beer in the sunshine. You know, enjoying the weather and people-watching – and we got chatting. The amazing coincidence was that we were all bound for Tuscany the following week, so after that, we stayed in touch.'

Star has fallen silent and is studying her plate.

'Are you all right, love?' Susanne's voice is soft. 'It must be difficult, talking about Sander. I take it you haven't heard from him?'

Star shakes her head.

A silence falls, filled only by the scraping of cutlery as unsaid words hang in the air.

CHAPTER FORTY-THREE

Tuscany, September 2019

Brandon

There's a jangling in his gut and a mild headache over one eye. He can hear Susanne brushing her teeth; even when she spits, it's ladylike. Jesus, what was he thinking? As if he can get a woman like her to fall for him so hard that she'll go along with almost anything. And time is running out: only *two more sleeps*, as Star would say, before Susanne, Dale and Evie fly back to England.

And then what? He'll be banished to the farthest, darkest corners of her mind within weeks. Just a lovely, misty memory. A holiday romance with a boy seventeen years her junior; or so she thinks. Brandon longs to tell her that he's older, twenty-eight in November, which would surely help his cause, wouldn't it? Ah, but then again, the unravelling of the lies would begin.

Which is why he has to act now. Because once Susanne boards that plane, all his hopes of a better life for himself and Star will fly away with her. Thanks to bloody Veronica. Why did Harry's godmother have to be Susanne's *neighbour*? Why couldn't she have booked a holiday villa on the internet, all in good faith and totally anonymously, like everyone else?

Susanne returns from the bathroom, her skin clean and glowing.

'You okay, hon?' she says, sliding back into bed beside him, scrutinising his face, like a mother to a sick child.

'Actually, I do feel a bit rough.' Brandon sits up, pushes his hair back and rubs sleep from his eyes.

Susanne puts a hand to his forehead. 'Oh no. I hope you're not going down with something. You do feel hot.'

'Good to know,' Brandon says, with a suggestive smirk. 'Babe, I'm fine. The only thing wrong with me is knowing that you're leaving me soon. Susanne, I can't bear it, seriously.'

Their eyes lock, and it isn't a lie. Brandon pictures himself, waking up with Susanne every morning in a vast light-filled bedroom, her hair spilling across pillows dressed in the finest linen, before stepping into a double rainforest style shower together, where they'd fool around for a while before each dressing in elegant designer clothes. Then, they'd eat breakfast in a sleek modern kitchen that overlooks an exquisite, well-stocked, walled garden. Lunch would be consumed in one of Tunbridge Wells' smart brasseries and...

His reverie is interrupted by Susanne's phone, burbling from the nightstand.

A frown creases her brow. 'It's Colin. Wonder why he's calling so early. Harry, do you mind? I need to take this.'

'Sure,' Brandon murmurs, pulling on last night's discarded jeans and heading for the bathroom.

Covering his need to pee by turning the shower on, he considers Cody's father: rich, successful, well-educated, savvy. Even setting aside the Ronnie factor, no doubt Colin Campbell would have plenty to say about his ex-wife and the mother of his only son hooking up with a pretty-boy chancer with an uncertain past.

He considers all the wealthy older women he's serviced in the last couple of years. Simple transactions without preamble or promises – just sex in exchange for cash, with women who were often selfish, rude and bitter and, more often than not, lonely.

Susanne is none of those things. She is beautiful, kind, cultured and courteous – and from the moment he'd set eyes on her, he had bigger plans; an understanding that he'd be playing the long game.

Brandon steps under the shower head and turns his face towards the warm torrent, willing his head to clear so he can plot his next move.

*

He leaves Susanne sunbathing flanked by Dale and Evie, after vague mumblings about needing to visit one of San Gimignano's travel shops to plot the next leg of his journey. Without explanation, he takes Star with him; the original cover story of her being Sander's girlfriend no longer seems to matter. Soon Susanne would know everything – or at least an edited and fictionalised version of events – and it would all seem irrelevant.

Rumbling along in the jeep, Star is tight-lipped, her eyes fixed on the horizon.

'You all right, love?' Brandon asks.

Star nods. 'Yeah. I got my period this morning and my tummy hurts. Slow down, will you? It's worse when we go over bumps.'

Brandon sighs. 'You only had to ask. Are you sure that's all it is?'

'Isn't that enough? Like you'd know how it feels!'

'Sorry, you just seem—'

'Pissed off? Brandon, I'm scared. Those women are going home soon and then what? Why won't you tell me anything? You keep talking about this big plan you've got up your sleeve. Well, for Christ's sake, can you share it with me, please? Because as far as I can see, once they leave, we'll have to as well – and then what? Moving from place to place and staying in shitty two-star hostels again?'

Brandon changes down a gear and looks across at his sister; tears shine in her eyes and something else. Fear.

Star wrings her hands; her voice is almost a whisper. 'What happened… it'll all come out… I know it will… and then that's it. Game over.'

Brandon shakes his head. 'Stop it, Star. We agreed never to speak about it. Look, trust me. If Susanne—'

Star balls up her fists in frustration. 'If Susanne *what*, Brandon? If fleecing Susanne is your big career move to get us out of shit street, you're cutting it pretty bloody fine.'

Oh god, he can see the hysteria rising, the panic. Seeing a passing point up ahead, he slows down and manoeuvres into it.

'Okay, Star. Listen… listen to me! I know this has been really hard, on both of us – and after Mum and everything – but we have got to keep it together. We're nearly there. Because the thing is, I'm not going to rob Susanne. I'm going to marry her.'

*

In the jewellery store just off Piazza Della Cisterna, Star has cheered up immensely, eyes quick and darting like a magpie, mesmerised by all that glitters under the lights.

The salesman tenderly strokes the tips of his moustache. 'Please, take your time. Affairs of the heart cannot be rushed,' he says in his honeyed Italian accent.

Brandon gazes at tray after tray of cheap costume rings, feeling despondent and clueless.

'Star, please – help me with this. It doesn't need to be expensive – that's the whole point. It'll be a romantic gesture, to show her I'm serious, but with the promise of the real thing once we get home.'

'Only if I can have one as well,' Star pouts, trying on three rings in quick succession, watched by the salesman.

'God, you really are a little pain. Yes, all right. You can have a *small* one, only don't show the others, will you? It'll detract from the romance of it all.'

Ten minutes later, Brandon emerges onto the cobbled street clutching a smart carrier bag, its silky gold bow belying the modest price tag of the ring inside.

Star had insisted on wearing hers at once. With an indulgent smile, the salesman had cleaned it for her there and then.

'Oh, thank you! Have I ever told you what a *generous* big brother you are, Brandon?' Star says, laying her gratitude on with a trowel.

Brandon sighs. 'Small things… but I'm glad you like it.'

Star extends her hand and admires the bubble-gum stone in its silver setting. 'Do you think it's a real pink topaz?' she says, her eyes wide.

'Not at that price. But it was worth the thirty euros to see you smiling again, and I must admit it looks very pretty.'

'Yeah, well, I hope Susanne likes hers and she says yes. If she doesn't, I'll have her ring as well.'

'Oh, she'll say yes. I know she will,' Brandon says with more conviction than he feels.

CHAPTER FORTY-FOUR

Susanne

Susanne had expected to hear from Colin. After all, an Edinburgh to Gatwick airport handover stood between them and there were timings to sort. What had floored her was Colin's assertion that he'd be driving down from Edinburgh to Tunbridge Wells instead; a dual-purpose trip that combined the safe door-to-door delivery of their son and the opportunity for Susanne to meet Melissa. Which could only mean one thing.

Heart racing and palms clammy, Susanne had nevertheless managed to keep her tone breezy.

'Oh, okay. Well, I'm sure Cody will enjoy the drive. Has Melissa got family here, or are you two doing anything special while you're down south?' The pulsing in her ears had almost drowned out Colin's answer.

'No, nothing like that. We're specifically coming to see you, Susanne. It's important that you meet Mel. We've been together ages and I'm sure you're curious about the woman Cody has spent all summer with,' Colin had reasoned.

'Of course. I agree, makes total sense. Actually, Col, I have to go; the girls and I are heading out for the day and they're waiting for me,' she'd lied, fearing her emotions would get the better of her.

They'd skipped to the arrangements then. The day after Susanne landed, Colin would rock up at her home with Cody and Melissa in tow, then they'd all have dinner together in one of the brasseries in town before the visiting couple would check into the spa hotel on the common overnight.

Harry had considerately given her some space but is now mysteriously absent, after mumbling about going to the travel agent in San Gimignano. At this precise moment, his vagueness – and the fact that Star has gone along for the ride – couldn't matter less; Susanne is relieved that she can fall apart in relative privacy and pick over Colin's news with her friends.

As they lie draped on sunbeds, basking in the scorching sun in a last-ditch effort to top up their tans, Susanne fills them in.

Dale looks put-out. 'Bloody hell, Susanne, that's shitty. I'm really sorry.' She reaches for the sun cream and begins liberally applying it to her chest and shoulders. 'Thing is, I guess it was always going to happen. Are you okay with it?'

Actually, I'm not okay with any of it, Susanne wants to scream. *I'm not okay with meeting my ex-husband's new partner – especially when he's likely to announce that they're getting engaged, married or starting a family of their own. I'm not okay with the fact that I've been sleeping with my neighbour's godson, who is almost young enough to be my son, and most of all, I'm not okay with my oldest, closest friend stuffing my personal possessions under her mattress and lying to my face. So, no, Dale, I am not okay.*

Instead, Susanne swallows hard. 'I have a feeling they're getting married. And I'm fine – I just need to get used to the idea, that's all. Cody has already accepted Melissa, so now it's my turn to suck it up.'

'Easier said than done though,' Evie says, sitting up. 'It's like the final chapter to the fairy tale.'

Susanne scoffs. 'Think that came with the divorce, Evie, love. I'll be fine, really.'

Dale stretches like a cat and grins. 'I feel a bit sorry for Melissa, though. Just imagine, you're meeting your bloke's ex-wife for the first time… and then she looks like you, Susie,' she chuckles.

Harry's assessment of Dale echoes in Susanne's ears: *the woman's obsessed with you.*

'Well, clearly Colin prefers her,' Susanne snaps, her tone sharper than intended.

*

When Harry returns, he seems nervous and edgy, the tension visible in his face. He barely acknowledges Dale and Evie, moving past them and sweeping Susanne into his arms.

'Have you had a relaxing morning, Susie? Was everything okay with your ex when he rang?' His gaze is searching. Without waiting for an answer, he looks to the others. 'Girls, will you forgive me if I take Susanne out to dinner tonight?' He turns back to Susanne. 'I thought we could drive into Siena – get dressed up and go somewhere special, on me, of course. It's the end of the holiday, after all.'

Touched by Harry's urgency and extravagant display of affection, Susanne agrees.

Dale and Evie exchange looks. *What the hell?* It's only one evening; for once she can't be bothered to factor in Dale's approval.

'Harry, I'd love to – if you're sure,' Susanne says, suddenly shy and realising how much she longs to be alone with him so that he can take away the hurt caused by Colin.

'Oh, I've never been more sure of anything,' is Harry's earnest reply.

Star joins them, swigging cola from a can, her expression quizzical. 'Hiya, what have I missed?'

Harry beams at her. 'I've just asked Susanne out to dinner – just the two of us – and she said yes.'

Star's smile is radiant. She does a funny little skip, sending an arc of cola flying.

*

It's almost seven thirty by the time they arrive in Siena. The light is beginning to fade but the city's ancient stone retains its heat. Susanne glances down at her feet, grateful for her jewelled flats; between the winding cobbled streets and the temperature, her wedges would have slowed her down.

Strolling around Piazza del Campo, Susanne regards Harry's profile. With his mouth curved in a gentle smile and his eyes lively, he wears the expression of someone desperate to share a secret. Their conversation in the car had been disjointed and offered no clues as to why he had brought her here, to this romantic city.

Looking around her, Susanne is aware that Harry is several inches taller than most Italian men and easily as handsome. A sudden flashback to the night before, Harry's face contorted in ecstasy then soft as a child's as he'd fallen asleep beside her, adds a delicate flush to her cheeks.

'Hey,' Harry points ahead, 'I think I can see it. Yes, that's the one. Bar Il Palio. I read online that it's the place to be at *aperitivo* time. Come on, let's see if we can squeeze in somewhere.'

A glass of prosecco in hand, grazing on tiny delicious snacks and people watching, Susanne sighs with contentment.

'You look happy, baby,' Harry says, lacing his fingers into hers.

'I am, it's wonderful here. Good to be on our own, too. I love my friends dearly but being around them twenty-four seven has been a strain – for all of us.'

Harry's expression clouds over. 'I'm not surprised. Things must be very tricky between you and Dale after finding out—'

Susanne stiffens. 'Actually, do you mind if we don't talk about it? Sometimes the house feels like a tinder box waiting to go up. Let's not spoil tonight.' She finishes her wine. 'Shall we have another drink?'

Harry shakes his head. 'You can, but I'm driving, aren't I? There's a restaurant I want to take you to – trust me you'll love it.'

*

A short walk away at the Villa Marcello, Susanne agrees; Harry has made an excellent choice. Everything pleases her, from the charming trompe l'oeil of an olive grove, which gives the intimate restaurant a depth it does not possess, to the soft, flickering candlelight and the crisp white table linen. Glasses sparkle, the waiters are discreet and the food is mouth-watering.

'Oh my god, this antipasti is the best I've ever eaten,' Susanne breathes as zesty artichoke hearts explode in her mouth and prosciutto melts on her tongue.

Despite the perfection of each dish, Harry eats little, his eyes darting and watchful. Instead he seems nervous, sipping fizzy water and toying with his food.

After a main course of wild boar ravioli, Susanne rubs her stomach. 'Harry, I'm done. That was wonderful, but I couldn't manage another mouthful. How on earth did you know about this place? It's so… traditional… I mean for—'

'For a young guy like me? I researched it online. I wanted to take you somewhere special. You don't have to keep bringing everything back to age. There's so much you don't know about me. Age is just a number; it couldn't matter less, and really, we're not so different.'

Susanne's eyes are soft in the candlelight. 'Harry, we could scarcely be more different. Look, I know you think you have feelings for me, but you'll forget all about me once you get home. You've got an incredible new job waiting, and more than that, parents who love you and who want the very best for you. I've loved our time together, but—'

Harry shakes his head. 'No! Don't say it. Nothing has to change… Well, actually, it does. But going home doesn't mean the end for us.' His eyes blaze, and after taking a sip of water, he chews his lip.

Astonished by his outburst, Susanne's voice is gentle. 'Harry, what on earth do you think your godmother would say if we kept seeing each other? We can't go sneaking around once we're home, it would be just too weird.'

'Forget her! Ronnie doesn't matter… or the job… or any other fucking thing that you think is so important.'

Embarrassed, Susanne looks around. Anywhere else, Harry's raised voice might have attracted attention, but here, he cannot be heard over the boisterous hubbub of other diners. She changes the subject, asks him about the highlight of his summer.

Harry groans. 'No, please, not small talk. Susanne, I love you, and I can't let you fly home without making you understand that properly.'

Susanne breathes deeply; the heat has become stifling and her stomach has begun to churn. 'I think the world of you, too. But we need to get to know each other. Holidays are such a weird, intense bubble. The practicality of life would be so different. You're just twenty-five, and you need to do normal stuff like have lots of girlfriends, make your mark at work, then one day get married and have children.' Susanne's thoughts turn to Cody; the pang of missing her son is like a physical blow. She gropes for her water glass, aware of a rising nausea.

'Yes, yes, you're right. All those things. But with you, Susie. With you!' Then to Susanne's utter astonishment, Harry has slid from his seat and is on one knee before her, the other leg extended comically behind him, ready to trip up any passing waiter. In his hands: a small velvet box. He opens it up. A ring with a large, clear stone sparkles in the candlelight. His mouth is forming shapes – words that Susanne cannot hear for the pounding sea in her ears. She feels her face becoming hotter, her hands tingling… Black shapes float before her eyes before silence envelops her.

CHAPTER FORTY-FIVE

Dale

Going out for pizza had been Dale's idea and offering to treat Star and Evie, an attempt to be conciliatory.

Evie had been reluctant at first. 'Let's just split the bill. I suspect we've all run out of money by now.'

But Dale had insisted. 'No, please, let me. I've been such a vicious old cow recently, it's the least I can do.'

Star had been surprisingly gracious. 'Thanks, Dale – that's really nice of you. Have I got time for a shower and hair wash?'

Relieved to be forgiven, Dale had beamed. 'Of course, take your time, Star. Let's reconvene at eight.'

Now, feeling lighter at the prospect of going home and singing softly to herself while trawling her wardrobe for something clean, Dale can hear a ringing sound. Realising it is the bell of a landline, she opens her bedroom door and finds Evie in the hallway.

'Where's that coming from?' Dale says, walking towards the sound.

'From the study by the entrance. I answered it once before when Susanne's neighbour Ronnie called for Harry. Wonder if it's her again.'

'I'll get it,' Dale says, suddenly serious. In her experience, ringing landlines often carried bad news, and to her ears at least, the sound is ominous.

Inside the room, the blinds are drawn, and the temperature is a few degrees cooler; a fine film of dust covers the desk.

Dale reaches for the handset, Evie standing next to her. 'Hello?'

'Hello. Who is this?' An English woman's voice, waspish.

Dale makes a face. 'This is Dale, I'm staying here. Who do you want?'

An intake of breath. 'Is Harry there, please?'

'I'm afraid not, he's gone out for the evening. Can I take a message?'

'It's Caroline Klein. His mother. I really must insist that he rings me. I've been calling and calling his mobile and it just clicks straight to voicemail.'

Harry's lack of respect makes Dale scowl at the receiver; poor woman, it's not her fault that her son is rubbish at keeping in touch with his folks.

'I'm getting so worried. We've heard nothing for weeks, not even a phone call on his birthday – and just a couple of snippy texts since then. We're a close family. Harry wasn't brought up to—'

'It must be very frustrating, I don't know if this will help, but boys will be boys, as the saying goes.' Dale's heart is beginning to thaw. Clearly the poor woman is only now waking up to what a selfish idiot her son is.

'How does he seem to you, Dale?'

So many answers vying to be spoken, and yet... Dale collects herself. 'Er... perfectly happy and certainly very well,' Dale answers, wondering what else to add.

Evie's eyes are wide as she listens intently, filling in the blanks.

'Please get him to call me, will you? Sorry to bother you with this but I'm at my wits' end. Tell Harry if he doesn't phone me tomorrow, then I shall board a flight myself.'

'I'll tell him, but I'm not sure that—'

There's a catch in Caroline Klein's voice as she says a curt goodbye and hangs up.

Dale replaces the handset and stares at the silent phone. 'How weird was that? Evie, I've got a bad feeling about this. Let me think for a moment.' She paces the cool, still room, then spins round on her heel.

'Right, Evie – I'm sorry to do this to you, but I want you to go through Harry's old room. We must have missed something the other day.'

Evie's eyes are round. 'How am I meant to do that? We've just arranged to go out.'

'Say you feel ill; I'll back you up. You've got sunstroke and you had a funny turn in the shower. Then I'll keep Star out for a couple of hours… get her a bit tipsy and see if she'll let anything slip. Evie, please. I know I'm onto something. Those two are working together and meanwhile, our best friend is alone and vulnerable. I'll never forgive myself if anything happens to Susanne. Or to you,' Dale adds, placing a hand on Evie's forearm.

Evie pats Dale's hand and chews her lip. 'But what am I looking for?'

'Susanne's missing necklace, her blue dress, letters, photos… anything at all that might be interesting. Yes, I know it sounds daft, but why all the mystery? Maybe Harry's got himself into something illegal. You know he smokes weed, don't you? Well, who knows what else he takes behind closed doors?'

'Oh god. Poor Susanne, she never said. I know she hates drugs. What must—'

'Shh! The shower's stopped running in Star's room. Okay, you go – get into bed or something and I'll explain to Star why you've blown us out.'

*

'Such a shame Evie couldn't come,' Star says, biting into a crust of garlic bread, and not looking remotely worried.

Dale nods. 'I know, poor old Evie. She's very fair and we were baking in the sun the whole time you and Harry were in San Gimi. Did you have a nice time?'

'Oh, we didn't do much really, just walked around the shops... Harry treated me to a gelato.'

Dale groans with delight. 'Italian ice cream is to die for. Did Harry sort out his tickets?'

'Tickets?' A look of confusion crosses Star's face.

'For the next leg of his journey. Actually, I can't remember where he said he's going next.'

Their eyes lock for a moment. Star picks up her glass and takes a large swallow of Frascati. 'I don't think he's decided yet... he mentioned going back to London soon.'

A warm smell of garlic and hot bubbling cheese envelops them as a waitress arrives bearing two pizzas.

'Fab. I'm starving,' Star says, eyeing the food.

Dale laughs. 'Bloody hell, Star. Where do you put it all?'

'Oh, my mum was naturally skinny... my dad, too – although I don't really remember him. I was only a toddler when he took off.'

'Bless you, that must have been hard.' Dale refills Star's glass. 'Here, have a top-up. I can only have one glass so it's all yours, hon.'

Star beams. 'Cheers, Dale.'

'You know, Star, I really admire you,' Dale begins, her tone light, 'you're just so chilled about everything. You're eighteen, in a strange country, without a job and for all I know, pretty broke. You've split up with your boyfriend, who's out there somewhere, god knows where by now. And then there's Harry. You've only known him ten minutes, yet he's become your best mate. Star, I've seen the way he always pays for you – and he's very protective, too. I actually think you two would make a great couple.'

To Dale's surprise, Star's shoulders begin to shake with laughter. 'Oh, that's so funny, Dale – you don't even know how funny that is, oh dear...' Star dabs her mascaraed lashes with her napkin.

Dale smothers the irritation building inside her, knowing that Star could let something slip at any moment.

'No? Well, you tell me then. What's so funny?'

Star mimes shock, gasping and slapping a hand over her mouth before making a zipping motion and tossing away an invisible key.

Christ, enough with the pantomime. 'What's the big secret?' Dale asks, her face beginning to ache from smiling so much.

But Star shakes her head. 'Nothing,' she says, filling her mouth with pizza and clamming up. Realising that a new approach is called for, Dale changes the subject.

'So, Evie mentioned that you'd lost your mum. God, Star, that's rough. You must have been so young when—'

'Thirteen. I was thirteen years old when she… when it happened.' Star's eyes darken. 'Want to see a picture?' she adds, her tone brightening. Then she rummages in her handbag, finds her phone and scrolls through a mosaic of photos.

'Here, it's not that clear – it's a snapshot that someone scanned for me. But anyway, this is her sitting in our old garden, in the house where we grew up.'

Dale studies the screen, blows it up with her thumb and index finger. A thirty-something woman relaxes in a canvas chair, a cigarette held between her fingertips. The setting is a cheerless suburban garden, with worn patches on a scorched lawn. Just in shot, a child's bicycle leans against a fence, ribbons stream from the handlebars. With her fine-boned face, there is no mistaking the resemblance to Star, yet her mane of dark hair is a world away from Star's pale, fine locks. Dale hands back the phone, reminded of someone else, someone she cannot place.

CHAPTER FORTY-SIX

Evie

As the sound of the SUV dies into the distance, Evie springs out of bed and goes to Star's room, closing the drapes before daring to switch on the light. She looks around, reminds herself that although Harry openly shares Susanne's bed at night, his possessions vie for space alongside Star's in what used to be his room. It strikes her as odd that the two of them are so willing to share the space – a mark of their youth, perhaps.

As she'd expected, the room is a raggle-taggle of shoes and clothing. Star's scent, light and powdery, hangs in the air, and there's a fresh-looking spill of metallic blue nail polish on the rug. Ronnie is sure to be delighted by that!

Unsure where to begin her reluctant trawl through Star's girlish stuff, Evie's eyes rest on the small chest that doubles as a dresser. Brushing a hand over Star's still-warm hair dryer, Evie hesitates. Rifling through someone else's private possessions feels all wrong, so intrusive. She'd be mortified if anyone did it to her – not that they'd find anything of interest. Why on earth has she agreed to do this?

Think, Evie. Focus.

Dale had already carried out a rapid (yet quite thorough!) search of drawers and cupboards and the only suspect item she'd come up with had been the locked tin. Dale had been convinced that they'd find Susanne's missing necklace under lock and key, but then Harry and Star had interrupted them – which was excruciating to recall now – and things had quickly turned unpleasant. But then Evie had registered a degree of pleasure in Harry's smug expression, as he'd lifted the lid and revealed nothing more than a passport and a few coins in the tin's depths.

But what if Harry had called their bluff? And Susanne's pendant had been hidden beneath? Then again, why on earth would Harry and Star collude on the theft of a cheap necklace in the first place? The whole silly incident beggared belief.

All this suspicion and intrigue; because of a missing necklace, an errant frock – which Susanne had probably forgotten to pack in the first place – and the fact that Harry was selfish and forgetful about calling home.

And yet. A tiny doubt gnaws away in Evie's mind. There's no denying the strange atmosphere in the house and the thought of going home the day after tomorrow floods Evie with a relief so intense, she catches her breath.

Sod it. She'll take a look around – if only to reassure Dale that nothing peculiar has come to light.

Gently, methodically, Evie moves around the room, pulling back bedding, checking under pillows, opening drawers, feeling along shelves and finally peering into the cavernous wardrobe, where a rail of stylish, good quality men's clothes lines up beside a clutch of colourful, petite jeans, dresses and kaftans; Star and Harry's wardrobe merged into one incongruous collection. Beneath the hanging clothes, several pairs of men's shoes and an oblong, dust-free space where the tin had lived – until recently.

Now Evie's suspicions are aroused. She scans the high shelf, her eyes alighting on a folded scarf or sweater. Standing on tiptoe, she feels beneath the soft layers to something, cool, solid. And then the tin is within her grasp. It is locked, of course. She goes to the bedside table, feels to the back of the drawer and is amazed to find its tiny key.

Open the tin, Evie – just bloody get on with it!

She hesitates. What if the necklace is inside? Without answering her own dilemma, Evie inserts the key, feels a click and she's in.

As expected, a UK passport. Evie lifts it, but there is nothing else to see – even the handful of change has now gone. No necklace, no secret compartment or false bottom where one might languish. Without the passport, the tin is empty.

Suddenly, struck by a childish desire to peek at Harry's photo, Evie thumbs to the ID page. She frowns, perplexed. The name on the passport is Harry Klein, but the photo is of a person she does not recognise. She pauses, skims the details.

Date of Birth 28.08.94

Indeed, they'd celebrated Harry's birthday recently, but the young man in the photo looks nothing like him. The date of issue shows that the passport is four years old. Had his appearance really changed so much? Evie scrutinises the photograph. The eyes that gaze out at her are rounder and lighter in colour, the nose thicker and shorter – and where is Harry's trademark chiselled jaw?

None of this makes sense. Operating on instinct now, Evie grabs her mobile phone and snaps Harry's passport, zooming in on his face, before locking the tin and replacing it on the high shelf beneath the sweater. Then she returns the tiny key to the nightstand drawer, scans the room for anything else out of place, hopeful that it's such a mess that neither Star nor Harry will notice the difference.

Finally, Evie turns out the light, then half opens the drapes as she found them and shuts the door behind her. Exhaling audibly, she realises she's been holding her breath.

Heavens. What on earth is going on?

Evie's mind is racing now with questions that flash like neon signs. Firstly, if the young man in the passport photograph is Harry

Klein, then who has taken Susanne to Siena? Secondly, where is the real Harry Klein?

Goosebumps rise on Evie's arms as she reaches for her mobile and dials Dale's number, willing her to pick up.

CHAPTER FORTY-SEVEN

Brandon

He'd expected to sweep Susanne off her feet. Well, he'd done that all right. Now she is slumped on the tiled floor of the ladies' room, a pungent pool of vomit beside her, spatters visible on her dress and hair and it is all Brandon can do not to gag and leave her there.

Susanne is murmuring apologies and trying to sit up. He covers his shock and disgust. 'Don't try to move yet, give yourself a moment. You fainted. And then you threw up.'

Susanne groans. 'Oh, god… how awful, I'm so sorry… in front of everyone, in such a beautiful restaurant.' Tears well in her eyes and she pushes herself into a sitting position, edging away from the contents of her stomach, self-loathing visible on her pale face.

'It's okay, nobody saw anything. One of the waiting staff helped me half drag and half carry you in here before you were ill. How are you feeling now, darling?'

'Mortified. I've never eaten wild boar before… I guess it doesn't like me much.' She shakes her head, a look of dismay on her drained face. 'Give me a minute, will you – I need to freshen up and then we should go.'

Brandon nods. 'Of course.' He backs out of the washroom and pays the bill, adding a generous tip in lieu of someone having to clean the ladies' room. Then, deflated and mildly disgusted, he waits for Susanne to emerge before guiding her from the restaurant. A few people are staring – well, let them. It's not as though he'll ever be back.

Once outside, Susanne's colour returns. 'I'm feeling a lot better,' she says, 'now that I've ejected that lovely and expensive dinner. Harry, I'm so sorry… and I know my timing was terrible. I saw you… on one knee and everything, before I blacked out.'

Shit. This is not what he'd planned at all. Brandon attempts a joke. 'So, it's official. I literally make you sick. What a total idiot I am.' Why couldn't something go well for him? Just for once?

Susanne starts to protest. 'Harry, don't be ridiculous. Believe me, if I'd wanted to put you off, I'd have picked a far more ladylike way of doing it. Look, can we just go home, please? I reek of sick and I've managed to ruin the evening, for both of us.'

Brandon feels for the cheap costume ring in his pocket. The circumstances are far from ideal, but he needs to rescue the situation, make light of it somehow and finish what he's started.

They are almost back at the car, under cover of darkness except from the golden glow of cafés and bars, when Brandon spots a flower seller leaving a restaurant. He sprints forward and peers into the vendor's basket where a dozen or so individually wrapped roses languish, unsold.

'How much for all of them?' Brandon asks, fumbling for cash. Then he's striding towards Susanne, a huge grin on his face, the boxed ring in one hand, scarlet blooms in the other. Encouraged by her reaction as she rolls her eyes and giggles, her hand over her mouth, Brandon falls to one knee, ignoring the discomfort of the cobbles.

'I love you, Susanne. Will you marry me?' he asks in a clear voice.

'Harry, please get up!'

'Will you though? Just give me an answer, Susanne – we belong together.' A wheedling, begging tone has crept into his voice. He's asking the impossible and he knows it.

A grimace from Susanne. 'Harry, I'm really flattered, honestly. But I think you're barking mad. We're so different – what about your family? How will they feel when you—'

'I couldn't care less what my family thinks. You mean more to me than any of them and I'll walk away from them if I have to. You don't understand; there's nothing I wouldn't do for you. Cody sounds like an awesome kid and I know once I meet him, I'll want to love and protect him, too.' Brandon pauses. Susanne is eyeing the ring and has probably noticed it is a cheap fake.

'I know what you're thinking and you're right,' his tone is urgent, 'the ring is just symbolic. Put it on now and I'll have one made for you as soon as we're home. Together. Forget about all the obstacles… there's so much I need to explain but not here, not tonight.'

A cold numbness is creeping into Brandon's bended knee and a small audience has mushroomed around them as people have come out of bars and passers-by have paused to watch the spectacle.

Susanne hesitates; he can see the rise and fall of her chest as she takes a couple of deep breaths. She wrings her hands, her eyes becoming glassy with an emotion he can't read. 'My god, this is such a shock… I mean, a surprise. And I must be insane… but you make me happy, and I love you, too. So, I'm saying yes, Harry!' Beaming, she puts out her left hand and Harry slides the gaudy bauble onto her third finger.

'Yesss! Oh my God!' Brandon punches the air and throws his arms around her, mindless of the faint sour smell. Then ignoring the onlookers, he kisses her lightly and helps her towards the car.

*

Cloaked in blackness except for the beam of headlights on the road, Brandon feels a degree of relief. He steels a glance at Susanne, but she has fallen asleep, lulled by the bouncing rhythm of the jeep. He'll need a better car than this in England; it's Harry's pick after all, and far too basic for the likes of Susanne.

He can't afford to dwell on the details right now – details like how an unemployed, former model slash escort will ever afford a car, or a flat likely to ensnare a rich divorcee. As if jarred by his thoughts, Susanne stirs; her eyes flutter open, then close again.

He'll figure something out. He's good at problem-solving – he's smart, all his teachers at the Catford comp he'd gone to had said so.

Brandon's eyes flick to Susanne; she is breathing deeply now, her head lolling awkwardly to one side.

His proposal had been desperate, not to mention a total shambles. Susanne ejecting her dinner had been gross, but he'd pressed on with the plan regardless. And for one horrible moment while he was on one knee, cheap roses in one hand, fake ring in the other, he'd thought his charm offensive had failed him. So, he'd pulled out all the stops: he'd said how Susanne mattered more to him than his entire family and it had melted her heart. The stuff about Cody had been a gamble, telling her how he couldn't wait to meet him – like he gave a rat's arse about her spoilt brat kid – but Susanne had bought it hook, line, and sinker.

Of course, he'll have to tell her the truth. He smirks in the darkness, enjoying his own cleverness – or his version of it. He knows it would have to be soon, what with the complication of Ronnie the neighbour and everything. And if he says so himself, his cover story is utter genius.

He pictures Susanne's face: shocked initially, then won over by the romance of it all, when he explains that he and Harry cooked up a whole disappearing act, so that Harry can escape his rich, oppressive parents and be with the woman he loves. He's still fleshing out the finer details, but he knows they'll come to him. Better still, some of Susanne's neuroses about their affair will melt into insignificance, removing, rather than creating, obstacles to their domestic bliss. 'So, you see, babe,' he'll say, clasping her hands and gazing into those clear trusting eyes, 'you needn't worry about Ronnie, she's no relation. And as for the age gap between us, I'll be twenty-eight in November…'

The more he thinks about it, the more convinced he is that marrying Susanne will be a win-win. Either he'll grow to love her and the lifestyle they'll construct together, or he'll divorce her, take half of everything she owns, and simply disappear.

Brandon shields his eyes as a car flies towards them, passing them at speed on the narrow road, shattering his reverie.

Susanne will tell the other women about his proposal, of course; the ring is on her finger for all to see, and anyway, what woman would keep quiet about being engaged? Brandon pictures Dale: a look of horror on her beautiful, hard, slappable face, followed by a barrage of objections. Well, bring it on.

Just let her try and destroy things for the happy couple. His stunt hiding Susanne's necklace, dress and bikini under Dale's mattress had shocked Susanne to the core; he'd read it in her eyes, even though she'd been much too ladylike to confront Dale, saying she'd have it out with her once they were home. Yes, he'd done enough to undermine Dale, to shake her credibility and their friendship. He couldn't wait to see the crazy bitch's face.

Evie, on the other hand, would be sweet about it, even happy for them perhaps, offering her congratulations. He imagines Star, squealing with happiness, picturing her new lifestyle in posh Tunbridge Wells; a far cry from where they'd grown up in the terraced house opposite the bus station just off the South Circular, the roar of traffic echoing in their ears and the stink of diesel etched on their sinuses. No wonder both their fathers had fucked off without a backward glance, the losers.

Not that it mattered. None of it did now. Gone. All gone. His beautiful mother, who still came to him in his dreams, her mane of dark hair floating about her face. And as for Graham, his biological father – certainly never a *dad* – and then Ziggy, who'd barely stuck around until Star could walk, he had no idea as to their whereabouts and wasn't even curious. They might as well have been dead.

And if they were… he would dance on their graves.

CHAPTER FORTY-EIGHT

Susanne

Susanne fights her way through sleep. How long has she been out? Heavy-lidded, her eyes slide to Harry's profile. By the light of the dashboard, she can see his lips are curved into a smile, yet there's tension in his jaw that makes his expression hard to read.

She peers out, trying to penetrate the darkness. Undulating hills and a spine of cypress trees silhouetted against an indigo sky offer no clue to their whereabouts.

'Nearly home. How are you feeling?' Harry says, as if reading her mind.

With a slight shudder, Susanne recalls waking up on the tiled floor of the ladies' room. 'Sleepy. Embarrassed. Bless you, Harry. What a weird night you've had. First, I faint and throw up on you – and in a fancy restaurant at that. And then I snore all the way back. What marvellous company I've been,' she says, stifling a yawn.

It's too dark to see Harry's smile, but she can hear it in his voice. 'The only thing I'll remember tonight for is that we got engaged and I couldn't be happier about it.'

There's a feeling of something pressing on her chest, but she keeps her tone light. 'Me too. But Harry, we mustn't rush into things. There's a lot to sort when I get home and my priority will be Cody. I haven't seen him in weeks, and I can't tell you how much I've missed him.'

The thought of her son being back in her arms and under her roof almost catches Susanne's breath. All this craziness – her whirlwind romance with Harry – will all go on hold once they are home and Harry had better accept it.

Susanne frowns. Cody is not the only consideration. Dale and Evie will have to be told. Oh god, Dale. Her heart sinks at the thought of telling her, and she hasn't even had the conversation about the dress, bikini top and necklace yet. Clearing the air will be another priority.

Susanne considers her ex-husband's forthcoming visit with Melissa. Just thinking about it makes her stomach lurch. How much should she tell Colin while everything is so fresh and new? Perhaps she'll beat him to the punch, and casually let slip about Harry's proposal. Get Col's take on her forthcoming engagement to a rising star in the city – leaving out the fact that he's twenty-five years old and she's only known him for five weeks.

She knows meeting Colin and Melissa in all their loved-up smugness would be more bearable with Harry on her arm – and not only because of his model looks. Upping the ante is the fact that Harry's family are wealthy, that he's achieved a business degree at Cambridge and that he is on the brink of a career – while her ex-husband's has an imminent shelf life.

Susanne twists the cheap ring on her wedding finger. Bless Harry for going off in search of a pretty costume ring, how sweet and endearing of him. Almost weightless as his symbolic ring is, it feels natural for her third finger to be occupied again. She'd only recently removed Col's engagement ring: a tasteful solitaire diamond on a platinum band that now resides in the safe in her bedroom.

The anonymous roads take on a familiar shape as they drive through a valley, past the darkened pizzeria, and then begin their ascent to Villa Giardino. As they draw closer, Susanne sees the SUV in the drive and a single light blazing. She wonders who is awake.

Normally, she and Dale would huddle over tea or hot chocolate as she'd share the minutest detail of her evening with relish, but not tonight. Revealing Harry's surprise proposal and her bizarre mystery illness would only agitate her friend; plus, things were weird enough between her and Dale already.

'Harry, let's not say anything to the girls – about us, I mean. I just want to get home, get back to normal and let the dust settle before I go springing surprises on them. I've got a very difficult conversation with Dale ahead and telling her that you proposed tonight will be a red rag to a bull.'

'Wow, how to make a guy feel special,' Harry's tone is flat.

'Please, Harry. Dale doesn't get us, you know that, so just work with me on this.'

The house is silent as they let themselves in. Susanne groans with relief. 'I can't wait to shower and brush my teeth,' she whispers, mindful that the others may already be asleep. Discarding her shoes by the front door, she turns to Harry. 'I feel seriously grotty; do you mind if I sleep alone tonight?'

Harry makes a face. 'Why? What do you mean? So, we get engaged and now you're shutting me out?'

It's a flash of petulance that Susanne can do without. 'Surely you know why; I've just been ill,' she reminds him patiently.

'Oh, great. How will *that* look in the morning? I bet Dale will love the fact that we slept apart after our special night out.'

His jaw is set and miserable, his expression sulky. Is this a taste of life to come?

'Harry, forget about Dale, please. Look, I feel all yucky. Surely you can have the sofa just for one night?'

With an exaggerated sigh, he relents, heading to Susanne's room for a pillow and a spare duvet.

He puts his arms around her. 'Think I'll sit up for a while. I might even have another drink to unwind. I'm too excited to sleep yet. Get some rest, darling, and I'll bring you some tea in the morning. It'll be good practice for when we're married.' He releases her and studies her face. 'Tomorrow is our last day here and I can just about bear it, knowing that we'll be together in England, too.'

Later, in the shower, soothed by its piping hot needles, Susanne replays the evening in her head: images of Harry, dropping to one knee, first in a packed restaurant and later in the cobbled square with smiling onlookers willing them on. She tries to analyse her feelings, to label her emotions. She'd told Harry she loved him – and she hadn't lied exactly, but how can she be *truly* in love with someone she's only just met? Susanne is savvy enough to know that love and infatuation feel much the same during the first heady flush of romance. She considers the future: it's difficult to put Harry in the context of her life at home in Tunbridge Wells. Because between Cody, his godmother Ronnie and the fact that Harry is practically a generation younger than her, they'll always be facing obstacles. Thank goodness there'll be plenty of time to reconsider their engagement at home…

At last, feeling deliciously clean and relieved to be alone, Susanne puts on an oversized T-shirt, climbs into bed and is grateful when sleep overwhelms her.

CHAPTER FORTY-NINE

Dale

Wired, sleepless and still in her day clothes, Dale lies on her bed, fingers laced behind her head.

It has taken every ounce of her self-control not to rush at Harry – or whatever the hell his name is – and demand to know who he is and what he has done with the real Harry.

Hearing the jeep approach, Dale and Evie had scuttled to bed, leaving a light on in the hallway. Then Dale had listened through a crack in her bedroom door, at snatches of hushed conversation, as Harry and Susanne had moved through the house, before saying goodnight.

Why were they sleeping apart? What on earth had happened during their evening in Siena that had resulted in Susanne going straight to bed alone? Every fibre in Dale's body is screaming at her to go to her friend, to tell Susanne what she and Evie know.

Only hours earlier, Dale had waited until Star was digging into a large portion of tiramisu before reaching into her bag and stealing a look at her mobile. Seven missed calls from Evie. Seven! Jesus, what had she discovered?

'Star, Evie's been ringing us. Mind if I give her a quick call and make sure she's okay?' Then Dale had excused herself from the table and slipped out to the car park.

Evie had picked up on the second ring, before blurting out that Harry was not Harry, followed by a gush of garbled words.

'Evie, breathe… Slow down. Let me get this straight. You're saying that you've found a passport with Harry's name on it, but not Harry's face? Christ. Okay, I'll be back as soon as I can. I'm not getting anywhere with Star. She's just guzzled her way through nearly a whole bottle of wine and three courses – and still managed to give nothing away.'

'Please hurry, Dale. I'm really…' Evie's words had dried on the line.

'Scared? I know, love, me too. Keep it together – and not a word in front of Star. She's quite pissed so we'll talk as soon as she's gone to bed. Bye.'

Then Dale had hung up, feeling desperately protective towards Evie, who – good on her – had shown real initiative in her detective work.

*

Dale had tugged Evie's arm and led her outside onto the terrace. 'Come on, just in case Star's still awake – although I can't imagine it after what she's put away tonight.'

Then Evie had swiped through her phone, stopping at the incriminating passport photo she'd taken and handed it to Dale in silence.

'God, Evie. What the— Who *is* this?' Dale had gasped, scrutinising the defiant young face in Harry Klein's passport.

'Well, it's not the guy who's been living here all summer, that's for sure. Dale, what are we going to do? We need to warn Susanne, get her away from him and find out what the hell has happened to the real Harry.'

'Absolutely, but we need to tread carefully, because the thing is, right now, Harry – or whatever-his-name-is – thinks they're an item. He trusts Susanne… I mean, I don't know if he *really* loves her, or if it's all some elaborate ruse, but we've got to be careful that we don't tip him off.'

Evie had agreed. 'We're flying home the day after tomorrow anyway. Let's get Susanne on her own in the morning, tell her everything and then come up with an excuse for the three of us to leave straight away. We can spend our last night near the airport or whatever, anywhere away from *him*.'

Dale had agreed, impressed with Evie's thinking. 'All right. And as soon as we're somewhere safe, we'll go to the police. Evie, I've got a bad feeling about this. I think he killed Harry.'

Evie's hands had flown to her mouth, her eyes wide with shock. 'No! Please don't say that, Dale. We don't know… there could be a perfectly innocent explanation as to why he's not here and *what's-his-name* has taken his place.'

'Evie, come on. You don't really believe that any more than I do. He's got Harry's passport, which speaks volumes. Look, we've just got to keep it together now – nauseating and scary as it is, we'll wait until the morning to tell Susanne. Agreed?'

Evie had nodded her head firmly. 'Agreed.'

*

Dale reaches for her mobile phone: the digits glow 01:57 – only twelve minutes since the last time she looked. She'll never sleep tonight. How can she? How could anyone knowingly sleep under the same roof as a killer?

Get a grip, Dale – we don't know that yet. Innocent until proven guilty.

Someone is awake and moving around the kitchen. She can hear the clink of glass, of water running and the faint rattle of the terrace doors being opened.

Before she can stop herself, as if spring-loaded, Dale is up, forcing her feet into trainers and tying the laces. Hyper-alert, she moves along the corridor, and towards the kitchen, which is bathed in moonlight. She peers outside, sees the boy, a bottle of gin in one hand and a cigarette – or a joint, perhaps – in the other.

She opens the door, ignores the churning of her stomach and paces towards him.

'Hey, Harry. Can't sleep? I can't either. How was Siena?' Dale says, keeping her voice even, pleasant.

'Dale.' He drags deeply on the joint, screws up his face. 'Actually, it was very interesting,' he says with emphasis, adding, 'although it could have gone better. Susanne was ill. Food poisoning.' He feigns gagging.

'Oh! Is she okay? Poor Susanne,' Dale says, wondering if he's lying.

'She's sleeping it off. I'm sure she'll be fine in the morning.' The boy raises the bottle to his lips and swallows.

'Need a glass?' Dale offers, attempting to sound helpful.

'The bottle is just fine, Dale.' He eyes her coldly, pulls on the joint again, then lets his head fall back as he exhales a pungent plume of smoke, the arc of his throat reminding Dale of a serpent. He extends the weed towards her, but she shakes her head, revulsion lifting the fine hair on her arms.

Dale answers carefully. 'Cheers, but I haven't smoked that stuff in years. It doesn't go with being a teacher – although I know a few who might argue that point.'

'Oh, come on, Dale. Being coy doesn't suit you. You're pretty rock and roll beneath that disapproving exterior.' His laugh is unpleasant, high-pitched and gurgling with alcohol.

Dale longs for a drink to steady the jangling in her head.

'I was just enjoying the moonlight,' he says, looking up at the sky, 'but I'm glad you're here. We can have a chat, man to man.' Again, the high-pitched, unpleasant snigger at his own joke.

Her heart racing, Dale watches him walk ahead of her; loose limbed he stumbles against a chair in his path.

Why is he drinking with such abandon? Why tonight? Is their imminent departure making him reckless?

They are standing above the pool terrace, the shallow descent ahead of them. He takes a step down, then looks back at her. Dale follows, realising that in his current state of intoxication she can outrun him if need be.

'We should swim.' The boy's tone is decisive.

'You go ahead, Harry. It's a bit late for me.' Dale says, hanging back.

He sweeps an arm expansively, causing a shower of sparks to fall. 'Come on, Dale, where's your sense of adventure? Keep me company. We should get to know each other. Especially now. Seeing as Susanne and I are getting married.'

Before she can stop herself, Dale scoffs. 'Yeah, like that would ever happen.'

'Oh, it *is* happening. I asked her tonight and she said yes. Congratulations to me! So, as you can see, I'm celebrating.' He staggers slightly, eyebrows raised. 'What's the matter, Dale? Aren't you happy for us… or are you too fucking jealous that I got the girl and you didn't? I wouldn't be surprised if she cuts you off once you're home anyway.'

Dale lifts her chin. 'Susanne's my best friend, I'm not going anywhere.'

'You were her best friend, Dale. Past tense. You're not anymore. Not now that she's seen you for the sad stalker you are. You're pathetic. Following her around, always perving at her body, hoping she'll fall in love with you. Face it, Dale. You'll never be Susanne's type. She likes *this* too much.' He grabs his crotch, his face splitting into an ugly, mocking grin.

'Fuck you,' Dales seethes, and the words bubble out before she can choke them down: 'Where's Harry? What the hell have you done with Harry?'

CHAPTER FIFTY

Tuscany, July 2019

Brandon

By the time Brandon rises, Harry and Star are swimming. His sister's excited yelps carry; he can hear her from the kitchen. He doesn't call out, just takes the steps down to the pool terrace and watches as the two of them spring apart, their bodies blurred by the churned-up water.

He wants to punch Harry, teach him a lesson or roar at him: *touch my sister and I'll fucking kill you.* Instead, he greets them with a wave and a pleasant 'Good morning'.

Harry wears a shit-eating grin. 'Here he is – our resident top model,' he calls out, stupid and phoney to Brandon's ears. 'Sleep all right?' he adds, wading to the side and heaving himself out of the water.

Brandon glances at Harry's shorts and is gratified by their flatness. 'Yes, thanks. The bed was the most comfortable I've slept on in months.'

'Mine, too,' Star says, 'and I *love* having my own bathroom – and not having to share with *him*!' She slaps water in Brandon's direction, splashing his clean T-shirt.

He ignores her, can see she's acting up for Harry's benefit. What is she playing at? Does she fancy him or not? When they'd first met Harry in Rome, he'd been under the distinct impression that

Star was interested. But then, unprompted, she'd claimed that she liked Harry but that she could never sleep with him. In which case, she needs to stop winding the guy up and put some clothes on.

Sighing heavily, Brandon goes back up the steps, past pastel-coloured, sweet-smelling shrubs and fixes himself a coffee. Then he wanders from room to room, studying everything in the harsh morning light. Harry's words come back to him: *we'll all be Ronnie's guests and she's loaded...*

What must it be like to have so much money that you could buy and furnish a faraway house – and not even visit it every year? Who looked after all this stuff? Everything seemed to be clean and dust-free. How had Harry's godmother made her money? Had she married well? Invented something? Or worked her way up from humble beginnings? It interested him, how people created wealth. Once, when he was modelling, he'd done three fashion shows back to back at some weird arts club in Mayfair and had been paid fifteen hundred pounds. For an afternoon's work! It had been no more taxing than milling about in a few ridiculous looking outfits. It was the first, last and only time though. Other jobs had left him seriously out of pocket after he'd spent money on travelling and other essentials.

Harry's moaning about the public school he'd gone to had been inverted boasting. And his whining about not wanting to take the city job his dad had secured for him made Brandon sick. Didn't he realise how fortunate he was? Rich people just didn't seem to get it. They didn't understand how lucky they were; whatever they had, they always wanted more – or something else entirely.

*

The sky seems bigger than in Rome, and the heat less oppressive. It's already been a few days, maybe they can stick around for another week or two – it would certainly make Star happy. He looks across at her; lying on her stomach, legs bent and tick-tocking in the air, chin cupped in her hands while she reads one of those romantic novels she's keen on. As if feeling the heat of his gaze, she looks up, grins and carries on reading. Harry appears from the kitchen, carrying three Cokes that jangle with ice.

'Thank you, Harry,' Brandon says, wincing as the bubbles burn his nose.

Harry smiles. 'What do we fancy doing today? Anything specific, or just chilling by the pool?'

Star gets up, paces around, flexing her arms over her head. 'I'm easy. What would *you* like to do, Harry?'

He considers for a moment, suggests going into San Gimignano for lunch. 'We should give Joe and Sander a call, find out if they're here yet. If they are, we can meet them in the square and then I'll buy us all lunch.'

'Sounds good, Harry,' Brandon says, his eyes flicking to his sister, 'except that I'll pay; it's enough that we're staying here.'

Harry nods his approval. 'Okay, just this once. I'll call Sander.'

*

Brandon spots them at once, their new matching haircuts – dapper, retro style, with high quiffs and shaved temples – marking them out as a pair. Even their distressed denim jeans are in sync. They wave, Sander steering Joe's arm until they converge on the piazza. Four tall, striking males and a pretty blonde girl attracting attention like birds of paradise moving through a flock of pigeons. Hugs and air kisses are swapped before they duck into the nearest café for beer and pretzels while they decide where and what to eat.

Harry appraises the two travellers. 'You both look disgustingly well,' he says. 'Where are you staying?'

Sander's groan is dramatic. 'Oh, totally slumming it. It's fine though – means we can travel for longer.'

'It's not *that* bad,' Joe clarifies. 'It's a cheap and cheerful hostel at the other end of town, away from tourists. We've got a large room with a sofa in it and our own bathroom, and there's even a little corner kitchen thingy just down the hall; it's fine.'

'Oh, you should see where *we're* staying,' Star says, her eyes shining, 'it's got a pool and everything.'

Sander laughs. 'How the other half lives! Just rub it in, why don't you? We'll have to come and visit. Perhaps you can squeeze us in as well, Harry?'

Brandon catches something in Harry's expression – discomfort, perhaps – as he changes the subject, claiming he's starving.

Discovering that the bar they're in serves only snacks, the five of them drink up, pay and shuffle their way into the lanes, hindered by tourists of every nationality swarming the shops and walkways. Every bar and café is rammed with visitors; soon Brandon feels irritated by the crowds and miserable with hunger.

'I'm sick of people everywhere,' he growls, 'there must be somewhere off the beaten track, a place where the locals eat.'

And then he sees it: *Bar Montebello* says the faded, hand-painted sign that points them to a small courtyard.

Inside the cool, tiled restaurant, the frenetic throng of people is absent, although the lively buzz of conversation and unfamiliar Italian folk music playing in the background both add to the atmosphere.

'This is more like it,' Harry says, rubbing his hands and smiling at the young waitress as she directs them to a table. Brandon is aware of the collective head swivel as every diner turns to stare at them.

A man in an immaculate apron greets them warmly and invites them to sit.

'Welcome, welcome. We have some wonderful specials today,' he booms, adding, 'for such handsome gentlemen and their beautiful lady friend.' He gazes in Brandon's direction, a look of amusement on his face. 'You are famous, no? A model, perhaps? What is your name?'

Brandon grimaces, scratches his chin, embarrassed by the attention. 'Yeah, sometimes. I'm Brandon… Brandon Connor.'

'And I am Enzo. Is *my* restaurant,' he says, patting his chest with pride before disappearing back to the kitchen.

'You've pulled there, mate,' Harry says, sniggering. '*You are famous, no?*' he mimics loudly in caricatured Italian.

The others laugh politely.

Brandon imagines himself pushing Harry through the glass shop front. Instead, he fakes a smile and studies the menu.

*

The afternoon spent in San Gimignano with Joe and Sander flew by, their company light and easy, diluting the irritation caused by Harry. When it was time to say goodbye, they planned to meet again, promising to message each other in a day or two. Then, that evening at Villa Giardino, he, Star and Harry drank local red wine in the garden, snacking on ripe tomatoes, pecorino and focaccia – and Harry seemed to mellow with the fading light.

But the next day, he seems restless and impatient, rushing through breakfast and spending less time than usual on his morning routine.

A heavy reference book, *Great Wines of Tuscany*, lies open on the kitchen worktop. While Brandon sips his first coffee of the day, Harry paces, thinking aloud. 'I'd like to check out the vineyard I mentioned and the monastery ruins nearby; we can see those on the way. Then tonight, I thought maybe we can drive to Siena for dinner. What do you think?'

Brandon considers. 'Sounds good, but if you'd rather go alone, don't feel you have to schlep everywhere with Star and I,' he says, hoping that Harry will opt for a solo jaunt. Harry shakes his head, insists it'll be more fun if all three of them go.

'But I'd much rather chill by the pool,' Star whines when they're alone and Brandon pushes her to get dressed in more than a bikini.

Brandon shrugs. 'Well, that's the price you pay. It was *you* who wanted to come here in the first place. Harry may be an arsehole, but he's still our host – so unless you plan on offending him, or finding somewhere else to crash, I suggest you put some clothes on. I'll meet you by the front door in fifteen minutes.'

*

In designer sunglasses and scarlet polo shirt, his shiny hair blown by the wind, Harry looks every inch the wealthy traveller. He turns to Brandon and grins, before refocussing on the road ahead.

'Sant'Agostino – that's St Augustine to us,' he smirks, 'is only about fifteen kilometres from here. Veronica's book says it dates from the fifteenth century, and that Cistercian monks used it as a refuge for fallen women. Of course, it's been derelict for hundreds of years. Nobody goes there now apart from the odd goat,' Harry lectures, shouting above the wind and the car engine.

'Oh, that's interesting, Harry,' Star calls from the back seat, although Brandon knows that history of any description bores her senseless.

Christ, this could be a long day. At least they'll get to try some expensive wines at the vineyard later. As for dinner in Siena, he's heard how beautiful it is, so maybe a trip there could prove useful, even illuminating.

'Hey, there it is!' Harry says, making a sharp turn onto a narrow track that is soon replaced by stony ground, matted by grass and lichen as the crumbling ruins loom before them. They'd expected a car park, to pay at a kiosk perhaps, but if Sant'Agostino was ever on the tourist trail, it has long been forgotten.

Getting out of the jeep, Brandon realises they are at the top of a peak; the air is cooler, and he can see nothing above them for miles around.

'This place is creepy,' Star says, echoing his thoughts.

'It is a bit,' Harry agrees, striding towards what's left of the once-magnificent cloisters and gazing upwards at blue sky mottled by cloud, framed by crumbling arches.

'Soo boring,' Star mouths to Brandon, then out loud, 'I'm guessing you like history, Harry.'

'You guessed right,' he calls out, leaping from one stone ledge to another, arms spread for balance.

Then there's the irritating jingling of a mobile phone. Harry laughs, removes it from his jeans pocket. 'Can you *believe* there's a signal all the way up here? Incredible! Hello?' He is balanced awkwardly on jagged rock, the phone stuck to his ear, his eyes darting between Brandon and Star. The conversation is brief, bordering on formal.

Brandon frowns. 'Everything okay?'

Harry exhales, blowing out his cheeks. He finds a more secure footing.

'That was Ronnie. Listen, guys. I'm sorry, I was going to tell you tonight… over dinner in Siena. Bad news, I'm afraid; it's not going to work out.'

'What isn't?' Star frowns.

Harry grimaces. 'It's not possible for you to stay. Something's come up. Well someone, actually – *three* someones to be accurate.' Embarrassed, Harry can't look at either of them.

Brandon shrugs. 'Well, that's okay. We were only going to stick around for a week or two – that was always the plan.'

'Ahh, well, that's the awkward part. I'm sorry, but you'll have to leave tomorrow first thing. My godmother, in her wisdom, has promised the house to three ladies for the summer. One's a neighbour, apparently.'

'Tomorrow morning? You've got to be fucking kidding. We'll need a couple of days to sort something else.'

Harry shakes his head, his face set. 'No can do, Brandon. The women arrive tomorrow evening. I can't have any evidence of guests by then. Ronnie would freak if she knew I'd had strangers at the villa.'

And then Brandon realises: Harry has known for several days. The only reason he has told them now is because of the phone call – presumably giving him the women's ETA.

'How long have you known?' Brandon asks, a vein flickering in his temple.

'Couple of days.' Harry shrugs. 'Look, for Christ's sake, don't make a big deal about it.'

'A *big deal*? You practically begged us to come here. And now we're stuck in the middle of nowhere, without transport or—'

Harry cuts in. 'Suck it up, mate. I'll take you to San Gimi or something. Now if you don't mind, I want to take in this magnificent view before we leave. Look, up there,' he says, shutting down the subject as though they've been discussing the weather.

Fuming silently, Brandon watches as Harry scales steps worn smooth by age and the elements; they stop abruptly, leading to nothing but another narrow ledge.

'I'm cold,' Star whines from below, rubbing her arms from the wind. 'Are we going in a minute?'

'Yes, when this twat's ready,' Brandon seethes. He can hear Harry spouting something about the steps being a fire escape once, and how amazing the view is.

'You go... have a look,' Star says, stamping her feet and hugging herself against the chill.

Brandon takes the steps carefully, mindful of how easy it would be to overbalance. Harry is right; the view *is* incredible. A weird stillness amplifies the sound of the wind, creating a strange detachment in him. He can see Star looking up at them now, shielding her eyes from the sun. He gazes out at hills marked by soldier lines of cypress trees; it reminds him of a painting he's seen somewhere.

Miles away, the medieval towers of San Gimignano rise through the haze; only yesterday they'd enjoyed lunch there and everyone had been in good spirits. But now, he and Star are being dropped, like used tissues into a bin.

'You really shouldn't treat people this way,' Brandon growls, his voice low, but Harry hears him all right, turning to him with a look of contempt.

'Come on, Brandon, don't make a fuss, there's a good chap,' he says, his tone mocking. 'You people are all the same. Wanting something for nothing.'

'*You people*? What the hell does that mean? How *dare* you, you stuck-up prick.

You only invited us because you wanted to shag my sister. Well, not on my watch.'

Harry laughs. 'Star's a sweetie, but as for "shagging" her, as you so charmingly put it… I'd have to be pretty desperate to—'

'Shut up. Just shut the fuck up!' Brandon roars, lunging forward, before he feels the flat of his palms connect with Harry's chest. Then he's watching in shock as Harry wobbles, comically at first, eyes bulging, his mouth slack and gaping as he tumbles backwards, his cries snatched by the wind.

CHAPTER FIFTY-ONE

Brandon

There had been a moment of calm – a second's suspension of belief before the screaming started. But then he'd had to slap Star to make her stop, before hugging her tightly and telling her that it was okay… it was all okay. That it had been an accident, just a bizarre, sad *accident*. There was nothing to be done, no point in calling an ambulance or involving the police. And how would it look? Best to get away, drive back to the villa, decide what to do next.

'But I saw you, Brandon… I saw the way you—' Star had continued to cry and snuffle like a child who'd lost a kitten.

'Star, you saw nothing. Do you understand? It was an accident. Those steps… they're not meant for walking on, and Harry… he just… fell.' *Say it, believe it. Move on.*

Then they'd left Harry's body where it had landed, facing skyward, eyes open, unseeing, within the bowels of the cloisters, sure that he could not be seen from the road, or by anyone driving up to the ruins and gazing at the outside. For someone to find him, they'd need to go clambering all over the site as they had done. And by the time Harry was found, they'd be long gone.

On legs he cannot feel, Brandon walks over to the jeep. Harry's keys are in the ignition, his sunglasses and mobile phone are on the dash – all waiting for his return. Except that Harry isn't coming back. He takes a deep breath. 'Get in, Star.' It's an order, not a request.

'Brandon, please… we can't just…'

'Star, we can. Come on, quickly. We'll go straight to the villa now and then decide what we're going to do,' Brandon says, putting on Harry's sunglasses and stashing his own in the glove compartment.

He'd stopped for Star to throw up at the roadside, then she'd limped back to the car, and spent the rest of the journey home clutching her stomach and whimpering softly.

Arriving at Villa Giardino, they'd gone into the kitchen – where Harry's coffee mug and breakfast plate sat unwashed in the sink – before they'd each swallowed several nips of gin and taken long, hot showers.

Afterwards Brandon had collected up the clothes they'd been wearing and piled them into the washing machine. He needed to take charge of the situation; he couldn't expect Star to cope with something like this. Seeing Harry's inert body staring up at them like that – it had brought back too many memories.

Now, dressed in fresh clothes, her hair still damp, Star has stopped shaking and is sitting on the sofa, a throw across her knees, waiting for him to tell her what to do.

'Right, listen to me. I know what happened is really awful, but we need to just get past it and carry on; keep it together, okay?'

'Okay,' Star whispers.

*

Waking early to the sound of birdsong, Brandon feels that something is off, but in a distant and fuzzy way that is almost comforting, like when he'd had the flu once, and had turned the corner after a week of sickness. Now, opening his eyes, he finds Star lying with her back to him, dressed in pink T-shirt and strawberry red knickers, her hair matted at the crown. Why is she in his bed?

And then it comes to him. The image of Harry falling; arms twirling and useless, his mouth a wet gash of fear. He breathes in sharply, sits up as the room seems to spin about him.

Star emits a soft moan as she emerges from sleep. 'Brandon? It really happened, didn't it?' she rasps.

'Yes, but it's fine and we're going to get through this. Come on, get up. We've got loads to do today.'

After a quick coffee, they tear around the villa, creating some semblance of order, before steeling themselves to go into Harry's room, where his fragrance, verdant and expensive, still hangs in the air.

Star's eyes become moons of despair. 'Oh no, I can't... Don't ask me to move his stuff, please,' she begs as Brandon begins decanting Harry's clothes into his own wardrobe. Feeling calm and industrious, he realises that Harry's things will be useful props in his deception, that is until he's unnerved by finding a black tin box, the key still in the lock, containing a wad of cash, some loose change and Harry's passport. Hands trembling, he swallows the bile rising in his throat, thrusting the tin into the depths of his wardrobe among shoes and sandals.

The arrival of Rosa provides the second shock of the morning. Silver hair forced into a bun, blue tabard over a shapeless dress, she manoeuvres past Brandon, wielding a sack of linen and a bucket of cleaning products.

'I clean for ladies,' she announces, brandishing a mop, adding, 'I 'ave shits and trowels.' It takes Brandon a moment to process *sheets and towels* but it's a relief that she seems unsurprised to see him or Star; further affirmation that nobody has a clue who Harry is or what he looks like.

After waving Rosa off at the door, he steers Star into the shower, helps her to pack her stuff and then loads the car.

*

Brandon swallows hard. The man looking back at him from the rococo gilt mirror is smart and preppy – a student on holidays perhaps, or a young intern starting out in business. He glances at the salon floor and the long shining tresses that will soon be swept up and thrown away – years of growth; his precious hair. Oblivious to Brandon's inner turmoil, the stylist fusses round him, crooning his approval and admiring his creation.

Brandon pays the bill, puts on Harry's sunglasses and goes outside to find Star, her eyes still puffy from crying. 'You look nothing like him,' she pouts, chewing her thumbnail.

'Of course not – but at least with the same haircut I could pass for him on paper. We're about the same height and build. Star, don't forget these women have never met Harry, and I'm guessing they know nothing about him. Come on, let's have a coffee and some gelato for lunch, then we need to get you fixed up for a few days.'

Star's face crumples. 'Can't I stay with you? Please, Brandon, don't leave me here,' she begs, her voice cracking.

'Shush, Star. Get a grip! People are looking. We talked about this last night. I thought we'd agreed to try and get you in at the hostel where Joe and Sander are staying. They said it was clean and comfy, and you'll have them for company when I'm not around.'

Star nods, her mouth a downturned crescent. It breaks his heart to see her like this. 'Look, it's just for a week or two, then I'll come and get you and we'll fly home together.'

'But why can't we go home now?'

'Star, I've explained this once… Listen to me,' Brandon pulls his sister into a narrow alleyway, looks around to make sure they are out of earshot of tourists and shoppers. He lowers his voice. 'If I pretend to be Harry, nobody will miss him. The women won't know the difference, will they? But if I'm *not* there, they'll raise the alarm to Harry's godmother, Veronica. Thank God Harry talked about her a bit… enough that I can blag it for a week or two.'

'But then what?'

'It's simple. I'll say I'm bored with Italy and that I'm moving on, and by then I'll have them eating out of my hand and they'll cover for me – for Harry, I mean.'

Star frowns. 'What about phoning home? Are you going to impersonate Harry's voice as well?'

'Now you're being silly. Of course not. I don't think twenty-four-year-old blokes ring Mummy and Daddy every day, do they? Anyway, I dumped his phone. I dropped it inside the hollow of a tree while you were being sick at the roadside. No one will ever find it.'

Star's eyes widen, then she shakes her head and clamps her mouth shut.

'Good girl,' Brandon says. 'Big smile, you can do this. Come on, let's find a café and we'll give Joe a call, get the name of where they're staying and book you in.'

CHAPTER FIFTY-TWO

Tuscany, September 2019

Brandon

Brandon shifts his weight awkwardly on the lumpy sofa, replaying his weird marriage proposal in his head. It hadn't been quite the evening he'd planned. Then again, when did anything in his life ever go to plan?

What even *is* his plan? Trying to figure out the logistics of what comes next makes his brain ache. And recently, the lies have been getting harder to manage. Some mornings, it takes him a minute or two just to remember who he really is and who he is meant to be.

Harry's 'accident' bothers him surprisingly little. He'd managed to convince Star that poor Harry had lost his balance and toppled to his death nine or ten metres below. And sure, for a few nights afterwards, Brandon had woken with a start, heart pounding and bathed in sweat, picturing the two of them suspended in mid-air, spitting venom and bile at each other like tomcats on a garden wall, the wind whistling around them. Harry, two steps above him, his mocking face an ugly twisted sneer. Star below, shielding her eyes from the sun, straining to catch what they were arguing about. Then he'd roared at Harry to shut up – to just shut the fuck up – before he'd lunged at him, his hands connecting with Harry's chest.

Because all control had deserted him as he'd listened to Harry's insinuations, implying that he and Star were freeloading losers.

What a fucking nerve the guy had. Harry had deserved it. End of. No wonder Brandon rarely thinks about him.

But Star worries him. They'd made a pact right away to never speak of it. And they'd stuck to it, but Brandon saw what it had done to his sister, her nerves already shot from finding their mother on the carpet of the flat, vomit caked around her mouth and chin, an empty pot of sleeping pills beside her and a dry vodka bottle still in her right hand.

Thirteen-year-old Star, arriving home from school and using her own key, then screaming so loudly for her mummy to wake up, to please, *please* wake up, that the neighbours had broken down the door to help.

Christ, had they ever had just *one* lucky break in their whole lives? Growing up in London, fatherless, after Graham had gone out for cigarettes on Brandon's third birthday and had never returned. His mother Ingrid, beautiful enough to attract good-looking losers, but not bright enough to elevate them out of poverty and desperation. Office cleaning and the occasional handout from Grandma kept a roof over their heads, food in Brandon's belly and vodka in Ingrid's drinks cabinet.

And then, a brief window of hope in the form of Ziggy, a gigging bass player from Peckham who'd moved into the flat in Catford as soon as the baby was showing. For the first time, eight-year-old Brandon had someone to kick a football with on Saturday afternoons before the three of them would line up for burgers and milkshakes at Catford Island. Ziggy had even let Brandon hold his electric bass guitar once or twice, and he'd marvelled at its glassy smoothness.

Then one day, Grandma had met him from school and taken him to her house for tea. Brandon would always associate beans on white toast and Mr Kipling French Fancies with the day Star was born. *Star because she sparkles*, Ingrid had said, as light tripped from the baby's topaz-blue eyes and white-blonde hair.

Having a baby sister to cuddle and play with had made Brandon feel 'normal' for the first time, until one rainy Friday afternoon, Grandma was back at the school gates with little Star, only just walking, clinging to her hand.

'Your uncle Ziggy's gone away with the band for a while, and your mum's feeling poorly,' was her only explanation as they'd walked the five blocks to her house for more pink cake. Surprise visits to Grandma's became a regular feature of Brandon and Star's lives after that, as Ingrid took to her bed, sometimes for days on end.

Yet at the comprehensive school he went to, other kids called Brandon lucky – *jammy*, they said; all because he was several inches taller than the others in his year, and the bones of his face hung a certain way.

By the time poor Ingrid checked out of the world, Brandon had a model agent, a decent portfolio and a shedload of ambition. But over time, the dream had been diluted until he was spritzing perfume in department stores by day and escorting women older than his mother to the theatre several nights a week.

'Screw this shit,' he'd said one day to Star, for whom he was now wholly responsible thanks to a stroke that had confined Grandma to a care home. 'If this is all I'm doing, we might as well live somewhere warm.'

And he'd made it happen, kicking off with three months on the Costa del Sol one balmy summer, where they'd slept on the beach for a week before meeting Tracey, the vivacious landlord of an English pub, and it wasn't long before Brandon was pulling more than pints.

It was fun at first – naughty, harmless; a few weeks here, a couple of months there, and an endless supply of Deirdres and Dianes, of Jackies and Janets, Sandras and Simones. A swirling sea of women, sometimes pretty, often wealthy and usually lonely.

Ah, but Susanne. Susanne was different – *top drawer,* as his Grandma would say. A beautiful, middle-class mother used to the finer things in life; not from Brandon's world at all.

At first, she'd treated him not as a hustler or a gigolo, but like the spoilt rich kid she perceived him to be. But the more he revealed himself to her, the warmer her response. He'd held it together pretty well, all things considered – had made a decent fist of being Harry, adopting his superior manner, mimicking his accent, wearing his clothes and driving his car – even using his aftershave.

Not that Dale had been convinced; she'd had a sixth sense about him all along, the cynical bitch. Between her buzzing like a mosquito in Susanne's ear night and day and the incessant whining from Harry's family about the lack of contact, it was amazing he'd pulled it off.

Brandon shudders beneath the thin duvet. A low point had been on the afternoon of his fake-birthday party when he'd driven out to the monastery and parked up on the hillside where he'd once stopped to let Star puke. It had taken him half an hour to identify the right tree trunk, before getting scratched and filthy trying to retrieve Harry's phone. Then he'd driven to San Gimignano, charged the handset at a mobile network store and used Harry's contacts list to text Mrs Klein a few words of love and contrition.

He'd done it for Susanne. She'd seemed so sad – outraged, even – that a son could neglect to ring his parents, no doubt thinking of Cody; did the spoilt brat know how lucky he was?

Shit. He is too wired to sleep, and anyway, he should be celebrating. Toasting his engagement to Susanne, drinking to his new life. With a flicker of hope, Brandon remembers the last joint he rolled, which surely remains hidden away at the back of the cutlery drawer. A little weed, a couple of shots of gin… maybe three: he doesn't need a hangover for his last day with Susanne, not when he needs to pull off an Oscar-winning performance about the shining future they'll have together.

Throwing off the duvet, Brandon puts on the clothes he'd worn in Siena and pads next door to the kitchen, the moon lighting his way.

Then reaching for the gin bottle, he drinks it neat, feeling his eyes burn as its sweet oiliness hits the back of his throat. He slides open a drawer and feels for the joint. Perfect, exactly where he left it. Elsewhere, he finds matches used for lighting candles. Then, mindful of waking the women, he opens the French windows and steps onto the terrace to wander the garden, inhaling the scent of dew and jasmine. The shallow steps are just ahead. He hesitates, looks down at the pool below, which tonight is spilled ink, spattered by stars.

Faraway, he hears the bark of a fox, or a wolf – did wolves live in Tuscany? Perhaps it has found Harry's remains; a macabre but satisfying meal for the night. He pushes the grisly image from his mind, feels the weed permeate his nerve endings. The gin is sweet and pleasant as he swigs it straight from the bottle.

'Hey, Harry. Can't sleep? I can't either.' Dale's voice. He is startled to see her, tension visible on the bones of her face.

'Dale,' he sighs, irritated that she has interrupted what is developing into a very pleasant buzz. Never mind, he'll play the game and make small talk for a while if that's what it takes. But then, whether it's the weed, or the gin, or even the moonlight that have loosened his lips and resolve, for some reason, Brandon cannot resist sparring with Dale, goading her, before dropping the bomb.

'We should get to know each other. Especially now. Seeing as Susanne and I are getting married,' he brags.

Dale's dismissal is instant, as if he's a liar or a fantasist. Brandon wounds her again and again, twisting the knife, enjoying her pain and confusion; telling her that Susanne sees her as a pathetic, sad stalker, and that she plans to cut her off once they are all back in England.

Pick, pick, pick… all restraint vanished as they stand a few metres apart, regarding each other with utter loathing, until Dale's words silence Brandon, and freeze the blood in his veins.

*

'What the hell have you done with Harry?'

Her words slice through the night air, silencing his mocking laughter. He raises the gin to his lips, then changes his mind.

Why had he baited her, winding her up until she'd snapped? What had he been thinking? No! No way. He cannot have this – not now…

'*What* did you say?'

Dale stands her ground, her eyes fixed on his. 'You heard me. Who are you and what have you done with Harry? And don't even bother to deny it. I've seen Harry's passport.'

Shit! Think, Brandon. Think.

He eyes her with distain. 'How dare you go snooping through my stuff. That's not very nice, Dale – but I'd expect nothing more from you. Who else knows?' He's encouraged when Dale merely purses her lips and shakes her head.

So it's time; time for his cover story. The one intended for Susanne once she'd flown home and being Harry was no longer tenable…

Brandon sighs as though exhausted, beaten. 'Yes, the passport,' he says, his tone regretful, 'that was an oversight. Harry forgot to take it with him. I've been keeping it safe.'

He sees confusion register on Dale's face. *Keep going…*

'Dale, I don't know why you assume I've done anything with Harry. The fact is, we're friends and he asked me to help him.' He'd aimed for crisp, matter-of-fact, but he can hear the hesitation in his voice and the slur of his speech.

Dale shakes her head, a deep furrow between her brows.

'Fuck it. It will all come out sooner or later,' Brandon says, embellishing his story. 'Poor Harry – all that money but almost no freedom. His parents suffocate him,' he pauses, checks Dale's reaction; her expression is impassive.

'Anyway, he met a girl in Rome, Marika. She's Dutch, beautiful, but a complete space cake and not from Harry's world at all.

He was going to bring her here to party *per due* all summer, so to speak, but then he got word that you and the girls were coming and he asked me to cover for him by pretending to be him.'

'Why on earth would you do that?' Dale asks.

'Because he paid me to. Look, I'm not proud of it, but Harry gave me five thousand pounds to stay here all summer, just so his family don't find out about Marika. Easiest five grand I've ever made.' Brandon smirks.

'I don't believe you,' Dale says, folding her arms over her chest.

'Well, don't, then, but it's the truth. Jesus, I shouldn't have told you – I've really let Harry down now.'

'Then why haven't his parents heard from him all summer?'

'Because he's angry with them. His father's a control freak, a complete tyrant – always on at him to nail a career and threatening to cut the money off if he doesn't. Hippy-dippy Dutch girls were never in his family's plan for him, I can assure you. You should see them together, the guy's absolutely smitten; he's talking about never going home. Imagine that… *poof!* Like he just disappeared.'

Dale is shaking her head. 'No… *no*! I don't think that's what happened; it just sounds… If Harry's gone away, why is his passport here with you?'

'Oh my god, Dale – you've got such a suspicious mind. Because he doesn't need it. Harry and Marika are staying in a villa about ten miles from here. God, if I hadn't drunk so much gin, I'd take you there myself.'

He can see Dale is weighing up his story. *Keep it together, almost there… win her over.*

His tone softens. 'Dale, I'm sorry for being such a wanker. I hate that you don't like me. It's a blow to my ego. I'm normally so popular with women. Believe me when I say there's nothing I'd like more than for us to be friends, especially now that Susanne and I are engaged.'

'Yeah, I wouldn't count on that happening. Even if Harry's fine and all loved up, the fact is, you've lied through your teeth all summer.' Dale lets out a cheerless bark of laughter. 'I don't even know your name.'

'It's Brandon.'

'Brandon what?' Dale snaps back. He watches her expression harden. 'I don't believe you… not a single word. I don't think you were even friends with Harry. I see right through you, "Brandon". A guy like you – a hustler – you wouldn't even be on Harry's radar. He'd never—'

A bomb goes off in Brandon's head. *A guy like you. A hustler.*

Tossing the gin bottle into the grass, he feels a surge of adrenaline, his body powered by pure rage as he draws back his fist and punches Dale square on the jaw. The defiance in her eyes is replaced by fear and shock as she staggers backwards, stunned, and almost crashes to the ground before Brandon grabs her by the shoulders and hauls her upright. His hands are on her throat now, encircling, tightening, until her eyes bulge, and then she's pummelling his chest and shoulders, scratching his forearms, her feet lashing out at anything she can reach, until her limbs stop flailing, her eyes close and she is slack in his arms.

Panting hard, Brandon releases Dale as she slumps to the ground.

CHAPTER FIFTY-THREE

Susanne

Someone is beside her, rousing her from sleep. Susanne forces her eyes open, but except for a shaft of moonlight that slices through a crack in the drapes, the room is in darkness.

'Susanne, please wake up… you've got to wake up.' Evie sounds frightened, desperate.

Susanne sits bolt upright. 'Cody!' It's a reflex; an instinctive part of her since the day her son was born.

'Cody's fine. You've got to come. Something awful— It's Dale, she needs our help.'

'What's happened? What time is it?'

'Not sure… but it's well after two. Listen, something happened last night while you were out and we were going to tell you in the morning… only now it can't wait.'

'God, Evie, what the hell is going on?' Susanne's eyes are beginning to adjust as she gropes for her bedside lamp.

Evie grabs her wrist. 'No! Leave the light off. Just listen.'

And then Susanne is wracked with confusion and horror as she strains to catch Evie's hastily scattered words. Words that make no sense. A story – for it surely must be fiction – about Harry not being Harry, and that Dale and Evie have found a passport to prove it.

'But Evie, who else would he be? People change their appearance, don't they?'

'Not that much,' Evie hisses, producing her mobile phone and zooming in on a photograph of a youth whom Susanne has never seen before.

Susanne studies the boy's face, taking in his soft rounded features, and swallows hard as a rush of vertigo hits her.

'So, who have I been sleeping with all summer? I feel sick...' Susanne shudders, but pushes her revulsion aside. 'God, Evie. Where is Harry and what has happened to him? What the hell do we do now?'

Evie's grip tightens on her arm. 'I don't know, but I heard Dale get up and I'm frightened she'll try to confront him on her own. You know what she's like, so brave—'

'Or stupid, some might say.' Susanne is out of bed now, pulling on jeans and sweatshirt, hunting around for trainers.

A thought occurs to Susanne as she ties her laces. 'What about Star?'

'Dale is convinced that's Star's in on it, too. I have to say, I agree with her. Look at the way she just appeared out of nowhere and how close they seem.'

'Then we mustn't wake her,' Susanne says, before she and Evie creep through the house, holding their breath as they pass Star's room, across the main hallway and through into the kitchen. They pause at the French doors and peer outside where the moon silhouettes Dale and the boy deep in conversation.

'They don't look happy... Do you think they're arguing?' Evie whispers.

Susanne shivers. 'I don't know. But Harry – or whoever he is – looks so drunk! Look at the way he's weaving about and swigging from that bottle. Poor Dale, she was right all along. Why didn't I listen to her?'

Evie shakes her head. 'Don't think about that now.'

Susanne strides through to the sitting room, suddenly decisive. 'Evie, I'm calling the police. The number will be in Ronnie's folder. We've no idea who that... *person*... is – or what he has done to Harry.'

Using the torch on her mobile, Susanne finds Veronica's ring binder and there, behind a tab marked 'IN CASE OF EMERGENCY' is a list of phone numbers.

Then Susanne is punching out 112 as Evie hovers, arms wrapped tightly around herself.

Susanne hears the burr of a ring tone. 'Shit! What if they only speak Italian? Oh, hello? Do you speak English? Police, please. It's an emergency.'

There's a click on the line, then relief courses through Susanne's body when a male voice answers in heavily accented English.

'Thank god,' Susanne sighs. Then, keeping her voice low, she sums up their situation. 'That's right. Yes, there are three women in danger here. No, we have no idea who this man is, but we believe he's already killed at least one person,' Susanne looks at Evie and grimaces. 'He has a knife – please hurry.'

'Why did you say he has a knife?' Evie asks.

'To make them come quickly.' Susanne darts back to the windows.

The boy is walking away from Dale now, in the direction of the pool, but she is keeping pace, stalking after him.

'She's going to have it out with him – I can just tell,' Susanne says. 'Come on, let's follow.'

Keeping to the shadows, Susanne and Evie move along the terrace. Crouched down, they peer through the stone balustrade to the pool area below, listening for snatches of conversation that puncture the night air. The boy's voice; hard-edged and mocking, as he swaggers around, and Dale's; clear and challenging as she stands her ground.

Susanne stiffens. 'They're talking about Harry... about his passport... I just heard him say something like...' Susanne trails off as she and Evie strain to catch his words.

Evie gasps. 'His name's *Brandon*!' she whispers, trying the word out for the first time.

Then, propelled by fear, the women are on their feet, running towards the pool area as Dale, sent flying by a devastating punch, is being shaken by her throat; she struggles, raining kicks and blows on her attacker – a man who is no longer the sweet boy whom Susanne has tenderly caressed all summer, but a vicious assailant, driven by rage.

At the bottom of the steps, Susanne hesitates, caught in a web of fear and indecision as Dale is flung limply to the ground. But Evie powers past her, arms and legs pumping, and with a banshee wail, she flies at him from behind, landing on his back and sending them both flying into the water with a resounding splash.

'Help me, Susanne!' Evie cries, thrashing in the water, as Brandon bears down on her, spluttering threats; he shakes her by her shoulders, before grabbing her throat with both hands and forcing her head beneath the surface with a guttural roar.

For one frozen second, Susanne is torn between the heart-breaking sight of Dale's inert crumpled form and Evie's urgent need for help. Galvanised by instinct, she leaps into the water, barely registering the chill, and strikes out towards her friend. The effect of her sudden appearance shocks Brandon and he staggers back, losing his balance as he cries out her name.

Breaking the surface, Evie's eyes are red moons of terror and desperation as Susanne roars at Brandon, a sudden wave of anger unleashed.

'Look what you did!' she screams, her eyes darting first to Dale's body, then to Evie, who is scrabbling for the side. 'I trusted you! Oh, my god, I slept with you... I... To think that I let you get between me and my oldest friend. You evil, lying bastard! I hate you!'

Brandon hesitates, a look of dazed exhaustion on his face. Susanne expects him to strike her, but instead he reaches for Evie, this time grabbing her by the hair.

Susanne leaps on his back, forcing him to release his grip on Evie. Over his shoulder, she meets Evie's eyes. They exchange a look, the message as clear as if it has been spoken: *let's finish this.* Together they grasp Brandon's head and shoulders, forcing him below the surface. Already weakened by alcohol and exhaustion, Brandon's struggle is brief, all resistance leaving him as he sinks beneath Susanne and Evie's grip.

Hindered by their wet clothes and weeping, the women help each other out of the water and lie slumped and exhausted.

'Are you both okay?' Dale rasps, sitting up and massaging her neck, which is livid with puce finger marks. 'I thought playing dead was my only option...' Tears shine in her eyes.

'Oh, my god! You're alive!' Susanne cries, hurling herself at Dale, before Evie drags herself over and collapses beside them and the three of them hug each other in disbelief, breaking apart only at the sound of a piercing scream.

'Noooo! Brandon?' Star howls, dropping to her knees beside the pool, her hands clawing her hair at the sight of Brandon's body as it sways below the surface.

'Star!' Evie calls, going to her, but Star pushes her aside and with an ungainly flop, she's in the water, before jack-knifing below and trying to gather Brandon's dead weight in her arms.

'Help me!' Star shrieks, her tiny frame barely stirring Brandon's.

'Star, it's no good,' Evie cries, squatting at the side and reaching out to her. 'We've already tried to help him. Please, come out, he's gone.'

Susanne and Evie's eyes meet. 'She's right,' Susanne says, putting an arm out to Star, 'we tried to save him. But he... he was very drunk and he must have inhaled too much water,' she lies, willing Star to take her hand.

As Star's strength ebbs away and her screams become a hiccupping whimper, Susanne and Evie drag her from the pool, rubbing her trembling body for warmth.

'Star, listen to me,' Susanne says, managing to control the bubbling hysteria that threatens to overwhelm her. 'Harry – Brandon… whatever you knew him as – he went crazy and tried to kill Dale and Evie. We pushed him into the water to make him stop, but he was so drunk, he just… Love, I'm so sorry, I know you were good friends.'

Star is on all fours now, sobbing uncontrollably, fending off Susanne and Evie's attempts to comfort her. She lifts her head, her face blurred by tears. 'He's not my friend – he's my brother!' she wails.

'That explains a lot,' Dale croaks, struggling to her feet and joining the others. 'Star, I'm so sorry, but it's true – he tried to strangle me.'

'No! He wouldn't do that!' Star rages. 'Brandon wouldn't hurt anyone… not on purpose.'

Susanne shoots Dale and Evie a warning look; when she speaks, her voice is gentle, measured. 'We know that, Star. Things just got out of hand. Tell us what happened to Harry. Please, it's okay, we're here for you sweetheart.'

Star chokes back tears, wiping her face on the hem of her T-shirt. She lifts her eyes to Susanne's. 'Harry's dead. It was an accident. He fell off a ledge – at the monastery. Oh god, it was so awful. I wanted to get help, but Brandon said no one would believe us, that they'd think we killed him, so we just left him there on the ground,' she finishes, dissolving into fresh sobs.

'Christ, I knew it,' Dale says, finding her voice again. But Susanne silences her with a look.

'Let's go inside – we've all had a terrible shock. We need blankets and sweet tea. Come on, Star, we've got you,' Susanne says, as they limp back towards the house to the wail of police sirens, their blue lights electrifying the sky.

CHAPTER FIFTY-FOUR

Tunbridge Wells, Christmas Day, 2019

Susanne

At noon the doorbell rings.

'I'll get it!' Cody's gruff voice calls out, followed by the rumble of his size-nine feet on the stairs and the sound of the front door opening.

Susanne and Dale exchange looks.

'You know he fancies her,' Susanne says.

'You think?' Dale feigns surprise before erupting into giggles.

'Hey. Ooh, something smells yummy,' Star says, sweeping a blast of cold air in with her, still wearing her coat and a rose-pink beanie. 'All right, Cody?' she says, flipping off her hat and shaking her pale hair loose.

Cody is transfixed. 'Fine,' he gulps, his cheeks flushing.

'Happy Christmas,' Evie steps in after Star and beams before hugging Susanne and Dale. She looks around, delight visible on her face. 'Wow, Susie! You've been busy. It looks absolutely beautiful in here. Oh, I bought some bits and pieces from me and Star. It's not much, just some wine and whatnots,' she says, setting down a carrier bag of goodies.

Susanne smiles. 'Evie, you shouldn't have, thank you, love. Cody, take their coats, will you? Is it still trying to snow out there?'

There's a buzz of small talk as coats are removed and hung up, and Susanne's festive interior is admired in all its twinkling glory. And despite the fact that she's been cooking since dawn, her kitchen is as immaculate as ever, thanks in no small part to Dale, able sous chef and washer-upper for the day.

'Okay, a toast,' Susanne says, filling the last champagne flute as Dale hands them round. 'Cody and I want to thank you – Dale, Evie and Star – for choosing to spend the day with us, and making it so special.' She raises her glass. 'So here's to friendship, and to a happy, healthy and joyful Christmas. Cheers, everyone.'

The room is bursting with goodwill, love and generosity. Suddenly moved, Susanne looks around at the ring of glowing faces, and marvels at how far they've all come in just a few months.

*

The night Brandon drowned had scarred all their memories, try as the women might to forget. A pair of armed response officers had escorted three well-dressed detectives who'd produced photo ID – unnecessary given the circus of marked *POLIZIA* vehicles parked askew across the villa's drive.

Despite her ordeal, it was Dale who had taken charge, going into teacher mode, directing the officers outside to the pool, introducing the women by name and creating a snapshot of context for each of them.

The senior officer in charge, a woman who'd introduced herself as Claudia Vincenzi, had been otherwise tight-lipped. Two male officers had walked the house and garden, exchanging their observations in Italian before all three agents had converged on the pool terrace where the grim discovery of Brandon's body awaited them. Then there were phone calls in Italian, and the arrival of more vehicles as forensics swarmed the scene and Brandon's corpse had been removed.

Susanne had heard of people having out-of-body experiences, and it had happened that way as the indigo sky had ebbed away to coral, followed by a wash of morning blue; the sun rose, the birds sang, but everything had changed. Two young men were dead. And not just any young men, but the godson of her neighbour, whom Susanne would have to face at home, when (if!) the nightmare ended, and a boy whom she'd welcomed into her bed and to a degree, her heart.

The women had been questioned, separately. They'd closed ranks nonetheless, sticking rigidly to what they'd managed to piece together: that Brandon had posed as Harry after the incident at the monastery, keeping up his pretence all summer.

Susanne had admitted to being *involved* with him. Had she imagined one of the detectives' mouth's twitch at that revelation?

Then she'd described Dale's suspicions, which had resulted in the discovery of the passport, and finally, Brandon's desperate attempt to strangle Dale. So *naturally,* Susanne and Evie had done their best to help their friend. Pushing Brandon into the pool had been a reflex but then the situation had escalated as Brandon had turned on them, too, attacking Evie and holding her under the water. What choice did they have but to defend themselves against his psychotic behaviour? It wasn't their fault that he'd suddenly gone limp in the water. Too much alcohol and the strong weed he'd smoked had seen to that. And with Susanne, Evie and Dale's matching accounts, everything was straightforward, neat and consistent.

Only Star's story differed as she'd wept hysterically, insisting that Brandon had never intentionally killed anyone. Harry had fallen – she'd seen it with her own eyes – and she and her brother had simply panicked. And as for Dale, she'd been winding him up for days and he'd lost his head, high on booze and the strong weed he'd been smoking. Woken by shouting, Star had gone outside to see Evie and Susanne hauling themselves from the pool after Brandon had spun out and attacked the women. And despite that, they'd tried to save him, but it was too late.

Desperate to go home but forbidden to leave Tuscany, the women had relocated to a modest hotel in San Gimignano. Two days later, Vincenzi had arrived unannounced.

'Mrs Campbell, I am here about the alleged death of Mr Klein.' She'd paused, looked around at the small air-conditioned lounge that had been hastily cleared of guests before settling on Susanne, her eyes like search-lights. 'There is no body.'

No body? What did that mean? Susanne had shaken her head in confusion and disbelief. 'But that doesn't make sense. Star was clear about what happened. You must have been looking in the wrong place.'

Vincenzi had pursed her lips. 'We examined the whole site. Our search was very thorough, very *professional*,' she'd said with emphasis, as though mildly insulted by Susanne's assertion. '*Allora*, no body. Traces of blood, yes, between the ruins and the road – but nothing more. Mr Klein's family arrive later today. We are treating him as a missing person.'

'Really? That's… that's brilliant news. It means that Harry's still alive, that he could be found, doesn't it? Does that mean we can all go home now? Detective, I have a son who needs me. We were supposed to fly two days ago and there's nothing more we can tell you.'

'About Harry Klein, no. But we are waiting for a full coroner's report on how Brandon Connor died and until then, we must ask you, signora Morgan and signora Jones to remain in San Gimignano.'

It had been a demand, not a request. Terrified of being bugged or overheard, the women had hiked into the hills beyond the city walls, just to speak freely.

Halfway round a vineyard groaning with golden grapes ready for harvesting, gripped by panic, Evie had become tearful. 'They know, don't they? We're going to prison – I just know it.'

Susanne and Dale had done their best to talk Evie down, reassuring her that nobody except the three of them could possibly know exactly what had happened that night. Even any marks on Brandon's body where the women had held him down could be attributed either to Dale's struggle, or their fight in the pool, they'd reasoned. And anyway – it was self-defence. They'd had no choice in the matter.

The coroner's decision had been mercifully quick. Accidental drowning had been the verdict, underpinned by a toxicology report that revealed Brandon had been drunk and stoned by the time he'd entered the pool. And with this news came the women's instant release; freedom to fly home and return to their lives, changed though they were.

Susanne and Dale had boarded the first flights available to Gatwick, collapsing into narrow budget seats with relief and emotional exhaustion. It was Evie who had stepped up to support Star, liaising with the police and British Consulate officials so that Brandon's body could be flown home to London.

Star had been beside herself, hyperventilating with despair, telling Evie that a life on the street awaited her.

So Evie had taken Star home to Tunbridge Wells where she'd looked after her like a daughter, wiping away her tears and comforting her in the night when she cried out for her brother.

'I've told Star she can stay as long as she likes,' Evie had confided to Susanne over coffee on her third day back. 'She can give me a hand doing Mum's place up, it'll take her mind off things and make her feel useful, starting with her own room – we'll soon make it nice for her.'

'You've got such a good heart, Evie. But what will you do for money while you're not working?'

'Apart from my inheritance, you mean? Actually, I thought I'd temp part-time, at least until the house is how I want it. Then I'll start looking for something more permanent.'

Touched by the notion of Evie taking Star under her wing, Susanne had wanted to do her bit, and had offered Star two mornings a week cleaning. But Star had declined, preferring instead to waitress at The Gallery restaurant nearby, saying it gave her a little independence.

*

Dale sighs with contentment and places her knife and fork together. 'I have news,' she announces, her cheeks pink from champagne.

Susanne is all ears, 'Well, go on – don't keep us in suspense.'

Dale pauses for dramatic effect, her eyes sparkling by the light of a dozen candles. 'From January, I'll be head of English and Drama at school. How bloody grown-up is that?'

'Oh, Dale, that's wonderful… Congratulations!' Susanne jumps up from her seat to hug her friend.

'Brilliant,' Evie says, raising her glass.

Star nods her approval. 'Cool bananas, Dale.'

'Wish you were *my* English teacher,' Cody mumbles, filling his mouth with yet another roast potato.

*

Overhead, the ceiling vibrates with explosions coming from Cody's room. Evie raises her eyebrows, tea towel in hand.

'PlayStation,' Susanne explains, 'I bought him a couple of new games. You should see them, it's like being in a movie. Not sure how fascinated Star will be, though. Bless her, she's so good with him. I think Cody just wants to sit close to her… all those hormones racing. God, I feel for him.'

'When does he leave for Scotland?' Dale asks, loading plates into the dishwasher.

'December twenty-ninth – in plenty of time for Hogmanay. Then the next time he goes up there, it'll be for the wedding in March. *Hey!* Stop it, I can see you two, giving each other knowing looks. I'm fine, really.'

'Seriously?' Evie leans her head to one side. 'It's okay not to be fine. Your ex is getting married. It's a big deal.'

'No, not to me. Not now. After everything that happened in the summer, I just want a quiet life. No drama, no more adventures. We all need to move on. When I think what could have happened...' Susanne shakes her head, reaches for her wine glass.

'That reminds me. How's Ronnie doing?' Dale asks.

'Okay, considering. She's a tough old bird. I see her around town sometimes, driving her Porsche and looking immaculate, but Harry's still missing and it must be horrendous for his whole family. I don't know how I would cope if Cody disappeared.'

Dale shudders. 'Don't think about it, Susie. It will never happen. It's weird, isn't it? We spent all summer thinking we were living with Ronnie's godson. Turns out we never even met him, and we probably never will.'

Susanne nods, the sadness that is never far away clouding her expression. 'Poor Harry. At least he has parents who love him and who are still looking for him.'

CHAPTER FIFTY-FIVE

Star

Tongue protruding with concentration, Star removes the vanilla-scented sponge from the oven and sets it down on the cooling rack.

'Yay! My first cake. It looks good, doesn't it?' she says, clapping oven-mitted hands together and beaming with pride.

Evie smiles. 'It looks fab, Star, well done. Wait until we do the icing later – that's the best bit. I'm really proud of you.'

Star grins, fills the sink with hot soapy water and starts clearing up.

'I'll dry,' Evie says, grabbing a tea towel. 'I love that you're learning to cook... Not that I'm an expert or anything, but I used to watch my mum so I can do all the basics.'

Star's tone is wistful. 'Don't remember Mum making much; spaghetti hoops and pot noodle were about the limit in our house. After she died and it was just me and Bran, we mostly lived on sarnies and takeaways.'

She can see real affection in Evie's eyes. Kind, patient Evie. So eager to share her time and her home with poor little orphaned Star. All alone in the world, just like Evie.

Perhaps that was why she'd helped so much in Tuscany; dealing with the police and other assorted officials – their names, titles and what they actually did had gone straight over Star's head, as she'd descended into shock and despair.

And then, like a light switching on in her fuzzy grief-stricken head, it had occurred to Star that *she* might go to prison. After all, she'd managed to convince the police that Harry had fallen from that crumbling ledge – locking away the image of Brandon shoving him hard with the flat of both hands – but there was no denying that they'd failed to get help. That they'd left Harry's body where it landed. Evie had spoken up for her, painting her as some sort of halfwit. An innocent child, who'd been swept along with her brother's actions in a state of shock and confusion.

And then, in an incredible twist of fate, the police had been unable to find Harry's body. What did that mean, exactly? Had he only fainted, or been stunned, and had at some point woken up and limped off into the hills? In which case, where was he now? None of it mattered to Star; all that counted was that there was no body. No body meant no murder, which meant there was no one to blame. Because even if Harry turned up in the future – which seemed highly unlikely – she'd stick to her story; that she'd seen Harry fall and had gone into shock, right there and then. Just like Evie said.

So Evie had taken her home to Tunbridge Wells – by far the nicest place Star had ever lived, with its pretty, expensive shops and lively bars and restaurants – and together they were doing up Evie's mum's house: pulling up old carpets, stripping off faded wallpaper, then bringing the rooms to life with airy, new paint colours and pretty curtains bought in the posh shop nearby. Evie had even talked about replacing the kitchen and bathroom, but she'd be leaving that to the professionals.

To Star's surprise, she could be very practical when she set her mind to it. And not just in the house. Evie was teaching her how to use computers, too; starting with Word and Excel, which Evie said would be useful in getting a good job one day. She'd even treated Star to a tablet, quite possibly the best present anyone had ever given her. Then Evie had added the Kindle app and shown Star how to use it for reading all the romance books she enjoyed.

Online banking had been a total revelation, and it was so convenient now that Star had a part time job waitressing at

The Gallery. She could access her modest wages easily, just like Evie did with her inheritance; a few clicks and *poof!* – it was all there on the screen, plain as day.

And it didn't take a genius to figure out Evie's password; a postcard of the *Birth of Venus* was pinned on the wall beside her computer, and Venus it was. So, Star had tested the water. Ten pounds here, thirty pounds there… Soon Star's nest egg would run into thousands, before one final sweep of Evie's account.

But there was no rush. Evie rarely checked her statements, and anyway, Star had other items on her agenda. 'Agenda': it was one of Evie's words and it sounded so grown-up and impressive that Star had adopted it, setting out her own on a notepad that she kept under her bed.

Next on Star's list, after relieving Evie of her inheritance, was Cody. Soon she would educate him, let him know what a scheming old slapper his mother really was. How she'd spent all summer in bed with a young man not much older than Cody himself. Gross! No kid wanted to hear that. Star had watched Susanne with her son; the way she mollycoddled and suffocated him, treating him like a child, when he was almost a man. It would be easy to sow a seed. Wouldn't Cody be better off living with his dad in Scotland? At least there he'd be allowed to grow up, have a life of his own one day – and he'd be able to bring friends home without worrying that his mum might try and get them into bed.

And while that was happening, Star would sort that other lanky bitch in London. Being promoted to head of department in a school that size was a big deal. To Star, it felt like a gift. Because it wouldn't take much to drip-feed a little poison, a few rumours on social media about Dale's inappropriate behaviour among some of the young, impressionable female students. And it wouldn't matter that the rumours weren't true. People remembered, gossiped. What was that expression? No smoke without fire.

Of course, some might say that it wasn't nice to cause chaos for three women who had helped her – especially Evie, who'd given her a home and a fresh start in a posh area. But that was because they didn't know the truth.

Well, Star knew. The only truth that mattered was that those three stuck-up bitches had killed her brother. Goading him into attacking them like that, then pushing him into the pool when he'd been too drunk and stoned to know what he was doing.

They said it had been an accident. That there'd been a struggle in the water after Brandon had gone crazy and tried to kill them all. But Star didn't believe them. All Star knew was that she missed her kind, funny big brother, who'd done everything for her since she was thirteen.

Those women – they'd taken away the one thing Star had left and the only thing she'd loved.

Now it was payback time.

EPILOGUE

San Gimignano

Seated at a pavement café, muffled against the chill, a young man finishes up scrambled eggs and coffee. His right hand strays to the band of white skin on his left wrist, to the vacuum left by his watch. In the shop where he'd sold it, the two men had been friendly enough, eager to trade his Rolex for a fat roll of notes.

The watch had been all he had, and something told him it had been important to him once. But right now, he has other priorities. Like filling his stomach when it growls and finding a comfortable bed for the night.

He considers his most recent home – the only one he can remember. The bed had seemed hard at first; basic, like all the other furniture in the little stone house, yet oddly comforting, with its view of the hillside and the sheep and goats that wandered past: he'd liked falling asleep to their bleating.

The elderly couple had been so kind, especially given they weren't his people. He knew that because he couldn't understand a word they said, but the woman had looked after him with such care that they might as well have been family.

And thank god that the old man had come along. How long had he lain there? On the stony ground, with the wind whistling through the cloisters? An hour? A day? A *week*? But apart from a searing headache – which the matted stickiness of his crown explained – a swollen ankle, and a thirst the like of which he'd never known, he didn't feel so bad; well enough, in fact, to limp as far as the nearest road.

It felt like he'd only been walking an hour or so when a farm truck slowed behind him and the driver had offered him a ride.

'Luigi,' the old man said, patting his chest and expecting a reply. Which was when he'd realised that he hadn't a clue who he was or why he was there. So he'd smiled, pointed to his injuries and hoped the man would take him to a hospital.

The rocking movement of the truck was pleasant and the sun warm through the windshield, but when he woke, there was no hospital, just the stone house, with sticks of furniture and a stove.

Luigi's wife, Marta, had welcomed him. She'd cleaned him up and bandaged his ankle, then poured him bowl after bowl of the best soup he'd ever eaten, all the while revealing what few teeth she possessed in a warm smile and chatting in a language he could not understand.

Then she'd given him clean (if loose and scratchy) clothes to wear, and he'd begun to feel human again until exhaustion overtook him, and he'd woken up in the tiny room on the hard bed, to the sound of animal grunts and whinnies outside his window.

Using the sun, he'd counted the days, which soon became weeks and then months, until one morning as the days were growing cooler and shorter, a row erupted between the man and woman. There were tears from her and shouting from him, and the clang of tin pots being thrown against stone walls.

The following day, their dispute over, Marta had handed him a parcel of clothing – including a bright red shirt which looked oddly familiar – and some food from the larder, before hugging him as tears spilled down her wizened cheeks.

This time in the truck, Luigi had been silent except for the odd remonstration with other drivers as they'd approached San Gimignano (according to the sign they'd passed), where he and his package had been deposited outside the city's walls.

A memory stirred. He had been here before. And not with Luigi or Marta.

So, he'd wandered the steep narrow lanes, their sounds and smells fragments of a dream just out of reach…

Hunger satisfied for now, the young man pushes his plate aside and fingers the wad of cash in his pocket. His head may be empty, but some things make sense. Food must be paid for; money is currency and now he has some – but soon it will run out. And then what?

He strokes his beard. Every day it becomes less itchy and more part of him. He wonders if his hair has always been this long: almost as long as the other boy's. The one who often comes to him in the mornings during his first few seconds of consciousness: a flickering image of a tall, handsome young man and a blonde girl with eyes the colour of a swimming pool.

A vision of his family, perhaps? The thought is comforting. He hopes they are looking for him.

A LETTER FROM BEVERLEY

Dear Reader,

Thank you so much for choosing to read *The Perfect Liar*. If you enjoyed it and want to keep up to date with all my latest releases, just sign up at the following link. Your email address will never be shared and you can unsubscribe at any time.

www.bookouture.com/beverley-harvey

The Perfect Liar was my first thriller and it was a joy to write. The beautiful location was inspired by several trips to Italy over the years, but I wanted to take that Italian dream and turn it into a nightmare, by adding someone dark and mysterious into the mix. We women are – for the most part – loyal and trusting, and our friendships endure, so it intrigued me to create a world where a young man could burst into a close-knit group and create total havoc. I hope you found yourself rooting for Susanne, Dale and Evie, anxious to know what could possibly happen to them next. I also hope that the blue skies of Tuscany provided a temporary escape from life's mundanities – if only for a little while.

If you loved *The Perfect Liar*, I would be most grateful if you could write a review. I'd love to hear what you think, and it makes such a difference helping new readers to discover one of my books for the first time.

I love hearing from my readers – you can get in touch on my Facebook page, through Twitter, Goodreads or my website.

Thanks,
Beverley Harvey

 Beverley Harvey Author

 @BevHarvey_

 beverleyharvey.co.uk

ACKNOWLEDGEMENTS

With sincere gratitude to all at Team Bookouture – thank you for choosing my novel. Special thanks to my editor, Therese, for shining up my ruby in the dust; to the tireless efforts of Kim and Noelle for letting readers know it exists; and thank you to Peta for helping bed in an initially confused author. You're all fab and ridiculously hard-working.

Love and thanks, too, to my wonderful partner Mark – who sees only the good in every situation – and to my family for their encouragement (wish our parents could have read and enjoyed this book).